PAINTED WOLVES

A NEW MODEL OF LEADERSHIP FROM POWERFUL WOMEN

Kelsey Medeiros

For information, contact Hogan Press
11 S. Greenwood, Tulsa OK 74120
hoganassessments.com

979-8-9856452-2-4

Cover design by 99designs
Typeset by Progressive Publishing Services

HOGANPRESS

PAINTED WOLVES
A NEW MODEL OF LEADERSHIP
FROM POWERFUL WOMEN

Her mother told her
she could grow up to be
anything she wanted to be
so she grew up to become
the strongest of the strong
the strangest of the strange
the wildest of the wild
the wolf leading the wolves

—Nikita Gill,
from *Fierce Fairytales*

Contents

Preface

In my leadership course, I ask students to select a biography or autobiography about a leader who interests them. After reading the book over the semester, they must analyze the leader's style and approach according to the theories and topics we've covered in class.

Each semester, inevitably, *multiple* students select the following leaders:

Elon Musk
Phil Knight
Adolf Hitler
Steve Jobs
Jeff Bezos

Notice any similarities?

Each semester, the gendered homogeneity of student selections, frankly, drives me nuts. Are there good and bad lessons about leadership to be learned from these male leaders? *Of course.* Are they interesting to read about? *Of course.* I fault none of my students for their choices. In my personal leadership journey, I too once loved reading about the Elon Musks and Steve Jobses of the world. I once even had a crush on Elon Musk! But as I have improved my knowledge of leadership, understanding of the world, *and taste in men,* so too have I improved my views on who should lead.

As I changed, I became more familiar with the persistent gender gap in leadership and began to ask the same question that I now ask when reading my student papers. In the words of David Guetta, "Where Them Girls At?"

Only a small handful of students each semester selects a woman. And it's nearly always the women in the class who choose to read about another woman.

What do my students' papers have to do with this book? To put it simply, I'm tired of reading papers about men. I'm so tired of it, in fact, that I embarked on the idiotic challenge of writing a book about women in leadership to diversify our exemplars of leadership and make these leaders more accessible to my students, to you, and to me. Reader, I simply cannot read another paper about Elon Musk.

There are important lessons to be learned from all leaders—good and bad, charismatic and mundane, male and female. However, as I will describe in the pages that follow, the overreliance, overabundance, and oversaturation of examples of men in leadership severely limit the lessons that can be learned. As a result, these men limit the way in which we lead.

Women, be it for biological or social reasons, lead differently. They develop their leadership approach differently. They face unique challenges. They form different relationships with followers. They choose distinct priorities from their male counterparts.

Throughout the COVID-19 pandemic, we saw women's unique way of leading during crisis. We saw women in head-of-state positions limit the spread of the virus, keep deaths to a relative minimum, and encourage preventative measures and vaccine uptake. For a few brief months at the start of the pandemic in early 2020, their success gripped the world's attention—making headlines around the world. Over time, however, while women continued to successfully manage the virus, our interest waned.

This book strives to reignite that interest, to celebrate the successes of the women, and to provide more examples from which we can learn how to lead differently—*and about which my students can write their papers.*

COVID-19 brought us death. It ravaged our mental health. It fundamentally changed our social relationships. To put it scientifically, *it sucked.*

As I wrote this book while battling my own COVID-19-induced depression and physical illness, the women featured in these pages brought me hope. They reminded me that the potential for a better world exists. But it's up to us to choose it. It's up to us to choose a different kind of leadership. It's up to us to choose women.

We can start by reading about women in leadership. *Or anyone other than Elon.**

In this book, you will meet several women from around the world who demonstrated the value of a unique set of skills distinct from those occupying the pages of many famous leadership texts. As you read about these women and their skillsets, I hope you reflect on your own approach to leadership and consider how you can be part of a change to create a better way of leading and a better world.

As you read, please bear in mind that not *all* women are suited for leadership. Just as not all men have the skills, values, or desire to lead, not all women have the skills, values, or desire to lead. The purpose of this book is not to suggest that blindly choosing any woman to lead us is a recipe for success. Rather, this book argues that our views of suc- cessful leadership are fundamentally shaped by the way men lead. As a result, our assumptions about who can lead and what leadership looks like are bounded by men's approach to leadership. By looking to success- ful women in power, we can challenge our views of leadership and learn to lead differently.

You'll note that my own language throughout this book is bounded by an outdated binary view of gender. This book does not speak about openly transgender, non-binary, or gender fluid leaders. This is largely because, at the time of writing, there are no heads of state that openly hold these identities. Additionally, because these individuals have histor- ically been silenced and excluded from positions of power, the research on leadership and gender from a non-binary perspective is extremely lim- ited. Recently, however, an increasing number of non-binary, transgender, and gender fluid persons have overcome the systematic challenges holding them back from leadership to obtain positions of power. For example, the

---

*At the time of writing Elon Musk was single handedly destroying the popular social networking website, Twitter, being accused of illegally covering up the firing of 8 SpaceX employees who wrote an open letter calling out his inappropriate behavior including sexual harassment,[1] and facing legal actions against his compa- nies SpaceX, Twitter, and Tesla.[2] So yes, I'm not a fan.

sitting Prime Minister of Serbia, Ana Brnabić, is the first woman and first openly gay person to hold the position. And in 2021, she became the first openly gay head of state to have a child while in office.[3] When appointed as the US assistant secretary for health in 2022, Dr. Rachel Levine became the highest serving openly transgender person in the federal government.[4] As more non-binary individuals reach these positions of power, we must similarly look to them for lessons on leading effectively.

At this point, it bears recognizing the subjective nature of the word *effective*. What does effective leadership actually mean? Depending on the intended outcome, *effective* can carry a number of meanings. In the case of COVID-19, a definition of effectiveness, at times, divided scholars, leaders, and the public. In this book, I choose to define *effective* by COVID-19 case and death rates. I consider leaders of countries with lower case and death rates as more effective than leaders of countries with higher case and death rates. But there are other metrics by which to judge these leaders. The economy, for instance, can be used as a measure of leader success during COVID-19. As research on the impact of COVID-19 continues, we will undoubtably encounter more diverse metrics of success and be challenged to think about how each benchmark shapes our views of the leader. From an oversimplified moral perspective, it can be tempting to argue that COVID-19 case and death rates are the superior outcome to consider— the idea of letting people die is morally repulsive to many. Given the rapid spread of the virus, the health risks associated with contracting it and the pressure felt by health systems, particularly prior to the vaccine, a decisive, coordinated, scientifically-driven approach that limited the spread of the virus should produce the most positive long-term outcomes when compared to other approaches.[5] Additionally, countries without strict decisions to limit the spread of the virus early on would likely continue to face continuing restrictions that will have a large economic and health impact in the long-term.[6] From a more complex standpoint, however, one must consider the long-term effects of shutting down a country to limit the spread of the illness on jobs and mental health. Bearing this in mind, I use COVID-19 case and death rates as the primary metric for determining leader effectiveness.

To understand what made these women particularly effective leaders during this time, I took a thematic approach to analyzing their actions and decisions as reported by media outlets throughout the pandemic from 2020 until late 2022. Of course, with any media reporting comes a bias. And one can argue that we don't have the full picture of a leader's thinking or even who made the final decisions when it came to government policy. In some instances, women have even been attributed with a country's success when that woman has very little "real" power. With that caveat in mind, we can still draw conclusions in the similarities of actions among the women leading their countries during COVID-19—actions that reflect scientific findings and expert advice—and expose important lessons for leading effectively.

Painted Wolves vs. Lions

I never expected to receive a masterclass in organizational leadership on a South African safari. But as our eight-seater Toyota Land Cruiser crunched over the sundried Kruger Park brush—it happened.

The morning sun woke over the horizon as we climbed into our seats for our morning game drive. There were seven of us in the car that morning, each eager for the day, keeping to ourselves as we allowed the coffee to take hold. Joe, our safari guide, and the tracker, Quolani, were the last to board the car and take their positions, Joe in the driver's seat and Quolani on the edge of the hood. "There are reports of lions on the eastern boundary," Joe said, "so the plan for this morning is to head that way and see if we can track them."

We set off through the park, passing zebras, giraffes, and the punk rockers of the bush—warthogs, before pulling up to three teenage lions lying in the open plains. Another safari Land Cruiser idled nearby as occupants snapped pictures. Everyone in our car beamed with excitement and held our breath in collective anxiety, quietly oohing and ahhing at the majestic sight. After a few minutes passed, one of the male lions stood up, stretching his long body out to nearly double in size. He shook. A sign, Joe explained, that the lions would be on the move shortly.

As Joe predicted, within minutes, all three lions had stood, stretched, and began their morning stroll. We followed the lions a few steps before they stopped to take stock of their environment, scanning their surroundings, looking left to right. One slowly turned its head in my direction. My heart stopped. We held our eye contact and I held my breath for several long beats before the lion moved its gaze to the brush to my right. They then lay back down for a morning nap and I exhaled in relief that I would not be the lion's breakfast.

This pattern of walking, scanning, napping continued for nearly an hour before the morning took a dramatic turn.

A mother and baby impala entered the scene from stage right. The lions, the impala, and all of the heartbeats in the Land Cruiser froze.

The mother clocked the lions. The lions clocked her. And we clocked the danger, the hunger, the fear.

The mother tucked her baby into a bush and raced off. Joe quickly explained in a hushed wildlife documentary narrator tone that leaving the baby alone in the bush was the baby's best chance of survival. The baby was likely less than a day old and was still learning to use her stilts of legs. By running off, Joe continued, the mother hoped to draw the lions away from her young.

The lions, however, didn't fall for her ploy and the baby missed mom's cue. Sensing danger, the baby ran and the lions followed, with our Land Cruiser trailing closely behind. We kept our distance while keeping pace. The lions and the baby weaved in and out of bushes and brush, making it difficult to see whether the baby was outrunning the lions or the lions, with their speed and agility, were bearing down on the newborn.

At one point in the chase, the lions took a rest! We stopped with them, ourselves taking a breath from the intensity. In the pause, I scanned the area, seeing the resting lions, brush, trees, but no baby impala. There were no signs of her—dead or alive.

Like the lions, we waited. After 20 minutes of little action aside from some rolling, moaning, and a bit of pacing from the lions, the scene changed again.

They spotted the baby. The race reignited.

They made their way through rough terrain that made it difficult for the Land Cruiser to follow in their path. As Quolani thrashed branches with his machete and Joe bulldozed over bushes, we managed to follow their trail. When we reached them, they had already caught the baby impala and were now enjoying a midmorning snack. I'll spare you the rest of the details.

As a pescatarian with a strong vegetarian tendency, I could hardly stomach the sight. Joe read the sadness on my face and explained that he also found these scenes upsetting. But, he explained, that there is a circle of life (cue Elton John), and it's important that, as humans, we allow nature to take its course and to limit our influence in their systems. *Okay, okay,*

okay, yadda yadda, I get it, I thought. And I did. But soft tears still began to swell as I thought about that mother who had given birth only hours ago. And that poor baby. So innocent and unaware.

As I held back the waterworks and covered my eyes to the scene unfolding in front of me, Joe narrated the scene like my personal David Attenborough. "Lions are selfish animals," he said. "The female caught the baby, so this is her meal." As Joe spoke, almost as if on cue, one of the male lions approached the female to grab a small bite from her plate. She immediately snapped, like you might when someone tries to steal the last bite of your favorite dessert.

Joe continued: "Lions are selfish. Whoever gets the kill, keeps it. They don't share it with the group." (*How rude,* I thought.) "Businesspeople always talk about how leaders should be like lions," Joe said, "but this is a terrible analogy. Lions are selfish. Leaders should be more like painted wolves. They hunt in packs, and regardless of who makes the kill, they share the meal with the whole pack. Leaders shouldn't be selfish. They should share the reward of their goals with everyone. Businesspeople should really talk about how we need more leaders like painted wolves— not lions."

There I was, a leadership scholar, in the back left corner of the Land Cruiser, in the middle of Kruger National Park in South Africa, receiving a profound lesson on leadership. As others moved on to questions about eating and hunting, I sat there, gobsmacked, reflecting on Joe's lesson. *We do teach people to be like lions,* I thought. Books have been written about leading like lions, and whole companies are dedicated to helping leaders embrace the "power and grace" of lions. I've seen pictures of leadership development programs with cubs staring into mirrors only to see a ferocious lion staring back. Certainly, that is the Western cultural. We see this archetype portrayed regularly in our media as well. On HBO's hit TV shows alone, we see Logan Roy of *Succession,* Joffrey of *Game of Thrones*, and Selina Meyer of *VEEP* displaying (or attempting to display in the case of Selina) these lion-like characteristics. Ideal of leadership that we have perpetuated—powerful, majestic, selfish.

But do lions make good leaders? Or to Joe's point, should we consider an alternative animal role model?

The painted wolf, also known as the African wild dog or the cape hunting dog, lives in sub-Saharan Africa. Although they share similarities with wild wolves and your couch loving Fido, painted wolves are typically leaner and have longer legs. You can also easily distinguish them by their oversized rounded ears and the way their brown, black, yellow, and white fur brushes across their skin as if an artist's canvas. Below is a picture I was lucky enough to capture while on safari.

In comparison to the lion, wild dogs are much smaller size. The painted wolf weighs a mere 40 to 70 pounds (wwf), whereas the average male lion weighs anywhere between 300 an 550 pounds and the female lion between 250 and 400 pounds (discovery uk). Despite the painted wolf's size, they outperform lions when hunting. The painted wolf boasts an 80 percent kill rate (thornybush), meaning that a hunt leads to a successful catch approximately 80 percent of the time. But the lion, as strong and mighty as they be, successfully catches and kills their prey only 30 percent of the time (lion alert).

What makes the painted wolf so successful compared to the lion? Researchers who have observed painted wolves in the wild note that packs have a collaborative plan for every hunt. Whereas lions are most likely to hunt opportunistically and on their own or in pairs, painted wolves hunt as a coordinated pack of 5 to 15. With a three musketeers mentality—all for one and one for all—each painted wolf is given a specific role in the hunt, equally contributing to the overall success (live science). For example, an injured pack member may be given the role of babysitter and remain at the den to look after the pups while the others hunt. Adding to their success, the pack also regularly communicates throughout a hunt with physical touch, gestures, and grunts. Researchers in the field have even noted that the pack may vote on their next moves by sneezing (live science 2)!

The painted wolf's three musketeers attitude continues even after they make a kill. If, for instance, a kill is made too far from the pack's pups, then other members will overeat and regurgitate the food for the pups when they return. In contrast, hungry lions will gorge themselves, even at the expense of their young. If limited food is available, mother lions are likely to keep it to themselves rather than share (lion alert).

If lions are less effective hunters than painted wolves, why do we hold the idea of being a lion-leader in such high esteem?

There are clearly alternative ways to be effective than simply being the biggest, most selfish animal in the bush! But don't take my word for it (or even Joe's), lets look at the research on leadership effectiveness.[1-6]

If the lion leadership model works, then we might expect to see an abundance of great leaders, especially considering the number of Simba-focused leadership programs available.

Statistically, scholars estimate that anywhere between 50 percent and 75 percent of leaders fail.[7] This implies that the majority of our leaders fail in their roles. A majority! What's more, a good portion of these leaders fail quite quickly. Compiling data from multiple studies, McKinsey & Company[8] reports that 27 percent to 46 percent of leaders were viewed poorly within the first two years of taking on a new role.

These are spectacularly impressive numbers. To put this in context, imagine for a moment that an airline has a 50 percent rate of crashing due to pilot error. Would you buy a ticket to fly with that airline?

And these failures don't come cheap. Early research in the 1980s and 1990s suggested that the estimated price tag on leader failure was

$500,000.[7] But by the 2000s, that estimated cost reached multiple millions of dollars.[9]

What are we doing wrong when it comes to leadership?

It's not an issue of an investment. Globally, organizations spend more than $350 billion annually on leadership development programs.[9] Despite the dollars spent, these programs are clearly not cutting it. In response, scholars and practitioners have called for a broader approach including improved training and development programs, more rigorous evaluation, clearer strategies, and refined competency models. All of these steps are undoubtably important. But another critical step, a much more difficult step, must be undertaken if we are truly going to improve leadership around the globe. To fundamentally change who we attract to, and who we select for, leadership positions, we must question our understanding of what it means to be a good leader. We must change our underlying beliefs about what it means to lead. To paraphrase Joe, we need to stop thinking about leaders as lions and start thinking about leaders as painted wolves.

To this end, we must take stock of how we have arrived at our definition of leadership in the first place and consider how we might disentangle ourselves from the lion perspective. Over time, our idea of what good leadership looks like has evolved substantially. The dawn of leadership research in the late twentieth century ushered in the belief that leaders are born, not made. Known as the great man theory, these early ideas emphasized the innate traits that made someone a leader. First and foremost on the list? A penis. The idea that women could be leaders seemed to be so far outside the realm of possibility that the researchers need not even mention this trait, instead simply including it in the theory's title: great *man*. Obviously, leadership wasn't for "the ladies" (despite evidence of their leadership throughout history in both human and animal kingdoms). Other important and stated traits included physical features such as height and personality characteristics such as extroversion. The great man theory largely perpetuated sexist and racist beliefs that white men—and only white men—were born to lead.

As research evolved, so too did our understanding of the qualities of what makes an effective leader. Although traits such as height influence who we are likely to *see* as a leader, these traits have little to do with who will be *effective* as a leader.[10] With little empirical evidence supporting the link between the traits outlined in the great man theory and leader effectiveness, researchers returned to the drawing board, turning their attention away from traits and toward skills. Skills can be taught, which fundamentally challenged the idea that leaders are born. Instead, the skills approach introduced the dominant view of leadership today—leaders are made. The research revolved around a new question: What skills do leaders need to be effective? Core skills identified included human skills (e.g., relationship building), technical skills (e.g., analytics, field-specific activities), and conceptual skills (e.g., problem solving, creativity).

Running with the idea that leaders are made rather than born, researchers then expanded their line of questioning: What skills, behaviors, and styles do leaders need to be effective? For instance, one area of research focuses on the impact of charismatic leadership, a style, on leader performance and follower reactions. Others focus on the effects of leaders' interactions with their followers, whether leader authenticity helps or hinders leader performance, and how effective leaders balance managing tasks and people.

Modern questions on leadership reflect the complexity of leadership and the need for more nuance. Now, our understanding of leadership focuses on the intersection of how and when: How should leaders behave, and when is that behavior most useful? What external factors interact with a leader's style or skills to produce more effective or less effective leadership? What role do followers play in how effective a leader is at accomplishing their goals?

Despite these major advancements, one area continues to lag behind: diversity.

Although researchers have asked questions surrounding diversity in leadership, research progress remains hampered by lagging progress in society. White men remain the dominant occupants of leadership positions in many countries around the world. This is especially true in the global West. Consequently, as research often reflects the current world—the good and the bad—our understanding of how the world functions is limited by the data samples available. When it came to leadership research, this meant that our understanding of leadership was limited by who held leadership positions—white men. As women and people of color were largely kept out of positions of leadership at this time, the idea that they could lead wasn't even considered, much less studied. The assumption that women and people of color could (or could not) lead wasn't tested until many years later. As was the case throughout the development of leadership research and theories, white men remain the dominant lens through which we understand what it means to lead.

However, as more women and people of color have advanced into leadership positions, they challenge our assumptions about leadership. Bringing new perspectives and ways of leading to the table, they challenge the status quo of what it means to be a good leader. And in doing so, they call into question the value of the lion-as-leader model and introduce new approaches such as that of the painted wolf. The idea that there may be a new and more effective model of leadership emerging from a historically overlooked pack took center stage in spring 2020.

In the twilight hours of 2019, Dr. Le Wenliang sounded the alarm on a rising pandemic that would fundamentally alter the way in which we lived. As we moved into the early months of 2020, most of us continued our daily lives as normal, with an eye toward peril in China and a Vegas-style confidence that what happened in China would stay in China. As winter stretched into spring, however, it became clear that we would each feel the impact of the COVID-19 pandemic. The viral outbreak flew around the world from China to Europe, Australia, North America, and later to Africa and South America, transfixing the world's attention on epidemiological facts and figures for months to come. It was in these early months that we received a crash course in the basics of epidemiology, learning the importance of Rd (the rate at which the virus reproduces), PPE (personal protective equipment), and accurate reporting of case and death rates across countries. Key phrases that had yet to enter global vernacular, such as "social distancing" and "flattening the curve," quickly became commonplace on news outlets, on Twitter, and at dinner tables. We debated the utility of masks in public spaces and ordered masks in designs that represented our personal tastes. We changed the meaning of personal space from one in which shaking hands, slight touches, and even warm familial hugs were mainstays of friendly greetings to a space in which we treated everyone—and everyone treated us—as a possible Typhoid Mary.

It was also in the throes of the COVID-19 pandemic that we recognized the power of women in leadership.

I remember the moment well. I was sitting in my bed, my dog, Luna—a bulgy-eyed chihuahua rescue mix—curled up like a cinnamon roll next to me, snoring, completely unaware of the health crisis unfolding outside. I was searching the Internet in hopes of calming my anxieties (*as an aside, I do not recommend this tactic*), looking for any semblance of an answer about what this virus was, how it behaved, and how it would impact my life in the time to come. In a state of desperation, I turned to Twitter for answers (*again, not a recommended approach*).

Once curated to reflect my academic and personal interests, my Twitter feed was now populated with virology facts and figures from epidemiologists and other medical professionals. At the time, Italy's cases and deaths surged, making it the center of the outbreak, and I scrolled endlessly, engulfed by the images of overrun hospitals, empty city streets, and an opera singer serenading Florence from his balcony. It was amidst this combination of both horror and hope that a particular tweet caught my eye:

The tweet captured my attention because of the vast differences across the four countries, spinning my brain as to why Italy was suffering such a harsh fate in comparison to the others. After a moment, however, my focus shifted to Germany: *How did Germany have so many cases and so few deaths?* I wondered. I turned my anxiety-driven Internet search into a quest for Germany's secret. It quickly became apparent that I wasn't alone in this question and, in the days to come as the death rate remained at or near zero, more and more people grew interested in exactly what Germany was doing to suppress the death rate to such a degree. At the time, many speculated that Germany's low death rate could be traced to who was getting sick. Some argued that younger Germans were the ones contracting the virus, and they were less likely to experience severe symptoms and more likely to make full recoveries. Others suggested that the German diet provided them the nutrients and resources needed to fight off the virus.[11] Some even went so far as to accuse Germany of fudging its numbers, hiding the true figures from the public to enhance Germany's reputation.

However, many also recognized the speed with which Germany responded to the crisis. Aiding them in this effort was an existing system that had been put in place in the event that Germany ever faced a crisis of this proportion.

It worked. Within a month of activating its epidemic strategy, Germany mobilized the development of 300 laboratories, a test that could detect the virus within 2.5 hours, and processes to test up to 160,000 individuals per week.[12] *Impressive.*

When the stories of Germany's success first emerged in March 2020, few mentioned Angela Merkel as a driver. As a leadership scholar, one with a specific interest in women's leadership, I'm embarrassed to admit that I did not make the connection myself. Instead, in concert with those discussing Germany's success online and in the news, I remained fascinated that a country could achieve such results in the face of adversity. Germany had developed tests, and Germany was succeeding in the fight against the coronavirus.

But was "Germany" making decisions? No. Merkel and her team of scientists, experts, and policymakers made these decisions. It was under *Merkel's* leadership that Germany reached such success in the early months of the pandemic, and it was under *her* leadership that Germany sustained this success, emerging from the first wave of COVID-19 with a stronger economy and lower death rate than neighbors such as France and Italy.[13] But the importance of the Germanic leader's gender was yet to be recognized by most.

Stories of Germany's relative success were soon followed by those of New Zealand's. In the early days of March 2020, New Zealand confirmed its first few cases of COVID-19. But as the country—with a population of 5 million—reached just over 200 cases and the death toll stood at 19, the country locked down. From mid-March until the end of April, New Zealanders, informally called Kiwis, lived in the world's strictest lockdown.[14] Jacinda Ardern, New Zealand's prime minister, instructed her citizens to "act like you have COVID-19."[15] Some viewed these actions as extreme, questioning why a lockdown was necessary with such a low death rate. But by mid-April, the world was championing New Zealand's approach, emphatically proclaiming that New Zealand wasn't "just flattening [the] curve. It [was] squashing it."[16] By June 2020, New Zealand had no active cases of COVID-19 and was ready to reopen for business, with appropriate precautions in place.

The rhetoric and discussion around New Zealand differed from that of Germany's success. Ardern had already received considerable attention and praise for her response to the Christchurch mosque shootings and the White Island volcano eruption, both horrendous crises that struck the small island in 2019. As the public's focus shifted to her in a time of crisis once more, some began drawing connections between a country's COVID-19 response and the leader's gender.

Taiwan, for example, typically in the spotlight for its contentious relationship with Beijing leadership, shone for Tsai Ing-Wen's approach to leadership, an approach that kept the number of cases under 450 and the death toll to 7, as of June 2020. These numbers stood in stark contrast to those of Taiwan's southern neighbor, Australia. Both Australia and Taiwan recorded their first case of COVID-19 on the same day—January 25, 2020. Both have similar populations of approximately 24 million citizens each. Both are islands. But by early April 2020, Australia had reported nearly 5,000 cases, while Taiwan's cases stood under 400.[17] Two years on in October 2022, Australia reported more than 1 billion cases and just under 14,000 deaths. At that same time, Taiwan had reported just over 54 million cases and fewer than 10,000 deaths.[†]

[†]All case and death rates reported by Worldometer.com.

What did Tsai Ing-Wen (president of Taiwan) and Scott Morrison (prime minister of Australia) do differently? Tsai quickly closed Taiwan's borders and enabled an impressive track-and-trace system to monitor and stop the flow of the virus from person to person. Businesses quickly began taking temperatures and providing sanitizer to customers. The government also controlled the face mask supply, allowing three masks per person per week. Morrison similarly took a rather hardline response to the virus, closing Australia's borders, instituting a track-and-trace program, and enacting social distancing and isolation policies. However, early decisions regarding the *Ruby Princess* cruise ship, from which 2,700 passengers were allowed to disembark despite many showing symptoms of COVID-19, in combination with some rebellion to social distancing policies on beaches and in parks, likely led to the higher infection and death rate in Australia.[18] Although Australia's numbers fail to impress in the same way as Taiwan's, the Oceania country's response still tops the charts as one of the most successful globally. The early misstep with the *Ruby Princess*, however, underscores the criticality of every decision made by leaders during a crisis.

Other countries with women as head of state have earned global recognition for the response, including Greece, Iceland, Finland, and Barbados.

What did all of these country's responses have in common?

They were led by women.

Within weeks, news outlets picked up on this underlying theme:

"What Do Countries with the Best Coronavirus Responses Have in Common? Women Leaders"[19]

"Why Are Women-Led Nations Doing Better with COVID-19?"[20]

"Are Female Leaders More Successful at Managing the Coronavirus Crisis?"[21]

"Why Women Make Better Crisis Leaders"[22]

"Are Women Leaders Better at Fighting Coronavirus? It's Complicated."[23]

The story was everywhere, and many people jumped to the conclusion that women were better at leading during a crisis. But the *Vox* article

"Are Women Leaders Better at Fighting Coronavirus? It's Complicated." is accurate—the relationship between women in leadership and the effectiveness of a country's response *is* complicated.[23] As North notes, the correlation isn't perfect, meaning that not all women in leadership positions have been praised for their response. In fact, some have received significant and valid criticism of their approaches. For instance, Belgium, led by Prime Minister Sophie Wilmes, had one of the worst mortality rates in the world, with 66 deaths per 100,000 people. When Wilmes visited a Belgian hospital, doctors and nurses greeted her by turning their backs to her as she passed by.[24]

As everyone who has taken an introductory statistics course knows, correlation does not equal causation. That means that there are many other factors to consider, outside of a leader's gender, that could be the real driver of success. Some people have suggested that the country size matters. Others have argued that the same cultural characteristic, namely, egalitarianism, that led to the election of a woman also led to the leader's success. Other factors, such as previous experience with pandemics, likely influenced responses. For instance, Taiwan and Singapore were heavily impacted by the SARS outbreak in 2003, leading many to speculate that a country's previous experience with a pandemic impacted its success in 2020.

Unfortunately, at the time of writing in 2022, it is empirically impossible to tease out these differences and identify the true sources of these countries' success. *Why?* There simply are not enough women in head-of-state positions to conduct robust statistical tests comparing them to men in the same positions. During the first two years of the pandemic, the number of women holding a country's top position ranged from 22 to 26. That number stands in stark contrast to the 173 remaining countries with men as their top leader. It's statistically inappropriate to compare two different groups of such drastic sizes. Any result we obtained would be unreliable and invalid.

Anecdotally, however, a trend does appear to emerge. Of the 11 countries noted in *Time*'s "Best Global Response to Covid-19 Pandemic," six were led by women.[25] Given that women make up a mere 11 percent of global heads of state, if they were performing similarly to men, one would expect to see a similar proportion of women represented on the "best of" response list. Mathematically, that means we should see only one female-led country on the list. Instead, female-led countries made up 54.5 percent of the list. Moreover, Nicholas Kristof, a former opinion columnist at the *New York Times*, compared 13 countries led by men and 8 countries led by women, revealing that female-led countries lost one-fifth the number of people to COVID-19 in the initial wave of the pandemic than male-led countries lost.[26]

Although by no means conclusive, the evidence leans in women's favor. And the evidence certainly suggests that the differences in actions between men and women on the world's stage are meaningful. By paying attention to their actions, we can glean leadership lessons and understand how those actions may have influenced leaders' effectiveness at managing COVID-19.

To quickly refresh:

Did *all* women respond perfectly to the pandemic? No.
Did *many* women respond well to the pandemic? Yes.
Are there lessons to be learned from these women? *Hell yes!*

There's another point raised by the *Vox* author, Anna North, that deserves attention. In her article, she has concerns that praising women for their handling of the COVID-19 crisis could lead to the overgeneralization that all women are better than men at managing crises.[23] In turn, this could set an expectation trap in which women are always expected to perform better than men. If and when women do not live up to these expectations, failure or missteps could lead to harsher criticisms than those that might be hurled at men for making the same decisions.

Although on the surface this claim seems reasonable, the fact is that women are already judged more harshly than men (*all the damn time*, might I add). Research conducted by scholars around the world consistently shows that women are penalized more harshly,[27] face greater obstacles to advancement and employment,[28] and are even more likely than their male counterparts to be put in precarious leadership positions[29]—simply because of their gender. This happens daily to women all around the world in nearly every profession at every level. This imbalanced treatment is a systemic issue of gender bias propped up by both men and women globally. More on that soapbox in the next chapter.

While North's concern over praising women for their COVID-19 response represents a real issue for women, I wholeheartedly disagree that our response should be anything less than shouting, "YOU GO, GIRL!" from the rooftops for many years to come. We celebrate men's success for much smaller wins (the lyrics of Taylor Swift's "The Man" provide a comprehensive review). Why would we stay quiet about this?

Equally as important, paying specific attention to the women who led us through the pandemic provides insight into effective leadership. Could we also do this by looking at how men led? *Sure.*

But there have been enough pages and text dedicated to men over the past 1,000 and more years that, frankly, it might be a bit refreshing to look at leadership from another perspective. The number of words written *by* men and *about* men, specifically with regard to leadership, is extensive and arguably exhaustive. A great example of this can be seen in a blog post titled "The MBA Reading List According to the Top Business Schools in the World."[30] The authors include 20 book recommendations derived from Harvard, Wharton, Stanford, and other well-regarded universities. All 20 of these books were written by men—and white men at that. In the academic literature, the vast majority of scientific articles investigating leadership focus on men, which means that what we understand about leadership is based nearly exclusively on the way men lead. This focus on men is largely driven by the fact that a majority of leadership positions are held by men, leaving men as our primary exemplars of leadership. In the past, when a researcher wanted to better understand leaders, they, appropriately, studied men. But as women increasingly rose in the ranks and took on positions of power, the response was to haphazardly apply existing knowledge about leadership to these women. Rather than give women the same attention as the men received in understanding leadership, women seemed to be treated as a special case of a man.

The dominance of men and therefore the near if not total reliance on the male prototype is not exclusive to leadership. For instance, in an episode of *Last Week Tonight* focused on bias in medicine, John Oliver plays an old clip of Larry Cahill summarizing the medical view that women are just men "with pesky hormones." In his typical satirical fashion, Oliver[31] then extends this argument: "Women are just men with hormones, children are just tiny men, dogs are furry men, and volcanos are just men who ejaculate lava."

To understand how women lead, we have squeezed them, along with their pesky hormones, into leadership boxes that were designed exclusively for men. It's the academic equivalent of asking women to try on men's jeans; noticing that they don't fit quite right around the legs, near the groin, and at the hips; adding a few safety pins to tighten them in some places; then looking at your handy work and saying, "Ah, that will do."

What? No, it won't!

This issue extends well beyond leadership, representing the general approach to understanding women. Caroline Criado Perez discusses it extensively in her book, *Invisible Women*.[32] She states,

> The presumption that what is male is universal is a direct consequence of the gender data gap. Whiteness and maleness can only go without saying because most other identities never get said at all. But male universality is also a cause of the gender data gap: because women aren't seen and aren't remembered, because male data makes up the majority of what we know, what is male comes to be seen as universal. It leads to the positioning of women, half the global population, as a minority. With a niche identity and subjective point of view. In such a framing, women are set up to be forgettable. Ignorable. Dispensable—from culture, from history, and from data. And so, women become invisible.

Women are no longer invisible in positions of leadership, but the way they lead remains hidden behind a failure to commit to identifying fundamental patterns in how women lead—free from the constraints of men's approach—and a wall of expectations of what leadership is supposed to look like, an expectation that time and time again has been shown to be male. This expectation appears so blatantly that if you ask someone to draw what an effective leader looks like, they nearly always draw a man.[33] As a professor, I've used this exercise in my class to introduce the topic of leadership, and I can attest, from personal experience, this bias still appears.

I also used this exercise at the start of a well-advertised campus work-shop on *gender* and leadership. Could the point of the exercise have been any more obvious? I must admit, I was nervous to use it because the cues were so strong. I normally try to suppress signs of gender when I use the exercise, doing so at the beginning of a class before the topic is even intro-duced. Surely, I thought, most of the attendees will grasp the point and intentionally draw a woman. Sadly, the exercise held true. Despite all of the gender-related cues screaming "DRAW A WOMAN!" approximately 75 percent of those in attendance still drew a man, showing just how deep these expectations run. Even when in a room full of cues contradicting and challenging the gendered expectation of leadership, the expectation won out.

Research tells us that one way to combat these expectations is to shine a light on women already occupying these positions who can serve as role models for other women as well as for men.[34,35] Each woman who cracks the glass ceiling and who leads effectively challenges our views of what leadership should look like and creates new opportunities for women and girls around the world. It's why Hilary Clinton's presidential campaign, as the first woman to earn the presidential nomination of a major polit-ical party in the United States, mattered so deeply and left many in tears on election night in November 2016. Clinton understood the gravity and weight of her campaign and what it meant to have a woman come so close to occupying the top position in the United States. Even in her loss, she acknowledged this, reminding "all the little girls who are watching this" to "never doubt that you are valuable and powerful and deserving of every chance and opportunity in the world to pursue and achieve your own dreams."[36] The same holds true for Kamala Harris's win as the first woman, and importantly, woman of color, to win the office of vice pres-ident of the United States. Stacy Abrams similarly demonstrated in the United States that black women are capable of leading effectively when she led the initiative that would ultimately change Georgia, a historically Republican voting state, in favor of Joe Biden, the 2020 US Democratic nominee and subsequent president of the United States.

The women in this book remind us of the same. Their successes provide us, both women and men, with cases of effective leadership and crisis management to learn from, to challenge our views, and to rewrite the script on what leadership means. Framed in the context of the unique challenges women face when they ascend to and hold such powerful positions, the pages that follow tell the stories of remarkable women, revealing the six skills that made them successful in managing a global pandemic:

1. Preparation
2. Issue-driven focus
3. Shared leadership
4. Willingness to learn
5. Emotion management
6. Risk-taking

Before diving into these stories, it's important to bear one caveat in mind. This book is *not* a tell-all on how to lead effectively *as a woman*. No, the purpose of this book is to shine a light on outstanding leaders who happen to share a gender and whose voices, despite being some of the most powerful voices in the world, may otherwise be drowned out by those with deeper tones and louder shouts. These stories provide lessons for all of us. They teach us how to lead effectively. Period. Full stop.

THE WOMEN

Let's meet the women who will teach us a thing or two (or six) about leadership in the coming pages.

Jacinda Ardern, *Prime Minister of New Zealand* (2017–2023)
This Kiwi began her political career immediately after graduating from university. Ardern served on the staff of multiple New Zealand members of parliament and the prime minister of New Zealand (at the time,

a woman) prior to moving to London where she worked for the Prime Minister of the United Kingdom, Tony Blair. In 2007, she took on the top position at the International Union of Socialist Youth. After traveling the world for her work, she became the youngest member of New Zealand's House of Representatives at the age of 28. Ardern continued to serve in parliamentary positions until 2017 when she became Labor Party leader in the leadup to New Zealand's general election. This leadership role launched her into the prime minister position later that same year. While occupying New Zealand's top role, Ardern tackled multiple crises, including the deadly mosque attacks, Whakaari/White Island volcanic eruption, and COVID-19.

Tsai Ing-Wen, *President of Taiwan* (2016–)
After earning her PhD in law from the University of London, Tsai taught law at universities in Taipei, the capital of Taiwan. During her academic career, she also worked with multiple governmental agencies such as the Fair Trade Commission, Mainland Affairs Council, and National Security Council. In 2000, she began her political ascent with an appointment as chair of the Mainland Affairs Council. Soon after joining the Democratic Progressive Party (DPP), she was elected as a legislator and became vice premier of the government. After a shuffle of leaders above her, Tsai left her government position to serve as a chair of a biotechnology company for several years. In 2008, she returned to politics when she was elected the chair of the DPP. After an on-again/off-again relationship with the DPP chair position over the following years, the DPP won a majority of seats in the 2016 election with Tsai at the helm. It was then that she became the first female prime minister of Taiwan.

Katrín Jakobsdottir, *Prime Minister of Iceland* (2017–)
Recognized globally for her feminism and environmentalism, Jakobsdottir is the second woman to hold Iceland's prime minister position. As a student, she studied literature and, in one of her many relatable moments, focused her master's thesis on crime novels. In 2003, Jakobsdottir became the deputy chairperson for the Left-Green Movement, a position which she held until 2013 when she became the chairperson. After a scandal

involving her predecessor in 2017, she became the prime minister of a coalition government consisting of three Icelandic political parties.

Sanna Marin, *Prime Minister of Finland* (2019–2023)
The youngest of the group, Marin became prime minister of Finland at only 34 years old. Immediately after graduating from university, Marin jumped into politics by joining the Social Democratic Party. Within a few years, Marin won a council seat and became council leader. A few years later, she won a seat in parliament. She then held a position as transport and communication minister before the prime minister resigned and she won his job. Immediately after beginning her tenure as prime minister, Marin faced the COVID-19 crisis and later faced off with the contentious Vladmir Putin during Russia's war on Ukraine.

Angela Merkel, *Chancellor of Germany* (2005–2021)
A scientist by training, Merkel earned her PhD in quantum chemistry in 1986. She worked as a researcher until 1989 when she entered politics after the fall of the Berlin Wall. In the time leading up to the reunification of Germany, Merkel began her political career as part of the East German pro-democracy political party—Democratic Awakening. This party later became part of the Christian Democratic Union (CDU)—the party Merkel would soon lead. She quickly impressed many leaders in the party and was appointed as the minister for women and youth, minister for environment, and then general secretary of the party. In 2000, she became the first woman to hold the chairperson position for the CDU. In a tight 2005 election, the CDU and the Social Democratic Party formed a coalition government with Merkel as prime minister. Merkel went on to serve four terms as prime minister. In her 16 years as prime minister, Merkel oversaw the resolution of many crises, including the European migrant crisis, the 2007–2008 financial crisis, and COVID-19.

Mia Mottley, *Prime Minister of Barbados* (2018–)
Mottley earned her law degree from the London School of Economics. Before becoming Barbados's first female prime minister, Mottley held multiple government positions, including attorney general; deputy prime

minister; and minister of education, youth affairs, and culture. The year Mottley became prime minister, her party, the Barbados Labor Party, won in a landslide victory, winning all House seats and nearly 75 percent of the popular vote. After calling a snap election in 2022, she won her second term in office in yet another landslide victory for her party. In addition to leading Barbados, Mottley served as chairperson of the Caribbean Community (CARICOM) in 2020.

Erna Solberg, *Prime Minister of Norway* (2013–2021)
Solberg entered politics at the local level when she served on the Bergen City Council beginning in 1979. She went on to win a seat in the Norwegian parliament before serving as minister of local government and regional development. In this role, she tightened Norway's immigration policies and earned the nickname "Iron Erna." Solberg served as deputy party leader of the Conservative Party before becoming the party leader. In 2013, the Conservative Party won the general election and Solberg became Norway's second female prime minister.

Halimah Yacob, *President of Singapore* (2017–)
After more than a decade of practicing law, Yacob entered politics as an elected member of parliament in 2001. Over the next 10 to 15 years, she held multiple different roles in government, including minister of state for community development, youth, and sports; minister of state for social and family development; and speaker of parliament—the first woman to hold the speaker position in Singapore's history. In 2017, she gave up her positions to run for president. In that year, the presidency was reserved for an individual of Malay decent—an effort in the Singaporean system to encourage representation across different groups. Yacob was the only candidate on the ballot. As a result, her election as the first female president of Singapore is both historical and controversial.

Sahle-Work Zewde, *President of Ethiopia* (2018–)
When she won the election in 2018, Zewde became Ethiopia's fifth president as well as the first woman to hold the position. Her career is storied, with work in the Ministry of Education and the Ministry of Foreign

Affairs in the 1980s. She went on to serve as ambassador to Senegal, Djibouti, France, Tunisia, and Morocco. Zewde followed the ambassadorships with a permanent position as representative to the African Union and director general at the Ministry of Foreign Affairs. In 2009, she began her work with the United Nations, serving in multiple positions before becoming the first African woman to become United Nations secretary general. Zewde was also the first woman to serve as special representative to the African Union and head of the United Nations Office to the African Union.

Myths about Women in Leadership

In the days following November 5, 2020, the world held its collective breath as election officials counted the US presidential ballots. Some held their breath in hopes of a continuing Trump presidency, while others held their breath in hopes of change. But many held their breath in anticipation of the first woman, and woman of color, Kamala Harris, to serve as vice president of the United States.

When the media announced the Biden-Harris win days after Americans headed to the polls, friends, acquaintances, and influencers flooded my Instagram with images and stories of Harris in a rainbow bedazzled jacket, in her cool girl chucks, and her viral "I'm speaking" GIPHY from the vice presidential debate during which she interrupted the interrupting Mike Pence to finish her point. Women were excited. Admittedly, not all women were excited, as some stood staunchly against her beliefs. But many women, including some who voted against her, understood the gravity of her win, a gravity perhaps best represented by a glass-ceiling-inspired post that took over the Internet in the days following the election victory:

Make sure to wear shoes, ladies. There's glass everywhere.

Marilyn Loden, a management consultant, first coined the term *glass ceiling* in 1978. Loden was serving on a panel in which the conversation focused largely on women's deficits and the impact of these shortcomings on their careers. In opposition to other panelists, Loden challenged the notion that the problem lay with women. Instead, she argued, women face invisible social barriers—stereotypes, biases, systems, rules—that hold them back despite their best efforts.[1] If you've ever accidentally attempted to walk through a glass door (*guilty*), you know that glass is deceptively invisible. But after you smack your head on it, you can take a step back, laugh at yourself and then open the door. Much like that door, the glass ceiling is invisible. But unlike that door, it has no handle that removes the barrier and opens possibilities. Instead, the glass ceiling, the barriers, must be shattered before women can progress.

Harris may not have completely shattered the ceiling, as a woman has yet to hold the US presidency, but her win shattered it in a way never before seen. America had seen women run for the vice president's office as well as for the presidency, but the glass ceiling always held them back. Harris's win showed that a woman could not only run for the second-highest office in the country, but she could also win. Harris signaled to little girls and to women that becoming vice president is within their reach. She signaled to girls and women *of color* that they too can have a place in leadership. They too can aim to become vice president of the United States. Of course, girls and women may have believed so before the 2020 election, but Harris's win made the possibility tangible.

Time reported on the reaction to Harris's success, telling the story of Mira Sawlani-Joyner and her daughter:

> Mira Sawlani-Joyner, a 38-year-old pastor in Arlington, Va., recalls that when she first told her 7- and 8-year-old daughters how significant it would be if Harris became the first woman of color to be Vice President, her younger daughter immediately asked, "Does that mean I can be president?"[2]

Harris recognized the historic and important nature of her own win in her acceptance speech, noting that her win signaled the possibilities availability for little girls everywhere:

> While I may be the first woman in this office, I will not be the last, because every little girl watching tonight sees that this is a country of possibilities.
>
> —Kamala Harris

I remember my own response to watching her take the stage and listening to her speak. Seated in a bar, sharing celebratory margaritas with friends, we raised our salt-rimmed glasses, cheering to progress. My eyes welled up with tears. I could physically feel the power that her win gave me and women like me. In that moment, I thought, *I can do anything.*

In retrospect, I probably had had a few too many margaritas.

A similar effect has been seen with other women ascending to positions of power. For example, during Jacinda Ardern's campaign in 2017, women approached her during town halls to express their admiration. To many New Zealand women and girls, Ardern was, and remains, an inspiration.

Although Harris had smashed that vice presidential glass and opened possibilities in the eyes of little girls, women, and certainly myself, I still question my response. Yes, her win is undeniably historic and important. But as I reflect on my rather dramatic (or perhaps drunken) response that night, I have to question, *Can I do anything?*

Progress has certainly been made, but the United States has still not seen a woman occupy the presidency. If we look more broadly, we see that the number of women holding top leadership positions is increasing, but the top remains a relatively lonely place. As of 2017, only 36 percent of countries have had at least one woman serve as head of state.[3] In 2022, 30 women served as head of state or head of government across 28 countries. More generally, women held 21 percent of ministerial positions across the globe with the most common positions for women in these positions focusing on family, social affairs, the environment, and "women's issues."[4] Although this marks progress, UN Women[4] argues that at the current rate, gender equality in the top governmental positions (e.g., head of state) will not be reached until 2150. Slightly more hopeful, they suggest that gender parity may be reached in ministerial positions in 2077.

In the United States, Harris remains the sole woman to win the vice presidency and join the ranks of an extremely limited number of women who have run in a primary presidential election. As of summer 2021, women make up a mere 23.7 percent of the US Congress, 18 percent of US governorships, and 25 percent of Fortune 500 board seats. In 2021, *Forbes* ran the headline "The Female CEOs on This Year's Fortune 500 Just Broke Three All-Time Records." *Exciting*! The actual record break, however, was not quite as revolutionary as the headline promised—the number of women holding CEO positions in Fortune 500 companies jumped from 7.4 percent to 8.1 percent in 2020—an increase of less than 1 percent.[5]

These numbers don't match up to the heralded attention that women in leadership received in response to COVID-19. This begs the question, *Why? Why aren't there more women in leadership positions?*

Women still face a number of staunchly engrained beliefs that influence how they act, how others respond to them, and the policies and systems that guide decision making and action. If we want to understand why there still isn't "glass everywhere," why women may *choose* not to pursue leadership positions, and why others *refuse* to accept women as leaders, we must start by acknowledging these beliefs. And if we want to see women progress to the upper echelons of leadership and to experience more equitable futures, we must constantly work to overturn these beliefs.

I must admit, I find it difficult to discuss these beliefs, as I wholeheartedly want to believe that they no longer exist. When I hear or think of them, they elicit a visceral eyeroll (*which I have attempted to temper throughout the following pages, but alas, one or two may have snuck in*). But the fact remains, these beliefs are real, they persist, and they impact the careers and lives of women around the world.

Myth 1: Women are not qualified for leadership positions

As Dwight from *The Office* would say: "False."

Multiple points dispel this myth. Let's start with education. Women have out-earned men in educational degrees at every level since 2010,[6,7] with a nearly 60/40 percent split. But this is not new—in the United States, women have earned more bachelor's degrees than men since 1981.[8] If we look to specific fields, women aren't just outnumbering men in the traditional "lady fields" such as nursing and education. Even in business, a field historically dominated by men, women are closing the gap. For example, the top 50 US MBA programs are approaching gender parity, as women now make up 40 percent of students.[9,10]

Education? Check.

But do they have the *skills* necessary to lead?

In 2011, Jack Zenger and Joseph Folkman were interested in whether women and men differed in the skills necessary for successful leadership. As consultants, Zenger and Folkman had access to a researcher's dream—spreadsheets of data about real leaders. Specifically, they obtained performance ratings for 7,280 leaders from the leaders' peers, supervisors, and direct reports. Of the leaders included, 36 percent were women and 36 percent were from outside of the United States. These leaders were rated on 16 competencies important for leadership, including task initiative, drive, inspiration, problem solving, communication, and building relationships. Women scored higher than men in 12 of the 16 competencies that were rated. In addition to scoring high on competencies stereotypically expected of women (e.g., building relationships), these women also scored higher than the men in more stereotypically masculine competencies, such as drive for results and taking initiative.[11] In 2019, the research duo repeated this work with a new crop of leaders and found the same pattern—women are as competent, and often perceived as *more* competent, in leadership than men.[12]

Myth 2: Women aren't ambitious enough for leadership
eyeroll

Research repeatedly shows that women begin their careers with just as much ambition as men, and while not all women want to hold positions of leadership (just as not all men desire to be leaders), many women do! In a longitudinal study, The Boston Consulting Group looked closely at the ambition levels of 200,000 leaders over the span of their careers.[13] They found that, at the outset women and men reported similar levels of ambition. However, as careers progressed, a chasm between men's and women's ambitions grew. As women's careers progressed, their ambitions typically declined—a pattern not observed with men. An oft-used explanation for the later ambition gap focuses on the changing roles of women. Women, some people argue, shift their ambitions from careers to children, leaving them less interested in pursuing leadership positions. However, the researchers ruled out this explanation when they found no significant differences in ambition between women who are mothers and those who are not. Instead, the data revealed that company culture and support for diversity influenced the emergence of a gender ambition gap. Specifically, in organizations with cultures supportive of diversity and that reflected this support in their policies, women reported higher levels of ambition later in their careers compared to women at organizations that lacked this support.

To bring this full circle, yes, women are as ambitious as men, but that ambition can be hampered by external organizational forces working against them as well as by complex societal expectations as to what a woman's ambition should look like.

Myth 3: Women's hormones make them unfit for leadership roles
Babies! Periods! Hot flashes! Oh, my!

Yes, women do experience unique biological activities that differ from those that men experience. Biology, however, is not the focus of this book. What is relevant to this book is work by scholars Alicia Grandey, Allison Gabriel, and Eden King, discussing how women's natural biological processes intersect with workplace expectations.[14] The researchers focus on three experiences: menstruation, maternity, and menopause, and argue that they are currently incompatible with workplace expectations.

While maternity in the workplace regularly receives media and public attention, we discuss menstruation and menopause at work with much less frequency. As noted by Grandey et al., however, both can similarly impact women's rise to leadership.[14] For instance, signs of menstruation and menopause are often viewed unfavorably in the workplace and may even be a source of ridicule. However, much of the perceived negative effects associated with menstruation and menopause stem from debunked yet persistent myths. For example, a mainstay critique of Hilary Clinton during her first run for the democratic nomination against Barack Obama in 2008 goes something like this: "What will happen when she has her period? Will she just nuke a country because she's angry?"

Although there are many, MANY problems with this statement, the most obvious problem is that the underlying principle is patently untrue. Women's moods do not vary in line with stereotypical menstrual cycle expectations.[15] *Nope.* And the best part (my absolute favorite part) is that men's moods varied just as much as women's! Worrying about the impact of a woman's menstrual cycle on her mood is a useless endeavor.

If, as the study suggests, men experience slightly larger fluctuations in moods than women, perhaps we would be better served worrying about men's moods. *But I digress.*

Menstrual cycles have also been inappropriately linked to decreased competency. Once again, however, research generally found no support for the relationship between cognitive performance and a woman's menstrual cycle.[16,17] Grandy and colleagues (2019) report similar patterns of incongruity between false beliefs about pregnancy and menopause and workplace performance.[14]

These false beliefs and inappropriate stigmas have led to the institutionalization of male-dominant workplace expectations and policies that are incompatible with the realities of being a woman. In response, women are systematically held back from leadership positions when they are otherwise capable. And by failing to make these still taboo topics central to workplace discussions, we continue to force out and remove highly capable, competent, and qualified women from the leadership talent pool simply for being women.

Is it a woman's fault that her biology is incompatible with our beliefs about leadership? Or is a biased and failed system to blame? *I'm team failed system.*

Myth 4: Women don't stick their necks out there for promotions

Historically, research suggested that women do not negotiate as frequently as men. Research conducted with MBA graduates in 2007 found that a quarter of men negotiated their offers, while only an eighth of women negotiated their offers.[18] This, and similar laboratory studies, have fueled the argument that women don't advance and that they don't earn equal pay because they don't ask for it. As business reviews and other news outlets heralded these claims across their front pages, this led to the generally held belief that women simply do not negotiate. These research findings are still being reported by top business news outlets today. For a recent reputable example, see *Harvard Business Review*'s "Why Women Don't Negotiate Their Job Offers." *(But don't bother looking it up because, spoiler alert, we are about to discover that this view is no longer correct!)*

Women responded to this misperception with a resounding *We can fix this*; giving birth to an entire industry now dedicated to supporting women in the negotiation process, empowering them with the tools to be good negotiators. Many of these programs are backed by scientific evidence demonstrating that certain circumstances improve the likelihood of women engaging in negotiations as well as the success of these negotiations.[19]

However, Artz, Goodall, and Oswald used the 2013–2014 Australian Workplace Relations Study, which includes all employees and workplaces in Australia, to examine how frequently men and women report attempts to negotiate for a better wage or promotion and whether these efforts were successful.[20] The data used in this study differs from data used in previous work in a number of important ways, including that the researchers were able to directly compare men's and women's negotiation attempts and successes within an organization. This allowed the researchers to eliminate potential alternative explanations driven by a specific workplace or industry. What they found is critical: women *do* negotiate just as frequently as men do, but women are less likely to be granted their requests.

Let me say that again for the people in the back: Women negotiate just as frequently as men do, but women are less likely to be granted their requests.

Each of these beliefs drives a larger narrative that the lack of women in leadership is a *woman's* problem. If she were just a little more educated, a little more prepared, a little more competent, a little more ambitious, a little less biologically woman, and a little more of a negotiator, then she would have earned that role. Come on, women! What are you waiting for? If you make these six lifestyle changes, you too can become a successful leader!

But as we've seen, women are just as educated, prepared, competent, and ambitious as men—and often more so. What, then, drives the lack of women in leadership?

The issue of why there are so few women in power can be traced back to engrained gender biases—biases held by both men *and* women. Much of the research on gender bias in leadership was initiated by Alice Eagly, a professor at Northwestern University. Her work largely revolves around the entanglement of gender and two attributes: agency and communion. Agency encapsulates several different qualities but generally refers to one's competence, confidence, dominance, and competitiveness,[21,22] traits typically associated with conceptualizations of effective leadership. In contrast, communion refers to more people-centric traits such as consideration for others, warmth, and bringing people together. Communal traits historically have not been associated with leadership, although that notion is changing.

The problem, of course, is that gender stereotypes drive the expectation that women demonstrate communality and men demonstrate agency. Because of these stereotypes, we are more likely to view men as leaders than we are to view women as leaders. A self-perpetuating cycle develops in which organizational systems, such as promotion expectations, encode these stereotypes and reward agency over communion. Consequently, more men than women are promoted to leadership.

One might logically propose that women should simply be more agentic, breaking the stereotype and the link between gender and leadership. Seems reasonable on the surface—so reasonable, in fact, that scientists tested this idea.

Results from the research, however, showed that women who displayed agentic traits were viewed unfavorably.[23] An oft cited reason for this negative reaction to women's agency, is that they are not meeting their communal responsibilities. In other words, more agentic women are "not nice enough"—a popular criticism of women in leadership around the globe.

Interested in how perceptions may have shifted over the years, Eagly and her colleagues examined US opinion polls on gender stereotypes from 1946 to 2018.[24] The polls included data from more than 30,000 US adults, providing a compellingly large sample of viewpoints over seven decades. In contrast to the early study that so strongly tied agency with men and communality with women, the 2020 study found that we now expect both men and women in leadership to possess agentic qualities. That's one check in the win column for women's progress! However, while our gendered expectations of agency have changed over the years, our expectations of communality have unfortunately remained the same. We still expect men to simply display agentic qualities, but we now expect women to be both agentic and communal. Men even receive a favorability boost when they engage in communal actions. But women don't receive the same bonus.[25] Instead, it is simply expected of women to be both agentic and communal if they are to be perceived as effective leaders.

Let's see what this looks like in action with ambition. Interested in the attributions of ambition regarding women in leadership, researchers analyzed press articles from the five days immediately following the election of Julia Gillard, Australia's first female prime minister, elected in 2010. In their review of the press's discourse surrounding Gillard and her ascent to power, the researchers found a familiar pattern: the press repeatedly raised problems with her ambition. Some of the press even made direct reference to the unfeminine nature of this ambition, stating, "A lot of people, including many women, were upset at Gillard's action in tapping Rudd, describing it as brutal and unpalatable. They expected a more genteel transition for Australia's first female prime minister."[26]

Evidence of a communal ambition also arose in Hall and Donaghue's analysis. Some of the press reporting on Gillard's ascent implied that she demonstrated the appropriate type of ambition *for a woman*—she was ambitious, but she waited her turn and did not demonstrate the "kind of naked ambition that defined Kevin Rudd before he got the job"—and that she "demurred, until the inevitable eventuated and the party's wise men and union and factional chiefs came calling." In other words, while she may have had ambitions for leadership, she did not overstep. She waited her turn "like a lady." *eyeroll*

"Act like a man" was, and largely remains, a dominant narrative in this space. Many leadership interventions focus on improving women's confidence, providing trainings in agile decision making, and course after course on leadership development to give women the skills they need to be effective leaders. Intentionally or not, *Lean In*, the popular book by Sheryl Sandberg in which she argues that women should "assert themselves," also falls into the category. To be a good leader, women must *lean in* to masculinized conceptions of leadership. Be confident. Dominate. Compete.

When I was living in Dallas in the late twenty teens, I met an outstanding woman who was working to improve the executive space for women. During one of our lunches together in the garden of Saint Anne

Restaurant, she shared one of her coaching stories. She explained that one of her executive clients recently brought the first woman onto his company's executive board. Although she brought diversity to the board-room, he had concerns that her thinking was not aligned with that of the rest of the group. He needed help, he explained, aligning her thinking to that of the other members.

If he wanted her to think like the others, was it diversity he really wanted? Or was it a "skirt" that thought like the men that he wanted? Although he explicitly stated that he sought diversity, he did not, in fact, want diversity at all. He wanted a woman, but only one who thought like the men. By making a woman act and think like the men on a team, we fail to leverage her unique perspective, her skills, her diversity. I fear this happens more frequently than one might hope—an overt statement that supports making space for women at the table, only to make them lean in so far that the team loses the unique value they offered in the first place.

But does teaching women to act like men actually work? Will it release her from the boundaries that womanhood places on her leadership prospects? To put it simply, *no*. When women act like men in leadership, they are not viewed more favorably and they are not more likely to be promoted. *But they are more likely to be called a bitch*. Further, companies lose out on the benefit of having a woman's perspective in the first place.

Another solution has been to focus on the "leaky pipeline," or the idea that not enough women are in positions at lower levels to justify parity in the upper echelons. Some have argued that there simply aren't enough trained women in the relevant field to create a sufficient flow of women into higher positions. This argument is most readily observed in STEM (science, technology, engineering, and mathematics) fields where women are historically and persistently held back. In the US tech industry, for example, women make up only 27 percent of the workforce.[27,28] What's more, white women make up approximately 14 percent, leaving Asian, Black, and Latinx women combined to make up the remaining 14 percent of the tech workforce. Similar numbers are seen when we look globally, with 29 percent of the STEM workforce being women.[29]

If the pipeline is the problem, then we simply need to unclog it! If we increase the number of women in these fields, then over time, we should see an increase in the number of women advancing into leadership positions. *Ta da!*

To some extent, we do see this transformation taking place. The number of women earning STEM degrees and entering the STEM workforce continues to steadily increase. However, women who do make it into the workforce often face a labyrinth of blatant sexism, sexual harassment, and sometimes assault in their pursuit. A report by Girls Inc. found that these types of behaviors begin early. In their survey of teen engineers, Girls Inc. found that girls reported instances of sexual harassment as early as their interview for an internship, leading many of the girls to decide that a tech career wasn't for them.[30] Further down the pipeline, we see instances of sexual harassment running rampant in the tech industry made famous in reports by women such as Ellen Pao when she sued Kleiner Perkins for gender discrimination and Meredith Whittaker who led a walkout in protest of Google's sexual harassment policies and response.[31,32] Research supports the idea that male-dominated, hierarchical cultures such as tech and medicine typically spawn these types of harassment cultures.[33] The inherent power imbalances of hierarchical organizations create an environment in which those in power use harassment as a tool to flex their power and remind those with less power who is in control. This hierarchical structure similarly keeps those lower in the hierarchy from reporting the harassing behavior. As such, women who want to advance in these cultures often face a barrage of physical and mental assaults.

To truly unclog the pipeline, we must examine why we have a pipeline problem in the first place. To recall an early question, is the pipeline problem a woman's problem, or is it a system problem?

We see the hoped-for effect of the pipeline solution predominantly for men entering stereotypical "women's work" at a rapid pace not observed for women entering stereotypical "men's work." The phenomenon known as the *glass escalator*, originally noted in 1992 by Christine Williams at the University of Texas at Austin, represents the quick advancement of men into leadership positions in "feminized" fields. Williams analyzed the themes emerging from a series of interviews conducted with 99 nurses, elementary school teachers, librarians, and social care workers between 1985 and 1991. She found a curious pattern. In these traditionally female-dominated roles, there was often an explicit preference for men, and these men were expected to advance in their careers.[34] Men joining these professions hopped on a glass escalator to promotion. When women enter traditionally male-dominated fields, however, we do not see an escalator, elevator, stairs, or even a damn step stool!

So, when do women become leaders? Under what conditions might we see them valued?

Michelle Ryan and Alexander Haslam suggest that women are often placed into leadership positions during difficult times or times of crisis. They termed this phenomenon "the glass cliff."[35,36] This theory first arose following an article in *The Times*,[37] which claimed that women in leadership had a negative impact on UK company performance. Researchers Ryan and Haslam at the University of Exeter were intrigued.[35] In their article, they point out many technical problems with the analysis conducted in *The Times'* piece—the biggest problem being that she didn't report any analysis. They argued instead for an alternative hypothesis. A negative correlation between women on boards and company performance could mean that women were causing the bad performance, but it was equally as likely that bad performance was causing the appointment of women to leadership positions. While *The Times* claimed the chicken, the researchers claimed the egg.[37]

To investigate this relationship further, Ryan and Haslam looked at share price performance of Financial Times Stock Exchange (FTSE) 100 companies—the same data examined in The Times article. But in their research, Ryan and Judge identified dates during which a new board member—male or female—was appointed. They then looked at the relationship between the addition of a new board member and company performance immediately before and immediately following this appointment. By doing so, the researchers were able to account for previous performance before the board member's appointment as well as for any *change* in performance following the appointment. They found evidence for the latter causal relationship: poorer performance was leading to the appointment of women to top positions.

Since this initial study, other researchers have replicated and extended this work. Some of the most convincing evidence for the glass cliff comes from a 2020 meta-analysis.[38] In their analyses, the researchers found strong evidence of the glass cliff effect, arguing that compared to white men, women and people of color are more likely to be placed in leadership positions during times of crisis.

Classic cases of the glass cliff can be seen in business. For example, Yahoo!, once an Internet giant, was nearing extinction when the board voted to appoint Marissa Mayer as CEO. Similarly, Carly Fiorina was brought in to usher in a new era for Hewlett-Packard, only to be labeled "one of the worst CEOs of her era."[39] But wait—there's more! JC Penney appointed Jill Soltau as CEO in 2018 as the company struggled through mall and box store closures. There's Meg Whitman at Hewlett-Packard, Mary Barra at General Motors, and Andrea Jung at Avon. Importantly, not all women appointed to these precarious positions fall off the cliff— some manage to hang on and dazzle in the process.

In the global political sphere, Ardern provides one such example. In Madeleine Chapman's biography of Ardern, she recounts Ardern's rise as the Labour Party's leader. At the time, the Labour Party was run by Andrew Little and was, in not so subtle terms, going down in flames. The party was polling the worst it had in its history. Approximately 8 weeks before the election, Little stepped down—and Ardern stepped up. Chapman writes, "Little stepping down looked like a desperate attempt from Labour to save the furniture. No matter who was leader, it was too late to turn around their polling. But someone like Ardern; young, energetic, fresh, may be able to shake things up just enough to save face. It looked like a desperate move, and one that may sacrifice her in the process" (p. 81).[40]

In other words, she was doomed. But Ardern shocked her party and her country by delivering positive results under impossible conditions. Although the Labour Party did not win a majority of the government that year, they far outperformed their initial expectations. New Zealand has a mixed-member proportional system, meaning every eligible New Zealander votes for their preferred candidate as well as their preferred party. Under this system, smaller parties can gain a larger number of seats compared to a straight vote. And in 2017, the distribution of results meant that no party would be able to govern without forming a coalition government with another party. After 3 weeks of debate and negotiations, the result was in: the New Zealand First Party and the Labour Party would form a coalition government with Jacinda Ardern at the helm.

The question I often ask when reading about the glass cliff is, What differentiates the women who fall off the cliff from those who hang on? The answer begins with a look at how these women make it to the upper echelons of leadership in the first place. When looking at women who do make it to the top, one commonality that consistently emerges is women's preparation. (That's your cue for the next chapter).

Preparation

When my husband and I first started dating, he surprised me with a trip to India (*this is obviously the moment I knew he was a keeper*). Although we were both living in Dallas at the time, he was working in London that week and had told me to board a flight from Texas and meet him at Heathrow. When I saw him at the airport, he explained, he'd share our next destination. Aside from the logistical nightmare of trying to pack for an unknown destination (and early on in a dating relationship, no less), I beamed with excitement. *Was I in a modern romance movie?*

After a short wait at Heathrow's UK border, the stern immigration officer stamped my passport and I crossed into the country to find Chris standing near the British Airways check-in desk. We walked over to the flight time board and he said, "Our flight leaves around 7:30 p.m. So, where are we going?"

I scanned the board and found four flights around that time—one scheduled back to America (*nope*), two scheduled to Europe (*maybe*), and one scheduled to New Dehli (*gasp!*). My eyes brightened and nearly burst out of the sockets as I turned to him and asked, "India?" He gently smiled with the subdued excitement characteristic of the Brits. In complete antithesis to his response, I dramatically and Americanly jumped at him, thinking I was Natalie and Chris was the prime minister at the end of *Love Actually* (a much less romantic moment without the swelling background music).

Having lived in India for 3 years, Chris knew exactly where to go, what to do, and where to stay. We spent a little over a week traveling through New Delhi, Udaipur, Jaipur, Agra, and Mumbai. During our visit to Jaipur, we stayed in one of the most magnificent hotels: Obaroi Japuir Villas. As we sipped our welcome drinks in the hotel lobby, the staff informed us that our room had been upgraded and we would be staying in one of the hotel's unique tents. This tent was pure luxury—including a king-size bed, a shower, a bathtub, closet space, and a sitting area. Can you say #roughingit?

Our first night, I awoke in our tent to a lost cat aggressively meowing at the door. *I'm jetlagged, cat! Shut up!* The cat proceeded to meow like a screeching violin for the next hour.

At some point, the cat quieted down and I fell back to sleep, awaking the next morning moderately rested.

Rolling over cumbersomely I asked, "Did you hear that cat last night?"

"Cat? No. Are you sure you heard a cat?"

"It was so loud; how could you not hear it?"

"Are you sure it was a cat?"

"Of course I'm sure it was a cat. I'm not an idiot, I know what a cat sounds like."

Unfortunately, dear reader, whenever I utter the words "I'm not an idiot," it usually turns out that I am, in fact, an idiot. And this was no exception.

Later in the day, I heard the same cat meowing in what can only be described as complete agony.

"There it is! That's the cat! Do you think it's okay? Should we tell someone?" I said, half concerned/half smug, now vindicated because there was obviously a wailing cat on the premises.

Chris laughed. "Kelsey. That's a peacock."

"THAT IS A CAT!" I nearly yelled.

Narrator: it was a peacock.

If you have never heard a peacock before, I assure you that they sound very similar to an ailing cat. But don't just take my word for it. Open your favorite search engine and type "cat peacock sound." (*Please do this now so I feel better about myself. Thank you.*) You will quickly see that I'm not alone in confusing these disparate animals.

To the point, it turns out that the cat whining at our tent door in the middle of the night was, in fact, a peacock. And as we toured the hotel grounds for the first time the next day, it became abundantly clear why my cat assumption was so obviously flawed—dozens of peacocks roamed the hotel grounds. They strutted across the garden, roosted on walls overlooking the fountain, and poked their beaks toward passersby. One morning, while we sat having breakfast in the private garden surrounding our tent, a peacock approached our table, eyes locked on my croissant. *Back off, bird.*

I tell this story mostly because I love peacocks. And India. But the secondary motive for telling this story is that I will eventually relate it back to leadership. Just stay with me a little longer.

Peacocks are some of the flashiest birds strutting the earth. Nothing compares to watching a peacock spot a peahen and unfurl its hidden feathered buttress to reveal a royal spectrum of blues and greens. They use this unparalleled beauty to attract attention, enticing peahens with their presence, their towering feathers, and their unfaltering swagger. They are shameless self-promoters, gliding by the peahens with their intoxicating beauty.

In stark contrast to this majestic peacock experience stands an enlightening moment in Queensland, Australia. In early 2020, my husband and I booked a room at an all-inclusive lodge in the secluded Swanfels hills. Our trip coincided with the disastrous fires raging at the beginning of the new year. The fires in Queensland, however, had largely passed—a fact evident as we drove through the windy, unbeaten path to the hotel, surrounded by scorched trees and debris.

One morning, we strolled through the crisped hills on a guided "walkabout," learning about the native plants and animals, as well as the importance of environmental protection to prevent fires like the ones Australia was experiencing at the time. We meandered through the acres of property, and I spotted a wallaby with a joey in her pouch, bounding away into the wooded forest.

As Chris and I walked back to our room after our walkabout, he stopped and pointed out a pile of sticks and trash lying beneath a tree. I snarked about how disrespectful some people can be by leaving their trash on the ground when Chris cut me off.

"It's a bower!"

"A what?"

He oohed and ahhed with intrigue, leaving me baffled and waiting for an explanation as to why this pile of garbage commanded our time.

"What is it?" I asked again.

"It's a bower," he stated, as if in the last two seconds I had come to know what that meant.

After his intrigue died down a bit and we approached this mysterious bower, he continued: "A bower is a structure that male bower birds build to attract a mate. They build it with sticks, and then they collect stuff in their favorite color and put it in the bower."

"They collect stuff?" I asked, intrigued.

"Yes, every bower bird has a favorite color, and they will find things in that color and bring them back to their bower."

"That's cool!" I said, using my extensive professor vocabulary.

"They can be difficult to spot because they hide them away." This particular bower was hidden at the base of a tree surrounded by bushes. "But this is definitely a bower. You can tell by the shape of the structure." The shape looked as if Moses had parted a sea of sticks that were now standing erect on either side of the barren ground to allow for safe passage. "And the collection of, basically trash, all in the same color. See? It's all blue!"

He went on to explain that not only do bower birds build these structures and collect these objects to attract potential mates, but they also do a special dance. Akin to a Saturday night at your local club, the bower bird shows off his smooth moves to attract the female passing by.

Had Chris not known what this structure represented, I would have walked past that tree disappointed in humanity (*again*) for our careless disregard for recycling and proper trash disposal. Thankfully, however, he is a bit of a bird nerd (more formally referred to as a *twitcher*) and enlightened me on the structural result of a small bird's hard work and impressive effort.

Now, unlike the peacock, many bower birds are not particularly pretty. Much like their bowers, you may likely disregard them as just another "generic bird" with little that makes them special. In doing so, you might miss (as I almost did) arguably one of the most interesting birds in the world.

The intrigue of a bower bird is much more subtle than that of the peacock, at least to the unfamiliar eye. Where the peacock shamelessly flashes its feathers and captivates safari goers and zoo attendees alike, the bower bird's effort may go unnoticed or, perhaps worse, be mistaken for a worthless pile of trash. It's not until you dig deeper and reexamine their structures that a bower bird's value and worth are revealed.

We see a similar dichotomy in human leaders. *(See? I told you this was relevant. Congratulations on your commitment to this chapter.)* You likely know a peacock leader—someone who shamelessly promotes themselves, rubbing their feathers in your face to attract attention. You likely also know a bower bird leader, someone whose talents frequently go unrecognized and overlooked. The peacock in your office captivates attention with their gravitas, while the bower bird works tirelessly with little notice. We might describe the office peacock as charismatic, as a strong presence, or as a natural leader. In contrast, the bower bird might be described as lacking potential, as bland, or even as forgettable.

Despite our initial attraction to peacocks, there's a growing narrative around the importance of not falling for the allure of peacock leaders. For starters, peacocks may look and sound like a leader, but there exists a deep chasm between who *looks* like a leader and who can in fact lead. Because of our stereotypes of leaders as confident, assertive, and charismatic, we implicitly believe that peacocks will make good leaders. These stereotypes then influence our decisions to listen to, to hire, to promote, to follow, and to vote for peacocky leaders.

These leaders are engaging, captivating. They often leave us feeling inspired. Further, a peacock's confidence and charisma will also make their desire for leadership more obvious. Confident that they are destined for greatness, they likely make their ambitions for leadership known. Because of these traits, these leaders both opt in to and are selected for leadership more frequently than their non-peacock counterparts.

However, just because we are more likely to *see* these individuals as leaders and they are more likely to promote themselves as leaders does not mean they actually make *effective* leaders. If you have been or are a leader, you know that leadership involves much more than showing off your feathers.

The formal definition of leadership according to scholars reads as follows.

Leadership: The process of influencing followers to achieve a shared goal.[1]

There are three critical components to this definition: influence, followers, and shared goal. Let's start with *influence*. When it comes to peacock leaders, their charisma and confidence help them assert their influence. Because we are naturally drawn to these leaders, they easily influence us. In some instances, a leader's confidence may blind us to their words or actions—leading us to rely solely on their presence rather than on their actual substance to draw conclusions about them. In this way, peacock leaders can influence us with their style and approach and not necessarily their message. That's not to say that all peacock leaders lack substance but rather that their substance (or lack thereof) can be obscured by their style.

The second important aspect of this definition is that leaders must have *followers*. Without followers, there is no one to lead, and therefore, an individual is likely just influencing their own behavior rather than the behavior of others. For peacocks, amassing an audience is another condition that they easily meet due to our tendency to quickly associate them with leadership. Our stereotypes of a leader allow peacocks to build a following relatively easily.

The final component, a *shared goal*, reminds us that leaders have an objective. Leaders must achieve something. *Shared* implies that followers also want to see this goal to fruition. As such, leadership focuses on achieving something for the greater good of the group—not just of oneself. This is where peacock leaders become problematic. Achieving an objective takes a complex set of skills that extends far beyond those necessary for influencing and amassing followers. It requires problem solving, decision making, planning, and creativity. And to recognize and achieve an objective that aligns with follower interests, not just self-interests, takes awareness and selflessness.

Peacock leaders can possess both the confidence that attracts us to them and the competence necessary to lead effectively. The problem, however, is that our tendency to be captivated by their confident feathered displays distracts us from asking important questions about their capabilities and skills for the role. We notice their confidence at the expense of competence. It's one of the reasons charismatic leaders are historically so dangerous. We focus on their style to the point that we miss their message, allowing them the power to lead us astray if left unchecked.

Researchers term this phenomenon the *confidence heuristic*. Broadly, a heuristic refers to a mental shortcut that is used to represent a belief or relationship. Heuristics are generally oversimplified understandings that allow us to quickly make judgments or decisions. In the case of the confidence heuristic, we use confidence as a sign of a person's competence, leading us to interpret confident leaders as effective or credible.[2,3] In contrast to this heuristic, other scholars have argued that unwarranted confidence, or holding confidence when one does not possess the appropriate knowledge or accuracy to justify that confidence, can backfire and result in decreased perceptions of credibility. This competing idea is known as the *calibration hypothesis*, which states that confidence uncalibrated to one's competence will result in negative outcomes.

Researchers compared these two ideas and their impact on our perceptions of a leader's message, specifically looking at perceptions of accuracy and persuasiveness. In their first study, researchers asked participants to view photos of individuals and estimate their weight.[4] After entering the estimated weight, participants were given advice from a third party regarding an approximation of the same individual's weight. The advice given by the third party varied in both accuracy and confidence. Participants heard from either someone highly confident giving accurate or inaccurate advice or from someone with low confidence giving accurate or inaccurate advice. For instance, advice could be, "I'm 95 percent confident [high confidence] that this 3-year-old child weighs 250 pounds [inaccurate]." Or, "I'm 40 percent confident [low confidence] that this 30-year-old woman weighs 130 pounds [accurate]." Participants were then asked to re-estimate the weight of the individual in the picture. After participants submitted the final weight estimate, the factual weight of the individual was revealed. Participants were then asked to rate the perceived accuracy of the advisor.

Overall, the results from the first study showed that participants rated those who were more accurate as more credible and those with high accuracy and high confidence as the most credible. However, results for those low-accuracy advisors are extremely important here. Advisors whose confidence aligned with their accuracy (i.e., low confidence/low accuracy) were viewed as more credible compared to those whose confidence and accuracy were not aligned (i.e., high confidence/low accuracy). For those of you who, like me, need help visualizing this, see Graph 1.

Based on this data, the calibration hypothesis is correct. Individuals whose confidence is appropriately aligned with their ability are viewed more favorably than those whose confidence is not aligned with their ability. From a leadership perspective, this tells us that leaders who are overconfident with respect to their own abilities may be viewed less favorably, potentially reducing their effectiveness.

The researchers also looked at how much the participants changed their estimates after receiving advice. They used the change in weight estimates as a proxy measurement for how persuasive the advisor had been. In contrast to perceptions of accuracy, an advisor's confidence did not significantly influence the advisor's persuasiveness.

If this were the end of the story, you might conclude that you won't fall for leaders who display unwarranted confidence—which is so obvious that you might think this whole chapter was unnecessary. But wait! Luckily, the researchers asked follow-up questions, and you haven't wasted your time reading about peacocks.

In the second study, researchers repeated the same series of events: view pictures, guess the weight, receive advice, re-estimate weight. This time,

Credibility

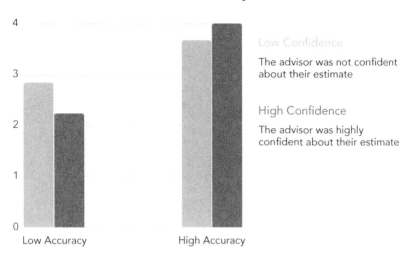

Low Confidence

The advisor was not confident about their estimate

High Confidence

The advisor was highly confident about their estimate

Graph 1. Advisors whose confidence aligned with their accuracy were viewed as more credible compared to those whose confidence and accuracy were not aligned. Data sources from Sah, D. Moore, and R. MacCoun, "Cheap Talk and Credibility: The Consequences of Confidence and Accuracy on Advisor Credibility and Persuasiveness," *Organizational Behavior and Human Decision Processes 121*(2), 2013.

however, after guessing the weight for a second time, participants were either (A) told that the advisor was correct, (B) given no information about the advisor's accuracy, or (C) informed that they could "pay" for feedback on the advisor's accuracy. For those who received feedback regarding advisor accuracy (group A), the results were similar to those seen in study 1, again suggesting that the calibration hypothesis is correct: we find those with confidence levels aligned with their competence more compelling.

However, when participants received no information regarding the accuracy of the advisor (group B), participants viewed highly confident advisors as more credible than advisors with low confidence—regardless of their actual accuracy. They were also more persuaded by high-confidence advisors than by low-confidence advisors (see Graph 2). This finding tells us that in the absence of information regarding a leader's accuracy, we are more likely to equate confidence with competence!

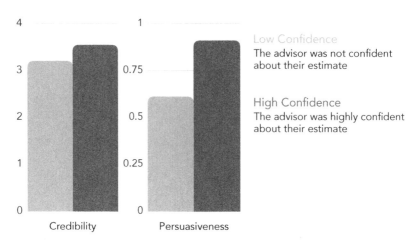

Graph 2. When participants received no feedback regarding the advice given, they were more persuaded by high-confidence advisors than by low-confidence advisors, regardless of their accuracy. Data sourced from: S. K. Carpenter, M. M. Wilford, N. Kornell, et al. "Appearances Can Be Deceiving: Instructor Fluency Increases Perceptions of Learning without Increasing Actual Learning. *Psychonomic Bulletin & Review 20*, 1350–1356 (2013).

To complete the story, we must also consider group C: those who could "pay" for feedback. Participants bought feedback more frequently when they received advice from advisors with low confidence (53%) compared to when they received advice from high confidence advisors (35%). But advisor *accuracy* did not influence how frequently the participants bought feedback. The real driver of "fact checking" was confidence!

Together, these studies provide several important insights regarding how we engage with high- and low-confidence leaders. First, if we have information about the calibration of their competence and confidence, a leader's overconfidence may backfire. In the absence of information of a leader's competence and confidence calibration, however, we are likely to interpret confidence as competence.

Second, results on paying for feedback tell us that we are less likely to question confident leaders. As followers often do not have detailed information on a leader's competence or knowledge, this is troublesome. In a crisis such as COVID-19, where information rapidly evolves and leaders require multiple types of knowledge to manage the crisis, it can be particularly difficult for a follower to interpret a leader's accuracy and effectiveness. Given the nature of a crisis, we may be inclined to following peacocks—relying on their confidence as a sign that they know how to navigate the situation.

Adding to this, overconfident leaders may breed overconfidence in their followers. In another research study, researchers asked participants to watch a video in which the lecturer either displayed confident characteristics (e.g., stood upright, made eye contact) or lacked these characteristics (e.g., hunched, relied on notes).[5] Participants then reported how much of the information they expected to recall. Those who watched the confident lecturer expected to recall more information compared to those who watched the less confident lecturer. However, when examining the actual amount of information recalled, researchers found no significant differences between the two groups. If we extend this finding to leaders, we might expect that highly confident leaders will similarly breed confidence in their followers. To a point, this may be beneficial for motivating followers to accomplish a task. But taken to the extreme, a group of overconfident yet undercompetent individuals led by an overconfident yet undercompetent leader can wreak havoc.

In this way, by falling for confidence, we set ourselves up for failure. We select leaders who look and sound good, without assessing whether they can perform a critical component of the job—achieve the shared goal. Broadly, this leads to the selection of leaders who are simply unfit. They are unqualified. This, in part, helps explain the failure in leadership we see today. In addition, our attraction to leaders with these feathery displays also dramatically limits our potential pool of leaders to those who possess overt confidence.

Unfortunately, this focus on confidence also acts as barrier to women's advancement. Related to our stereotypes of leaders as confident, dominant, and assertive, we know that men are more likely than women to display these characteristics. This isn't because men *should* have more confidence than women or even that men are innately more confident. The academic research on the topic largely suggests that the confidence gap between men and women emerges because of societal backlash directed at women who present themselves confidently through actions such as self-promotion, Research has long shown that women are punished for displaying the confident behaviors we expect of men (and leaders).[6] In response, women *learn* to hide or downplay these characteristics to avoid the negative outcomes that follow.

The classic adage that women should just "be more confident" should then be put to rest. It doesn't produce the intended effect for women or effective leadership. It's bad advice. It fails women. It fails all of us.

As I thought about this advice over time, advice I too personally received early in my career, I frequently found myself asking, Why do women have to be the ones to change? Why do women need to be more confident and men not less confident? Why are we using men as our confidence barometer and not women?

This "male-default thinking," as labeled by Caroline Criado Perez in *Invisible Women*, infiltrates our thinking on many levels.[7] I recently received criticism regarding my own male-default thinking in an academic research paper on the gender pay gap. When publishing an academic article, manuscripts go through a rigorous peer-review process during which domain experts review the paper and provide feedback and recommendations to a journal editor. The journal editor then decides whether or not the article should be published and if any additional changes should be made. In this instance, the paper focused on the gender pay gap in severance pay for executives. My coauthors and I found a $500,000 pay gap in which women in executive positions received $500,000 less in severance payouts compared to men in executive positions.[8]

Let's pause to take that number in: $500,000.

Throughout the discussion of this finding, we used language that suggested that women are significantly underpaid. In comparison to their male counterparts, this is of course, true. However, in using this framing, the editor argued, we revealed a fundamental bias in our thinking—we assumed that we pay men appropriately. Our implicit assumption led us to draft implications that we underpay women, and we hadn't even stopped to consider that we *over*pay men.

In this same biased fashion, we assume that men demonstrate an appropriate level of confidence, and we subsequently conclude that women are *under*confident. But what if the way society teaches women to manage our confidence is a more effective way to lead? And what if men's confidence, or perhaps more accurately, their *over*confidence, leads to ineffective leadership?

What if, instead of women having a shortage of confidence, men have a surplus?

There are, in fact, several downsides to overconfidence. For starters, when we are overconfident, we may be less likely to think critically about a decision or to question our own judgment. It can also result in our placing less effort to achieving our goals because we think, "I've got this." Or, perhaps it will limit our participation in learning opportunities, reducing our acquisition of new knowledge and skills. More dramatically, overconfidence has been linked to catastrophic decisions such as the sinking of the *Titanic*,[9] the Iraq War,[10] and the Chernobyl disaster.[11]

If we accept that overconfidence is, in fact, a negative and that women are not underconfident but are demonstrating appropriate levels of confidence, then perhaps the solution is to do a better job of keeping a leader's confidence in check.

If leaders were to have a more balanced confidence, what are some of the outcomes we might expect?

- Increased critical thinking
- Improved self-awareness
- Deeper introspection
- Improved solution monitoring
- More perspective-taking
- Actual competence

We can see these benefits pronouncedly in Angela Merkel's decision-making style. In response to the 2008 financial crisis, Chancellor Merkel needed to act to protect the German economy and people. In choosing the course, she took her a time—an approach heavily criticized by the German media. But Merkel believed in the importance of analyzing the situation and considering all possible consequences rather than act hastily. As noted by Matthew Qvortrup, who penned her biography, "she saw hesitancy as virtue. Analyzing every angle of the situation was a sign of strength and sure-footedness rather than the opposite, she said: 'I am quite brave when a decision has to be made.[12] But I need a bit of a run-up and I like—if possible—to think before I jump. I always like to know what will happen to me, even if this means that I am less spontaneous" (p. 39).

This desire to analyze the situation and make informed decisions was also on display in her response to COVID-19 in 2020 and beyond. She was largely praised for her attention to detail and collection of scientific evidence and information.[13] Her background as a scientist, holding a PhD in quantum chemistry, likely contributes heavily to this approach. As a scientist, she would have been trained to approach problems methodically, asking questions and testing hypotheses before drawing any conclusions. And this approach has paid off quite well, with Germany ranking highly for its handling of COVID-19, more successfully keeping deaths at bay compared to countries of a similar size such as France.[14]

As a scientist myself, I fully appreciate that the move-slow-and-investigate approach is not quite as sexy as the "move fast and break things" motto of Silicon Valley. A slow, investigative approach does not garner the same media attention as a confident, fast-acting leader like Brazil's prime minister Jair Bolsonaro, who was famously overconfident about the potential impact of COVID-19. On March 9, 2020, he stated, "In my understanding, the destructive power of this virus is overestimated." And on March 27, 2020, he compared COVID-19 to "a little flu or nothing."[15] Like the peacock he is, Bolsonaro grabbed attention and headlines. Meanwhile, Merkel continued to put her head down and work to solve the crisis. Her approach certainly lacks the peacock flair we instinctively crave in our leaders—a deficit that was regularly noted by German and global media. But importantly, it works. While countries with peacock leaders like Bolsonaro were largely still reeling from COVID-19, those with bower bird leaders like Merkel were faring better.

Another benefit of appropriate levels of confidence is observed in how women have responded to the confidence labyrinth they are expected to navigate—they know their stuff. Because women are penalized for their confidence, they typically cannot rely on the same gravitas that men can to get them ahead. Instead, they must be competent. And research tells us that these women must be *extremely* competent to make it to the top. In a study of 5,000 Australian workers, Leonora Risse found that women tend to "overinvest" or possess more than the minimum qualifications and capabilities compared to men.[16] Risse estimates that this equates to women possessing "one-and-a-half year's extra education, and nearly a full year's extra workforce experience than what is required for the job." In other words, women have more experience and are more prepared for their roles when compared to men.

These results are not surprising given the overwhelming evidence of biases against women in the hiring process. For example, one study found that male applicants were perceived to be more competent and hirable than women with the identical resume.[17] Then, once women have the job, the authors report, they are held to higher standards than their male counterparts again and face more backlash for mistakes. It's no wonder, then, that studies find women are likely to apply only for jobs that they are 100 percent qualified for—our biased expectations of women are such that women must be 100 percent (or more) qualified to be considered for a role. And even still, that doesn't guarantee that experience and competence will trump our confidence bias.

We can see this overinvestment in action once again with Angela Merkel. Qvortrup writes, "Her motto—which the other children found slightly annoying—was 'never show incompetence.' Annoying or not, it was a fair description of how she approached everything. Many decades later, when Angela had become Chancellor Merkel, her attention to detail and her obsession with getting the facts right became almost legendary" (p. 38).[12]

Similarly, Madeline Chapman writes of Jacinda Ardern, prime minister of New Zealand, "Ardern—for most of the negotiations the only woman in the room—had always been a policy wonk, always the one in meetings who knew the finer details on any given topic" (p. 124).[18] These women are good at their jobs because they are prepared and competent— skills that, because of our overly high expectations of women, we demand they possess in order to reach and maintain positions of leadership.

More broadly, we see this trend reported with the general population of women. Researchers at YouGov, a UK-based public opinion company, were interested in understanding the preparation gap between men and women that was so aptly highlighted during the 2016 US presidential election.[19] Following a quip from the then-Republican nominee for president, Donald Trump, Hillary Clinton responded, "I think Donald just criticized me for preparing for this debate, and yes, I did. You know what else I did? I prepared to be President." To find out whether this was a unique dichotomy or the preparation gap exists more widely, the researchers asked approximately 1,000 participants, "In general, do you tend to prepare for things or improvise as needed?" Take a moment to consider how you would respond to this question:

In general, do you tend to prepare for things or improvise as needed?

prepare   mostly prepare   a mix of both   mostly improvise   improvise

Results of the YouGov study reveal that of the 1,000 people surveyed, 32 percent of men reported that they typically improvise, while only 17 percent of women reported doing so. Along these lines, 60 percent of men reported that they "tend to prepare" compared to 74 percent of women. A similar pattern emerged across questions regarding job interview preparation specifically as well as feelings of respect for those who prepare. Generally speaking, then, it appears that women, compared to men, are more likely to prepare and men are more likely to improvise.

The moral of the story is *not* that to increase the number of women in leadership, we should lower our preparation standards and put the onus on women to try winging it more often. No, that is far from the desired message. What these examples demonstrate is that the competence women are forced to develop and bring to the table benefit them and us by making them more capable of solving problems and making informed decisions. Isn't that what we want in our leaders?

What we need to do is *raise* our standards for men! Rather than perpetuating a view that women should increase their *confidence*, we must expect and demand more *competence* of men. When we do that, we will see not only more women in leadership but also more effective leadership.[20]

Let's change the narrative from one in which women need to be more confident to one focused on changing the *system* that perpetually rewards male undercompetence and suppresses women's progress. To enact this change, we—leaders and nonleaders alike—must each be aware of our own biases. We need to critically reflect on what we value in a leader and take a hard look at our decision processes to understand how we can better align our values with our choices. If we value competence and preparation, how can we better hire, vote for, and follow leaders who come prepared with their magnificent bowers rather than fall for the ones who rub their feathers in our faces?

Issue-Driven Focus

In the time before crash courses in armchair epidemiology and before news of mutations and vaccines dominated the media, mainstream news ranged from spicy political dramas to blasphemous tabloid gossip. And the headlines in the months leading up to what Chris Harrison, former host of ABC's *The Bachelor* and *The Bachelorette*, might refer to as "the most dramatic season yet" certainly did not disappoint. In the United Kingdom, we read stories of Brexit and Megxit, and in Europe we watched as Notre Dame Cathedral burned. We witnessed a struggle for freedom in Hong Kong, and we watched the devastating Christchurch shooting in New Zealand unfold. In the United States, political dramas surrounding Russian interference in the 2016 election and the impeachment of President Donald Trump played out on television screens like a daytime soap.

Also making headlines that year was the divorce of Jeff Bezos and MacKenzie Scott. Mr. and Mrs. Amazon were calling it quits after 25 years of marriage. Reasons for their divorce occupied journalists for weeks. Rumors of an affair swirled as Bezos's alleged sext messages with his mistress leaked into the tabloids. Their dirty laundry splashed across Web pages and newspapers.

As the dissolving couple navigated both the media storm and the conditions of their split, they faced a problem I'm sure we can all relate to—dividing their $150 billion fortune.

The media weighed in with questions regarding how much of the Amazon fortune Scott would and should walk away with. And as the public started calculating her worth in dollars and stocks, stories of her role at Amazon began to emerge. It soon became clear that Scott, like so many wives of male moguls, played a critical, behind-the-scenes role in the formation of Amazon. While Bezos acted as the company's face and persona (#peacock), Scott worked invisibly to the public, pulling strings, managing contracts, and taking care of business that allowed Bezos the space to build their Amazonian empire.

In the end, Scott left with nearly $38 billion.

Thirty-eight billion dollars. *You go girl!*

As I dreamed of the vacations, yachts, and outfits I would purchase with my own 38 billion dollar fortune (*lol*), Scott proceeded to quietly give away her actual fortune with very few strings attached. In contrast, Bezos bought a 415-foot mega yacht that could house a small country and jetted off to space in his personal giant space penis. *Perhaps a difference in money management influenced their decision to divorce.*

The polar opposite ways in which Bezos and Scott were spending their fortunes reflects the distinct ways in which men and women spend their fortunes more broadly (or for those non-billionaires among us, our pennies). The underlying reasons for these differences provide insights into the contrast between the ways men and women lead, as evidenced by many world leaders during COVID-19, including Jacinda Ardern, Sanna Marin, and Katrin Jakobsdottir.

To learn more about leadership, then, let's follow the money.

Despite being a successful author, Scott remained relatively unknown to the general public before the divorce. Who was she? Until this point she had remained as elusive as *Gossip Girl*. But in 2019, as her dissolving relationship became media fodder, we learned of her essential role in forming Amazon.com. The *New York Times*, for example, reported that she was "clearly a voice in the room in those early years" and that she was "heavily involved in the business from the start."[1] Others noted that she played a critical role in the first freight contracts signed for the company.[2] As Scott pulled many strings behind the scenes, her husband became the face of the company. According to interviews with and reports about Scott, she preferred it that way. She never sought the spotlight and wanted to maintain her privacy and relative anonymity. While Bezos took to the radio and television to proselytize about his online book rainforest, Scott shared her views in private and worked behind the scenes to keep the company moving forward.[1]

When it came to spending their post-divorce fortunes, we witnessed a similar dichotomy between the estranged couple. Bezos spent his money on personal luxuries and funding his personal space tourism project, Blue Origin. (Blue Origin also made headlines that year for its reportedly toxic culture,[3] as had Amazon a few years earlier.[4]) And in 2021, Bezos, his brother Mark, 82-year-old Wally Funk, and teenager Oliver Daeman blasted off into space in Blue Origin's New Shepard rocket.

I remember watching the launch and thinking that we would be waiting hours to find out if they could successfully orbit the earth and land safely back in the Texas desert. I once essentially orbited the earth myself, flying from Sydney to Singapore to London to Los Angeles in a 30-plus-hour journey. Based on that experience (and not any space expertise whatsoever), I thought, *they won't be back until sometime tomorrow or the next day.* Much to my surprise, they landed in the Lonestar state within minutes of the launch.

Did something go wrong?

No, the only thing wrong was my expectation of what was being accomplished that day. Blue Origin and our dear friend Bezos were not, in fact, orbiting the earth. They rocketed up into the sky, passing the Karman Line (the internationally recognized boundary into space), and then returned to earth. The "mission" lasted approximately 11 minutes.

Following their decent, the four civilians turned 11-minute astronauts hosted a press conference that lasted significantly longer than their space experience. Bezos, donning his cowboy hat as if a space cowboy at a college frat party on Halloween, spoke of their success and its meaning for space tourism and the future of the planet. Much like listening to a Kanye West album, the god complex was palpable.

Meanwhile, Scott quietly began giving away her billions to historically underfunded charities. She donated her dollars to community colleges, historically Black colleges and universities, and organizations that help those who need assistance in paying off medical debts or purchasing food. In contrast to many donors, she required very little of her recipients. She didn't ask for buildings with her name on them, nor did she ask for strict reporting and evidence of how the funds were used and the results they produced. She was not concerned with a return on investment; she simply wanted to help. She formalized her dedication to supporting those in need by signing the Giving Pledge, a commitment to donate a majority of one's wealth signed by a handful of the world's wealthiest individuals.

In 2020, she posted the following on Medium:[5]

> Last year I pledged to give the majority of my wealth back to the society that helped generate it, to do it thoughtfully, to get started soon, and to keep at it until the safe is empty. There's no question in my mind that anyone's personal wealth is the product of a collective effort, and of social structures which present opportunities to some people, and obstacles to countless others.

Following through on her promise, Scott donated $6 billion to charities in 2020 alone. By October 2022, she had given away more than 12 billion dollars to more than 12 hundred organizations.[6] Importantly, Scott made these donations quietly, choosing to announce many of her donations on her personal blog. If not for the media's new fascination with her, these actions may have gone entirely unnoticed by the headlines. From what I can see, this understated approach reaches into all aspects of her dealings. For instance, it's been reported that she has no fancy office and no formal team. It's just her and a team of advisors making impactful monetary donations to those helping the most historically underfunded.

Is MacKenzie Scott the only billionaire to donate her fortune?

Of course not.

As of 2021, the Giving Pledge has 226 signatures, including several notable women such as Sara Blakely (founder of Spanx), Shelby White (investor), Judy Faulkner (CEO of Epic Systems), and Melinda French Gates (philanthropist).

Are women the only ones who donate their fortunes?

Definitely not.

We could sing the praises of many others, such as Mark Zuckerberg and Priscilla Chan, T. Boone Pickens, Michael Bloomberg, and Warren Buffet—all of whom have signed the Giving Pledge. Although Bezos has yet to sign the Giving Pledge and his two and a half billion dollar donations as of December 2022 pale in comparisons to those of his ex-wife,

MacKenzie's ex-husband has also committed to giving away a majority of his fortune over his lifetime.[7] So while we can criticize his donations relative to hers in the present, perhaps he will catch up with time.

A quick perusal of the Giving Pledge website reveals that a majority of the signatories are individual men or couples. At the time of writing, individual women make up only 6 percent of Giving Pledgers—a number far from the majority. When interpreting these numbers, it is important to understand the broader billionaire landscape. As of 2022, there were 2,668 billionaires across the globe, 327 of whom were women.[8] The math suggests that 12 percent of the world's billionaires are women. If we expected billionaire women to give at a rate higher than or equal to that of their male counterparts, we would expect to see them make up around the same percentage of signatories on the Giving Pledge.

But we don't.

There are two possible reasons for this: one, billionaire women don't give as much as billionaire men, or two, billionaire women give away their money but don't sign the Giving Pledge.

The research on women and charitable giving suggests the latter may be more likely. Researchers at Indiana University–Purdue University Indianapolis's (IUPUI) Women's Philanthropy Institute released a report examining gender differences in charitable giving.[9] They looked at data from three major sources on philanthropic giving and found that single women gave more money to nonreligious organizations compared to single men. Additionally, as a single woman's income increases, so too does her likelihood to give philanthropically.

The researchers were also interested in understanding differences in spending between married and single individuals. Although in some cases, they found no significant differences between men's and women's giving patterns, a few distinct patterns emerged. Broadly, they found that both men and women are more likely to give and to give *more* when married but that single women are still more likely to make donations to nonreligious causes when compared to single men and married men and women. When examining the giving patterns of married men and women, the researchers found that as a husband's income increased, so too did his likelihood of giving across the board. Although an increase in income similarly increased the likelihood that women would donate financially, their donations were more targeted. Instead of donating more across the board, married women focused on supporting particular sectors, including education, environment, and organizations focused on providing life essentials.

The results of the Woman's Philanthropy Institute study mirror those of an earlier study led by Debra Mesch from the Center on Philanthropy at Indiana University. Mesch and her coauthors wanted to understand whether men or women are more likely to give to charity and who is more likely to donate the higher amount of money.[10] In the case that differences did exist, they also wanted to explore the driving force behind any differences—the why. After collecting data from two US-based surveys of approximately 4,000 adults, they had their answer: women were more likely than men to donate to charity and to donate *greater amounts* of money. *You go girls.*

Addressing the why behind these differences, the researchers also asked survey respondents about two key values: empathic concern and the principle of care. Empathic concern refers to how sympathetic or compassionate one feels toward others. The principle of care reflects a general belief that we are morally obligated to help others in need. Both values explained giving behavior in men and women. People who reported higher empathy and care were more likely to give. Although these values similarly drove both men and women, women demonstrated higher levels of *both* values. By placing more importance on empathy and care, the researchers argued that women are more likely to make philanthropic donations when compared to men.

These value differences significantly influence the way in which women donate their money. Rather than herald their own praises, women more often leave their egos at the door and focus on the issue at hand. In an interview with the *New York Times*, Dr. Debra Mesch states:[11]

> If you look at the motivations for the way women engage in philanthropy versus the ways that men engage in philanthropy, there's much more ego involved in the man, it's much more transactional, it's much more status driven. Women don't like to splash their names on buildings, in general.

We also see this play out with how men and women spend money. In research on microloans, for example, research finds that women are more likely to invest money in ways that prop up the family, such as in education and business development. Conversely, men often use this money for more selfish means (e.g., restocking their beer supply).[12] Based on this research, the microfinance industry has made a big push to focus lending strategies on women—they produce a better return on investment than do their male counterparts.

When it comes to financial decision making, women appear to be driven by a focus on helping others, and this is reflected in their targeted, issue-focused philanthropy.

Caring, then, seems to be a major plus for women. For those of you making pros and cons lists, put a checkmark for the ladies in that pro column!

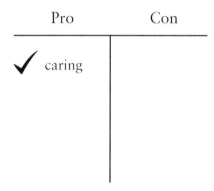

Unfortunately, the notion that women are more empathetic and caring is not always seen as a universal pro. This view has largely led to the under- and overrepresentation of women in specific industries. Aligning with our stereotypes, more people-oriented fields where caring is emphasized, fields such as corporate social responsibility and human resource management, tend to be more female-dominated. In contrast, fields such as strategy and finance that are stereotypically viewed as core business functions focused on the bottom line—not the needs of others—remain heavily male-dominated.

Anecdotally, I often hear that women "want to be" in people-oriented careers because they "want to help people." Women are just more caring, they say. They then relegate women to specific industries in which their caring can shine, because "that's where women belong." *Give the ladies what they want!*

Okay, great. But there are a few major assumptions here that need to be unpacked. First, do women *want* to be in these careers, or does society strongly suggest women should be in those careers? If you're rolling your eyes at my use of "society" and thinking to yourself, *Everyone is in control of their own decisions, Kelsey, what a load of garbage*, then I recommend you read *Nudge* by Richard H. Thaler and Cass R. Sunstein for a summary of the small ways in which we are influenced on a daily basis. A quick example: whether you are asked to opt *in* to something, such as organ donation, or *out* of it will influence how likely you are to do it. Our laziness often prompts us to take the path of least resistance. Meaning, if the default on our driver license application is to opt *in* and thereby make the default choice to *not* donate our organs, then we are less likely to donate our organs. If we flip the default to opt *out*, meaning that we automatically donate our organs, then we are more likely to donate them. The small change in wording, or where a tick box is placed on a form, dramatically influences organ donation patterns. Presenting organ donation as an opt out rather than opt in choice can increase organ donations and subsequently save more lives. The point being, "society" influences what we do on a microlevel on a daily basis. And when it comes to gender, there are blaring cues embedded in advertising and the toy aisle that markedly impact what we believe we can and should do from an early age.

The second major assumption is that caring only belongs in particular industries and not in business as a whole. Classic business texts back up this thinking. And business schools build this thinking by assigning books such as Sun Tzu's *The Art of War*. Of course, leaders can draw valuable business lessons from *The Art of War*, but the metaphor alone suggests a fundamental principle of how we see business—a battle. Business is a battle with a winner and loser, with the goal of destroying your enemy. *Ew*.

Relegating care to particular industries suggests that care should not be a major feature of business, politics, and leadership more generally. Caring is for the planet, but not for strategic decision making. Caring is for managing people, but not for finance. Caring is for tending to the needs of the sick or of children, but not for CEOs.

In perpetuating this false dichotomy, we leave entire industries devoid of caring. In much of the business world, we've created an *un*caring culture in which empathy and a moral obligation to look out for one another have no place. It's perhaps *un*surprising, then, that these industries attract, select, and perpetuate a selfish form of leadership that focuses on the leader's personal interests and concern for power. I'm sure it won't take you long to think of a leader you've met, a business leader or a leader of your country, who sought power for the sake of power and used it selfishly once they attained it. *I thought of five while typing this sentence.*

Many of the women taking center stage throughout the COVID-19 pandemic, however, present a counternarrative. Prime Minister Ardern of New Zealand, for instance, explicitly called out the need for more kindness in politics.[13] In reading the histories of many women in political leadership during the COVID crisis, they often express little to no interest in power early on in their careers. Many become involved because they feel an issue is not being addressed properly and they would like to do something about it. As opposed to deliberately seeking power for the sake of power, we see many of these same not seeking leadership roles at all. Rather, at least outwardly, these women vocalize their interest in change and their dissatisfaction with the current trajectory. In doing so, they propel themselves to the forefront of their political parties and ultimately take center stage in their respective countries. Generally speaking, these women then use their power to enact positive societal change.

In many of their narratives, women describe being pushed into leadership roles and even lacking ambitions for leadership entirely. Now, there may be reputational reasons for describing their ascent in this way, as ambitious women are still largely seen as taboo (**eyeroll**), so it is possible that they hold these ambitions at some level but know better than to express it. But it is equally as plausible that these accounts represent their true histories—women who took a role in government to make a difference on an issue, were effective, and subsequently were promoted.

Prime Minister Marin of Finland, for instance, noted, "I'm in politics because I thought that the older generation wasn't doing enough about the big issues of the future. I needed to act. I couldn't just think, it's somebody else's job."[14] Similarly, Iceland's Prime Minister Jakobsdottir described her displeasure with the slow advancement of environmental progress. As a result, she joined demonstrations against a hydroelectric plant, beginning her political career as an environmental activist. She stated, "I wouldn't say I was the most radical activist in town, but, yes, I began my political participation through demonstration because of a hydroelectric plant in the east of Iceland. It was probably the most controversial project that we have had in environmental issues in Iceland. That was the reason why I entered the Left-Greens, because of this struggle."[15]

Marin and Jakobsdottir join Ardern in describing an ascent to power characterized by the pursuit of positive change rather than political ambition.[15] For instance, after being chosen as party leader, Ardern stated, "I'm not here because of my own personal ambition. I'm not here because I want to be the big cheese or the top dog, I'm here because I want to bring in a team of New Zealanders who care deeply about making the country better. They just so happen to have chosen me to be at the lead."[13] Similarly, largely because of her role in environmental activism, Jakobsdottir describes being "pushed into" party leadership.[15] And Marin, in response to attention received because of her country's success with COVID-19, noted that the increased attention created more work for her: "Of course, it's also a great opportunity for Finland to present itself, and I'm grateful for that. But I think you focus on the issues, and not the person, it's easier."[14]

Focus on the issues and not on the person. Isn't that a novel idea? Well said, Prime Minister Marin.

In leadership researcher language, we compare these two groups of leaders as personalized and socialized leaders. Personalized leaders wield their power to achieve their own goals. They tend to be selfish and self-serving. Socialized leaders, on the other hand, focus on using their power for the good of the group. These leaders seek to serve others and may pursue a group goal at the expense of their own interests. When people seek power for the sake of power, in pursuit of their own, individualized goals, that is personalized leadership. But when people take on leadership roles to enact positive change, or simply to pursue a goal in the best interest of the collective group, we call that socialized leadership.

In line with observations of the women leading their countries through COVID-19, academic research generally suggests that women are more likely to display and value socialized leadership compared to men.[16] Regarding personalized leadership, we see the opposite effect—men typically display and value personalized leadership more than women do. Scholars argue that this is largely due to gender stereotypes that emphasize a similar pattern of values. For men, gender stereotypes emphasize dominance and influence, whereas for women, gender stereotypes more often focus on others and compassion. We can argue whether these are hardwired foci or are learned through deeply embedded social systems, but that is for another time and another book. The point is that women, regardless of their roots, much like how they spend their money, tend to adopt leadership styles that support the group, whereas men adopt leadership styles that support their own interests.

Let's pause there and reflect the following:

Which type of leader *do you* see more of?

Which type of leader would you *like to* see more of?

When it came to COVID-19, the benefits of socialized leaders can be seen playing out in real time.[17] Many took actions with other people in mind first. I suspect that these women's socialized leadership also led them to focus more squarely on the problem at hand compared to leaders with a more personalized leadership style. Because these women were not particularly concerned with obtaining and retaining personal power, they were free to focus on the immediate issues that had drawn them to their positions in the first place.

In contrast, leaders who were thirsty for power and, in turn, emphasized a need to stay in power added a second problem to every equation they attempted to solve. No longer were they simply trying to establish a healthy economy—they were trying to establish a healthy economy *and* appeal to their political base. (One might assume these always go hand in hand, but one would assume incorrectly. Most people are not expert economists.) Instead of trying to pass legislation that best served the country, they were trying to pass legislation *and* keep their followers happy.

Specific to COVID-19, while some leaders focused on the case numbers, others focused on both their case and their polling numbers. In this sense, they were attempting to solve two problems simultaneously—increasing the complexity of an already challenging situation. At times, these two goals had entirely distinct outcomes. For a simple example, let's look to an obvious choice—*Mean Girls*. Cady Haron, played by Lindsay Lohan, starts at a new school after being homeschooled to that point. A star student, Cady quickly stands out to her math teacher for her good grades in an advanced-level math course and is invited to join the "Mathletes," the school's competitive math team. But in the words of Damian, one of her first friends at the new school, joining the Mathletes is "social suicide." As Cady continues her journey at North Shore High School, her social status becomes increasingly important. As she tries to infiltrate and "ruin" the popular girl group at school led by Regina George, her goals change from simply being a good student to making friends to being the most popular girl in school. She even begins to fail her math class. (I won't tell you why in case you haven't seen this critically acclaimed film.)

Cady's problem becomes how to both succeed in school *and* still be popular. As these two goals are in conflict, one has to come out on top and drive her decision making. We see similar conflict with politicians who are trying to resolve complex issues such as controlling gun violence in America, reducing taxes, funding the United Kingdom's National Health Service, or keeping the power on in South Africa. Like Cady, leaders attempting to solve complex political, societal, or organizational problems face two dilemmas: how to solve the problem *and* win votes. When the focus is on gaining or keeping power, the actual problem can fall to the wayside.

I do not argue that women have no interest in their personal outcomes. Of course, they do. But women and men tend to prioritize their interests differently. We should therefore ask, What is the individual's primary motivator? Is it personal gain? Or is it the collective gain? For women, it appears to be a focus on the collective, emphasizing a concern and care for others.

Unfortunately, our stereotypes of leadership conflate with personalized leadership; consequently, we often select leaders who climb, punch, and kick their way to the top at any cost. The examples of women in this book paint a different picture. They show us that successful leaders emphasize the needs of others and the collective gain from their decisions. Their commitment to solving problems and addressing critical issues supersedes any need for power that they might have. In the end, choosing leaders who look out for all of us, rather than just for themselves, results in more effective problem solving that benefits more than just the leader.

When developing our own leadership, we should reflect on *why* we are pursuing a position of power in the first place. Is it because we want to promote ourselves? Is it because we want to solve problems for the collective we represent? Is it somewhere in between? As we continue to lead, it is similarly important to check in with ourselves and to understand what motivates us. If we are honest with ourselves, we can then choose how to move forward as leaders. Do you want to continue the path you are on? Or do you want to make a change that improves your ability to solve problems for those you represent?

Similarly, when considering who we want as a leader, we must ask ourselves questions about their motivations. We can design interview and debate questions that center around one's ascent to and desire for power. We can look for cues in a leader's speech—do they use words focused on the group (e.g., we) or do they use words focused on their own interests (e.g., I). We can choose to follow, give voice, and assign power to those who demonstrate empathy and care.

Collective Leadership

One person can never fulfill all of your needs. If I had to guess, you would need to date about seven people at once to feel that your dating relationship(s) met everything you actually need emotionally, mentally, physically, and so on. It's not fair or realistic to expect that of one person. You need lots of relationships in your life. Friends, family, romantic relationships.

—My therapist, 2014

In my early 20s, I told my therapist that I was *completely* dissatisfied with my romantic relationship and thought I was "destined to be single forever" (*In retrospective, that is a lovely option*). As we began to unpack that rather dramatic view, I explained that the people I dated were not enough. They didn't, in the words of Vicki Gunvalson from *The Real Housewives of Orange County*, fill up my "love tank." I never EVER (*cue the drama*) felt that they fulfilled all of my (*very reasonable*) expectations. NEVER!

I expected a lecture about continuously choosing incompatible partners and that the problem was, *obviously*, them. But in typical therapist fashion, she asked me to reflect on my own experiences and how they might shape my views and expectations of my romantic relationships.

Hold on, how could this possibly be my fault? Bear in mind, this was a decade prior to Taylor Swift popularizing self-ownership with her antihero lyrics, "It's me, hi, I'm the problem, it's me."

I was expecting one man to do too much and to be too much, she told me. I was still desperately clinging to my Disney princess fantasy where one person would sweep me off my feet and we would wander off down a quiet country road into the sunset together. We would then live happily ever after with 2.5 kids, never fight, and always make each other happy.

Perhaps if I had taken time to reflect on this view, even for a moment, I might have realized that no one outside of the movies (*and Instagram*) lives like this.

But alas, I was 23 and self-obsessed.

As a firm believer that we should have high standards for our partners, my therapist's advice sat uncomfortably with me. "I'm not going to lower my standards. Men need to rise to the occasion and treat me like the queen I am."

Like I said, 23 and self-obsessed.

I had seen my friends make excuses for bad and even abusive behavior in their partners. And I had done the same for years. To this day, friends tell me that what they like about their partner is that "they are nice to me."

Nice to you? That is the bare minimum!

Others say, "He doesn't abuse me like [insert previous partner name]."

Great, but that's a damn low bar.

From my own dating archives, a boyfriend in my late teens argued that the lies he told at work were okay because he "wasn't, like, murdering anyone."

Reality check: Comparing your actions to not "like, murdering anyone," sweetheart, is not the flex you think it is.

Over the hour-long session(s), my therapist helped me realize that lowering my expectations to accept "nice enough" or "not a murderer" is not, in fact, what she was saying. What she *was* saying, as I recall, sounds something like this: "Expecting our partners to be everything that we need, our hero, is not healthy. No person can fulfill *all* of your needs. You need to shift your expectations for what one person can do for you."

Let me say it one more time for dramatic effect: "No person can fulfill *all* of your needs. You need to shift your expectations for what one person can do for you."

Those words have sat with me for years of dating and now into my marriage.

They also sit with me in my own research.

Didn't think you'd get both leadership and dating advice in the same chapter, did you?

The more I think and read about leadership, the more I wonder how often we similarly expect our leaders to do and be too much. In the same way that I expected a 23-year-old boyfriend to be my end all be all, are we expecting too much from one leader? (*Please re-read that sentence in your best Carrie Bradshaw voice.*)

Caveat: Just as my therapist made clear regarding romantic relationships, I am not suggesting we lower our standards for leaders. How many times have you found yourself saying about a leader, "At least they are better than the last one?" or "At least they aren't Elizabeth Holmes or Bernie Madoff or [insert other shady leader here]?" or "At least they buy me lunch from time to time."

If you are having these thoughts about your leader, that person is NOT a good leader.

RUN, HON!

It is also true that expecting leaders to be heroes or to be able to solve any problem at any time is just as toxic as our "at least" attitudes. First, it's not realistic to expect perfection from any human being. Nor is it realistic to expect them to possess all the qualities we need to lead us through mundane times and through crises, to motivate us to be outstanding on our best and worst days, or solely and effectively resolve customer service, financial, strategic, and people-management issues. Being an effective leader requires a range of qualities and types of knowledge rarely embodied in a single individual.

Expectations that pressure leaders to possess all the skills and knowledge to be an effective leader can result in serious consequences. Research tells us that the combination of unreasonable expectations and substantial consequences associated with not meeting them can produce an environment where unethical behavior flourishes.[1]

As a now infamous example, Wells Fargo demonstrated how their unreasonable sales goals did just this. Between 2002 and 2016, thousands of Wells Fargo employees engaged in unethical and illegitimate sales practices, resulting in fraudulent fees and lines of credit for their customers.[2] Customers' identities were misused to "provide millions of accounts or products to customers under false pretenses or without consent," transfer money without customers' knowledge, sign up customers for new credit accounts, and more.

The question on everyone's mind echoed through the press: *Why?* Why did Wells Fargo employees engage in such rampant fraud?

The answer?

High expectations. Leaders within the company set unreasonable sales goals and pressured their employees to meet them to keep their jobs. As a result, employees felt they *had* to meet these goals. But given their unattainable nature, the only route to doing so was through unethical means (e.g., creating fake accounts).

On a more personal level, we can see this in other goals we set, such as exercise. Have you ever set such an unreasonable exercise goal that you push yourself too hard and hurt yourself? Or perhaps you try a new hobby and set your expectations sky high, only to be severely disappointed when you can't attain them and subsequently give up?

The same principle can be applied to leadership. When we set such high expectations for our leaders, expectations for them to possess super-human qualities and knowledge, we encourage bad behavior and set them up for failure. We encourage classic toxic behaviors such as bullshitting when you don't know the answer, hiding your weaknesses ("areas of improvement" for American readers), and striving to prove you can do it all yourself. Importantly, none of these behaviors are effective leadership attributes.

The likelihood of finding a leader who can do it all with their eyes closed while simultaneously rubbing their belly and patting their heads is next to zero. When we consider the rapidly increasing complexity of the modern world, the likelihood becomes a frigid 32 below.

As evolving technologies and globalization, not to mention world-wide catastrophes such as a pandemic, influence the way we live and shift the way our societies function, the need to recognize our own limitations becomes increasingly evident. As new ideas take hold, leaders must be willing to ask if they possess the capabilities and knowledge to solve new kinds of problems. The fact that they could solve old problems does not mean they have the ability to solve new problems or the skills to lead in a new and changing environment.

Enter *humility*.

Humility has many definitions, so before we go any further, let me clarify what I mean by the word.

Humility: The inner awareness that you might not be a legend at all the things and at all the times.

Thanks to inspiring women such as Brené Brown, who are changing the narrative around leadership, vulnerability, and humility, we are beginning to see archaic and seemingly impenetrable notions of leaders as heroes change. Humility, once seen as a sign of weakness, and placard for low self-esteem, is now largely seen as a strength, a sign of courage and self-awareness. With the likes of Forbes and Fast Company boasting of the benefits of humble leaders (#ironic), the idea of humility is gaining traction among leaders around the globe.[3,4] In addition, the notion that macho leaders are heroes is slowly being rejected.

Research speaks to the importance of humility in leadership. For instance, leader humility positively influences outcomes such as creativity,[5] project success,[6] organizational citizenship behaviors,[7] and team performance.[8] Research also highlights the importance of *authentic* humility, with misalignments between a leader's espoused humility and their actions potentially producing negative results.[9] Although, generally having a positive impact, leader humility, like margaritas, cookies, self-confidence, and stress, probably falls within the "Goldilocks Effect." This effect refers to the need for moderation, implying that extremes—too hot, too cold, too much, too little—can have significant downsides.[10] A balanced level of humility in which leaders can assert their knowledge and skills when appropriate while also recognizing their limitations may be most beneficial.

For leaders interested in or needing to improve their humility, the question then becomes: how do we become more humble leaders?

Scientific research on improving leader humility is limited with some research showing promising results and others less so.[11] However, if we look to observable skills and actions that humble leaders demonstrate, perhaps we can find some useful insights. If we approach humility development through this lens, we see two key behaviors that we can control and develop: seeking and giving help.

SEEKING HELP

What is with men and asking for directions?

—Dory, *Finding Nemo*

Have you ever found yourself wandering the aisles of Costco behind a man looking endlessly for the hummus and refusing to ask the red-vested worker for help? Or perhaps you've found yourself in the Dubai mall with a man who is sure he knows the correct way out to the Uber, but after 10 minutes still can't find the correct exit and won't ask the security guard standing next to you for help?

I have.

Although certainly a stereotype, the idea that men don't ask for directions seems to hold some truth, with research demonstrating that men are less likely than women to seek help.

Perhaps the starkest example of this reluctance to seek help is found in healthcare. Across leading causes of death, reports suggest that men die, on average, 5 years younger than women.[12,13] Death rates for men are also double that of women for suicide and liver scarring.[14]

What accounts for these differences?

One explanation is that men are less likely to engage in preventative behaviors such as seeking help from their doctor. In the 2012 National Health Interview Survey conducted by the US Centers for Disease Control and Prevention, men were nearly twice as likely as women to report having *not* visited a doctor in the previous 12 months.[12] Around the same time in the United Kingdom, researchers found that men consulted with their primary doctors 32 percent less than women did.[15] This gap was particularly pronounced during "working years" between the ages of 15 and 60. Logically, given that this age range encompasses women's primary reproductive years, the researchers hypothesized that this gap may be driven by women's increased likelihood to seek care for pregnancy and other related health concerns. However, even after taking women's reproductive health into account, men visit their doctors significantly less frequently than women. When it comes to mental health, we see a similar pattern. Women have more positive attitudes toward seeking help regarding mental health compared to men.[16]

Just as stereotypes of women as warm and communal can be harmful, stereotypes of men as strong and assertive can be deadly. In a study examining differences in help-seeking behaviors, researchers asked participants to solve a series of puzzles.[17] At the start, the researchers informed participants that, at any time throughout the experiment, they could ask for help from the researchers who would remain in the room. The participants were video recorded as they worked on the puzzles, and the videos were later assessed for how frequently the participants asked for help.

Researchers reported that 61 percent of the women in the study engaged in help-seeking behavior, while only 37 percent of men did so. A driving factor behind this difference was the participant's stereotypical views of gender. Specifically, participants who endorsed stereotypical gender attitudes on a survey taken prior to the study were less likely to seek help and sought help less frequently than those who did not endorse these same attitudes. When these individuals did request help, they sought it more slowly than participants who did not hold these same stereotypical gender attitudes.

The same researchers also measured puzzle performance. They wanted to know if asking for help had an impact on how well participants performed the task. In probably the least shocking news of this chapter, individuals who asked for help solved the puzzles faster than those who did not ask for help.

We often hear about the negative effects of stereotypes on women, but here we see clear negative implications for men as well. Our stereotypes of masculinity suggest that being strong means doing it on your own and not asking for help—even when circumstances are dire. As we see from these examples, this can lead men to perform worse, to die earlier, and maybe even to get lost in Costco and the Dubai Mall.

Why don't men just ask for help, you ask?

We find one answer in a set of studies examining the impact of leaders asking for help in both field and laboratory settings. Resarchers found that men in leadership roles who ask for help are rated as less competent by their followers compared to men in leadership roles who do not ask for help.[18] For women in leadership roles, however, there were no significant differences in perceptions of competence.

To put it simply, we penalize men for asking for help.

Digging into the data further, the researchers wanted to know why this was the case. They suggested two potential reasons. The first stems from role congruity theory, which argues that men are more likely to be assigned to leadership roles because our stereotypes of men as dominant and assertive align with our stereotypes of leadership.[19] Men asking for help violates our perceptions of a typical leader and therefore creates a misalignment between the men's behavior and perceptions of how a leader should behave. If men engage in behavior that is seen as less assertive or dominant, for example, by seeking help, it may sever the male-leader connection. As a result, men may be perceived as less effective in their leadership role.

The second potential explanation stems from the status incongruence hypothesis. This hypothesis argues that men are typically prescribed a higher social status than women.[20,21] If men demonstrate characteristics that more closely align with women (e.g., willingness to ask for help), their behavior may be associated with a lower social status and subsequently viewed as a weakness. If we consider the backlash that occurs when individuals violate the norms of their assigned gender, men in leadership positions who ask for help will be viewed as "weak" and rated less favorably than men who don't ask for help. *(Toxic masculinity much?)*

In their second study, the researchers tested both possibilities directly. They asked participants to read a short story about a leader who either asked for help or did not ask for help. They also varied the gender of the leader in the stories, meaning that participants read about either a man or a woman who did or did not ask for help. After reading the story, participants were asked to rate the leader's competence. In addition, participants rated how "weak" they perceived the leader to be as well as the extent to which the leader described represented a "typical leader." Using fancy statistical procedures, the researchers then examined whether weakness or leader typicality influenced participant perceptions of the leader's competence.

Perceptions of weakness did not explain why men were perceived as less competent after asking for help, but leader typicality did. In line with role congruity theory, then, we perceive men who ask for help as less competent because they violate our assumptions about how a leader (and a man) should act. This is unfortunate for several reasons, but perhaps the biggest reason is that seeking help is important for a number of activities related to successful leadership, such as learning and creativity.

The takeaway here should not be, "Sucks for the men! Guess they can't ask for help!" No, this research serves as another important reminder of how our gender stereotypes influence our perceptions of leaders and, in turn, perpetuate bad leadership behavior. *We* need to change our perceptions of leadership and challenge our views to allow space for leaders to ask questions. If we don't, we will continue to breed a leadership cadre of arrogant jerks who can't recognize their own limits.

Although this research highlights a rather negative phenomenon, a bright side does exist. While men were punished for asking for help, women were not. Women can and do ask for help. And if we look to women in power, we can see this in action.

At times, asking for help has been contrasted with decisiveness, or making effective decisions quickly. On one hand, if a leader stops to ask for help, they may act too slowly. On the other hand, making the wrong decision quickly won't produce desired results either. Are decisiveness and help-seeking behaviors compatible? Or do we have to compromise one for the other?

When it comes to examples of asking for help and taking decisive action, we can look to Taiwan's President Tsai Ing-Wen during the COVID-19 pandemic. Taiwan, by all accounts, was ripe for a struggle with COVID-19. Geographically, it sits just off the coast of China, setting it in close proximity to the source of the outbreak and making it a prime location for early export of the virus. In addition, travel between mainland China and Taiwan was heavy. As of February 10, 2020, a little over a month after the world became aware of the increasing risk of a virus emerging in Wuhan, 148 flights operated across the Taiwan Strait. Approximately 153,000 passengers made the journey monthly. According to *Taipei Times*,[22] the island welcomed nearly 3 million visitors from mainland China in 2019. Further increasing traffic between mainland China and Taiwan are the more than 800,000 Taiwanese citizens living on and more than 400,000 working on the mainland.

By all reasonable accounts, Taiwan was headed for disaster.

However, in January 2022, when many countries around the world were reeling from the Omicron variant, Taiwan's case total remained under 20,000. In a country of nearly 24 million people, less than 20,000 cases is an impressive number. That number implies that less than 1 percent of Taiwan's population had contracted COVID-19 as the virus approached the end of its second year. In comparison, Australia, a country with a similar population at nearly 26 million people, reached 2 million cases in January 2022. At the peak of its Omicron wave, Australia was reporting *daily* cases that were six times the number of Taiwan's *total* case count. If we look at another island, the United Kingdom, we see a similar contrast. With a much larger population than Taiwan—nearly 70 million people— the United Kingdom had reported 15.6 million COVID cases as of January 2022. Those 15.6 million people account for approximately 20 percent of the UK population.

Taiwan's success was overwhelmingly attributed to the leadership of Tsai and her science-driven response. The science behind her decisions was largely credited to her vice president, Chen Chien-Jen.[23] Chen is an epidemiologist by training and, prior to being tapped for the vice presidency, worked as an academic. Given his background, Chen was able to provide expert advice on how to respond. Whether he was awarded complete autonomy in the COVID-19 response or offered his perspective to the President, who then made the decisions, is unclear. However, the implications of either approach remain the same. Ing-Wen, a lawyer by training, did not possess the same epidemiological expertise necessary to keep COVID-19 at bay. Recognizing the need for scientific guidance, she sought the help and expertise of her vice president. In doing so, Tsai ensured that Taiwan responded to the crisis decisively and effectively.

It is important to recognize that by seeking the advice of an expert on managing a pandemic, she did not sacrifice decisiveness. In fact, paying attention to the experts led Taiwan to enact one of the quickest responses in the world. On the same day that the World Health Organization was alerted of an unusual pneumonia in Wuhan, China, Taiwan began screening all passengers from mainland China. On the same day! And by mid-January, they had already expanded their efforts to screen others who had recently returned from Wuhan.[24] Given Chen's expertise, as well as Taiwan's previous experiences with viruses, he knew they needed to act swiftly and exactly what measures to put into place. In her own account of Taiwan's response in *Time*, Tsai Ing-wen wrote:[25]

> Upon the discovery of the first infected person in Taiwan on Jan. 21, we undertook rigorous investigative efforts to track travel and contact history for every patient, helping to isolate and contain the contagion before a mass community outbreak was possible. . . . To prevent mass panic buying, at an early stage the government monitored market spikes in commodities and took over the production and distribution of medical-grade masks.

And those actions barely scratch the surface of the response. In a summary of Taiwan's actions, Wang, Ng, and Brook[24] provide a five-page table of detailed actions the Taiwanese government took between December 31, 2019, and February 24, 2020.

It's clear from Taiwan's response that seeking help does not mean losing time or strength. Instead, Tsai's response demonstrates that leaders can both seek help when needed and respond decisively. In addition, by gathering insight from those with relevant expertise and who may, simply put, know better than you, leaders can enact more effective decisions.

GIVING HELP

Women in leadership are not only more likely to *ask for* help, but they are also more likely to *give* help. In workplace research, there is a well-documented finding that women take on most of the office "housework."[26] In a 2014 *Washington Post* article, Joan Williams defined office housework as "the administrative tasks, menial jobs, and undervalued assignments women are disproportionately given at their jobs."[27] This includes tasks such as planning the office holiday party, cleaning the communal kitchen, and every woman's favorite task (*eye roll*), taking notes.

In my own experience at work as a university professor, I see the gendered split in office housework happen regularly. Although public perception of professors is often that their primary role is to teach the young, blossoming minds of tomorrow, in reality, the job entails much more. And in some cases, professors may engage in very little (if not zero) teaching. Depending on their role, professors may also be expected to engage in research (e.g., publishing scientific papers in academic journals, writing books) and service (e.g., working on special committees that help the department and university function). To be promoted, university professors need to meet certain expectations in all three areas—teaching students, publishing scientific research, and contributing to the university by serving on volunteer committees.

As part of my service responsibilities, I sat on a committee charged with reviewing each faculty member's annual reports of their activities in these areas. When reviewing service activities, the academic "office housework," the split in terms of *who* was doing the service could not have been more obvious. The women in the department took on four or more service responsibilities in a year, whereas the men rarely took on more than two. Some of the men in our department even attempted to claim some of their teaching responsibilities as service—teaching responsibilities that women with the same responsibilities did not claim as service. The committee consensus of these activities across both men and women was the same—they were all "exceeding expectations."

Men engaging in two service activities were viewed the same as women engaging double the number of service activities.

I am not alone in my experience. In a study examining more than 6,000 faculty members' responses to the 2014 National Faculty Survey of Student Engagement, women spent approximately half an hour more each week on service activities compared to men.[28] In the same study, researchers also examined data from approximately 1,300 faculty annual reports across two large US midwestern universities. Analysis of the reports revealed that women engaged in 1.5 more activities annually compared to men, which equates to approximately half an hour more time per week. Although the results varied slightly by field and professor rank across both datasets, the pattern generally held—women engage in more office housework than men.

A 2013 study analyzing the data of 1,399 political science faculty in the United States similarly examined gender differences in service.[29] In addition to understanding the gender gap, these researchers were interested in *why* this gap exists. Previous research had suggested that the onus is on women—women simply don't say no. The researchers found evidence that women do say yes to service more frequently than men do. Importantly, however, women are also *asked* to engage in more service compared to men.

(As soon as I finished typing this, I took a quick break to check my email and noticed a request to perform a service activity. I said yes. *Irony noted.*)

You might be thinking, *So what?* It seems great that women are more likely to help and to contribute.

Unfortunately, despite taking on most of the service or office housework tasks, women don't seem to reap any benefits. In a study on the effects of office housework, researchers found these tasks were related to promotion opportunities for men, but not for women.[26] Even though they are doing most of the office housework, women benefit the least.

One explanation is that women are engaging in these activities at the expense of other tasks. That is why some researchers aptly termed office housework a "non-promotable task." In the traditional academic world of big universities and tenure-track faculty members, research reigns supreme. Engaging in service takes away from research time, limiting productivity in this respect. Survey work demonstrating differences in service time have similarly shown that women spend fewer hours on research compared to men in similar roles.[29] Office housework pulls women away from other "promotable" tasks.

It's a catch-22 for women. If we want to meet expectations, we need to engage in office housework. But office housework isn't valued in the same way as other tasks. The devaluing of office housework, in turn, results in the devaluing of women.

And if women hand off the housework?

Women will similarly not be promoted because they haven't met the expectations of working women.

Damned if they do and damned if they don't.

But having colleagues who help others positively impacts our work experience. It creates a collaborative atmosphere where people work together to care for their spaces and for one another. Helping each other by collaborating with one another is essential to performance across most industries.

When it comes to collaboration, however, men and women seem to fundamentally differ in how they understand what it means to be a good collaborator. In a study examining these differences, researchers presented participants with a series of statements and asked them the extent to which they agreed with each.[30] Two example statements are as follows. Play along and circle your response to each.

1. "Being a good team player means helping all of my colleagues with what they need to get done."

| strongly disagree | disagree | neither | agree | strongly agree |

2. "Being a good team player is knowing your position and playing it well."

| strongly disagree | disagree | neither | agree | strongly agree |

Ready for the results?

Women were more likely to endorse statement 1 (helping colleagues), whereas men were more likely to endorse statement 2 (playing your position well). Neither is inherently a wrong choice. Rather, the statements imply something about what we value and how we see our roles in a team. Statement 1 suggests that collaboration is largely focused on the *we*. Statement 2, in contrast, suggests that collaboration is focused on the *I*.

Although no scientific studies that I'm aware of have directly tested how these gender differences in collaborative views impact leadership approaches, I have a hunch that they make a significant difference in the use of a collaborative leadership approach.

COLLECTIVE LEADERSHIP

There's a growing interest in a type of leadership called *collective leadership*, which argues in favor of a decentralized leadership approach. Rather than concentrating leadership with one person, collective leadership focuses on the value of a team or group of leaders. Given the complexities of leadership, particularly in modern society, the theory argues that one person simply isn't enough (*sound familiar? My therapist deserves a raise!*) and that successful leadership often takes a collective effort of multiple individuals.

If we look to many successful organizations today, we see how collective leadership plays out. For example, although CEOs largely attract a fair share of attention in the media, most companies are led by a leadership team, or a C-suite. While a CEO might put forth a strategic vision for a company, a CHRO (chief human resource officer) will lead the people aspect of the company and a CFO (chief financial officer) will manage the company financials. The CEOs themselves are not, in fact, making all the decisions about all the different aspects of running an organization.

Sometimes people raise creatives as a counter to this. Our stereotypes of the creative industry paint a picture of a lone wolf, such as Steve Jobs, working tirelessly in their Silicon Valley garage to develop the next big technological revolution. Although Steve Jobs did work tirelessly in his garage, he did not do so alone. Steve Wozniak worked closely with Jobs in the development of Apple and for many years thereafter. The pair succeeded by leveraging their individual, distinct skillsets to change the computer industry. Jobs has typically been credited with the vision for the company and Wozniak with the technical focus.

Research on creativity and innovation explains that this approach is common, demonstrating the need for different types of champions and leaders to help promote an innovation and overcome the typical hesitancy of introducing a novel product or service.[31]

We can see collective leadership in action in governments across the world. Cabinets, for example, provide presidents and prime ministers with a team of experts and support, each managing their own areas.

But perhaps the best example of collective leadership, or a team approach, can be seen in the Caribbean. The prime minister of Barbados, Mia Mottley, made international headlines for her response to COVID-19. From the beginning, Mottley emphasized the importance of a collective, global approach. As the leader of a small island nation, she quickly recognized her country's vulnerability to the emerging isolated approach to fighting the virus. Given the universality of this crisis, many countries turned their spending and focus inward, justifiably so, and smaller countries sadly felt the impact. This limited the access of other countries, particularly smaller countries, to some essential goods. As epidemiologists noted the necessity of a unified global response to end the pandemic, Mottley too called for a collaborative approach across governments at a World Health Organization press conference in spring 2021:

> If we do not get the fundamental development equation correct, if we do not work together, if we do not appreciate that we can only work together if we are to achieve a fair and healthier world, then we run the risk of seeing millions of persons die again in circumstances where policy responses can have a different result to ensure that less people become victim of epidemics and pandemics.[32]

Mia put her words into action. Individually, small, debt-burdened nations such as Barbados have little negotiating power, as they lack the capital and the demand to broker effective deals. The importance of a collective approach among these nations was recognized in the 1970s by the leaders of Barbados, Guyana, Jamaica, and Trinidad and Tobago. Together, they signed the Treaty of Chaguaramas that formed the Caribbean Community and Common Market, more commonly known as CARICOM. Although this treaty was later revised in 2001, CARICOM remained steadfast. CARICOM focuses on a coordinated effort regarding the economy, foreign policy, human interests, and security across 20 countries including the Bahamas, northern South America, and Central America.

As the head of CARICOM at the time of COVID-19, Mottley leveraged the community to lead a coordinated response. Through CARICOM, she was able to procure essential medical supplies from WHO and the Caribbean Disaster Emergency Management Agency. Member nations of the Pan American Health Organization (PAHO) in the Caribbean shared test kits to limit shortages. Along with Mottley at CARICOM, PAHO's leadership played a critical role in the coordinated response. (Intriguingly, three of the four directors for PAHO are women.) Through PAHO and their collaborative efforts with other bodies such as the Regional Security System and cooperative governments, the Caribbean nations were able to coordinate medical supply deliveries at a time when air travel was at a standstill, as well as to centralize testing in Trinidad while other countries developed their own testing capabilities. Led largely by Mottley and other women, such as the director of PAHO, Dr. Carissa Etienne, the collaborative response across CARICOM countries helped limit the potentially devastating impact of COVID-19 on these island nations.[33]

Mottley's response to COVID also highlights the importance of developing a well-rounded team. Early in her pandemic response, she named a COVID-19 czar to manage the response and serve as the public face of the government's response. The czar, Richard Carter, previously worked in Sierra Leone managing its Ebola pandemic, as well as with the Barbados National HIV/AIDS Commission. Mottley also appointed two others to oversee the development of treatment and isolation facilities and other critical infrastructure tasks such as training healthcare workers.

Mottley demonstrated her humility by recognizing the limits of her own expertise and her nation's capabilities, and in response, she sought help from experts who knew how to manage a pandemic and form a collaborative network of leaders. Together, these teams helped not only Barbados but all of the Caribbean avoid an economic and health catastrophe. Of course, like other countries, their response was challenged by new variants and the balance of priorities, but overall, by working together, these nations appear to have largely limited the negative impact of the virus on their communities.

When done well, collaborative relationships between leaders can produce more fruitful results than can a leader in isolation. Simply having a partner, however, won't suffice to meet every challenge. Truly collaborative leaders, or teams of leaders, must work together effectively to reap these benefits. The basis of these relationships rests on individuals' ability to recognize their limitations and weaknesses and their willingness to reach out for help and to collaborate.

When thinking about your own leadership development, consider the following:

1. How did you respond to the questions about what it means to be a good team player? How might this view influence your actions as a leader?
2. What holds you back from asking for help? How and whom can you begin to ask for help when you find yourself out of your depth?

Willingness to Learn

Learning occurs through a variety of experiences and activities. In grade school and university halls, we crack open our textbooks, absorb new ideas, challenge convention, and practice and test our knowledge through writing assignments and exams. In our offices, we participate in trainings to develop new skills, improve our performance, and become better leaders. In our houses and our communities, we watch television, read books, and gossip over coffee about what "he said" or "she did" and make mental notes to never do that ourselves. We learn from our own successes and failures. We read brightly colored inspirational posters about being lifelong learners, reminding us that we are never too old to pick up a skiing hobby or learn a new language.

We encounter learning opportunities daily. If not offered them in a formal, structured environment such as a job-related training session, we make decisions every day, observe the outcomes, and learn whether or not we want to repeat them.

Although we regularly encounter these opportunities to learn, *actually* learning from these opportunities it not a given. We must be willing to take the opportunity. We must sign up for that training course. We must do the work assigned. We must reflect on our own decisions to consider whether the outcomes were what we expected. And if not, we must consider how we can change our decision making in the future to avoid history repeating itself.

Easy, right?

As someone who considers herself an active lifelong learner, I'm regularly taken aback by just how hard it is to learn. Seemingly easy tasks, such as learning how to keep the newly planted flowers in our garden alive, deceive me regularly. *I got a PhD—how hard can it be to take care of some plants?* Turns out, pretty damn hard. (I killed them all within a month.)

A peak personal learning moment came recently when I went on a couples ski holiday in Austria. I had snowboarded once before and enjoyed the minute amount of boarding I actually managed. (Most of my time was spent sitting on my board searching for the abs I needed to stand up.) I was excited to get back on my board and try again. However, recognizing the 2-year gap in my experiences and the likely skill loss that had occurred, I started fresh with my snowboard learning routine:

1. I bought the snowboard, boots and bindings, jacket, pants, thermals, goggles, and helmet (all of which were obviously super-cute).
2. I signed up for snowboard school.
3. I showed up to class.

Based on my previous snowboarding experience, I held no false hope that I would be flying down the mountain by the end of the day or even the weekend. I set a modest goal to make it down the bunny slope without falling and to practice getting on and off the ski lift.

However, it had been some time since I last committed to learning an entirely new activity. And I forgot how much physical and mental effort it required.

In my 2-hour lesson, I spent more time sprawled on the ground than standing on my board. I hit my head at least four times *(wear your helmet, kids!)*. As a result, my legs burned from squatting worse than after a 2-hour barre class. My head hurt both from falling on it and from the sheer concentration required to *not* lean back when everything in me screamed "Lean back, girl!"

The 2 hours resembled a form of slapstick comedy: lean back, fall down, cry, flip over, stand up. Rinse. Lather. Repeat.

Learning to snowboard hurt.

Learning to snowboard was uncomfortable, difficult, and painful—both physically and emotionally.

With the patience of my partner and instructor, and the encouragement of my friends, however, I found the energy to keep going. By the end of the weekend, my snow-covered butt was falling down an actual piste.

Here's a picture of me *almost* at the bottom. The exhaustion was real.

Once, much to the horror of my partner, I fell in the middle of the piste—stuck smack in the middle of a bend between a blue (beginner—my route) and red (advanced—likely death) slope. I pushed myself up, arms, legs, and brain fatigued from the journey thus far, and leaned. The angle at which I landed, however, required me to lean forward into the red slope to turn myself toward the direction of the blue slope. The motion required defied all logic. As I stood up, my body betrayed me and leaned back— physically away from, but simultaneously turning my board toward, the red slope. Within seconds, I fell back on my butt, slamming my pelvis on the ground. As I repeated this process again and again, growing more desperate each time, I inched my way closer to the red slope.

After the fourth attempt, I quit.

I collapsed in the middle of the slope and cried.

Skiers and snowboarders came flying past, darting right and left to avoid me. At one point, a group of three-year-olds came flying down the slope hand in hand, laughing as they nimbly dodged the sad grown woman crying in their path.

Eventually, I unsnapped my bindings, picked up my board, and carried it to the edge of the slope where I sat in a snow chair and, you guessed it, cried some more. My partner put his arm around me and asked, "Why are you crying? That won't help you get down this mountain. Take a breath, and then let's do this."

After a few more tears, I stood up, and continued to fall my way down the mountain.

The next day, I woke up, made my way up the mountain, and repeated the process.

In each of those moments, I had a choice. I could give up at any time and retire from my wildly (un)successful snowboard career. Or, I could put in the effort and push my physical and emotional boundaries to become the next Lindsey Jacobellis (or simply make it 5 minutes without crying).

Obviously, I'm now well on my way to the Olympics.

I tell this story to share a time I persisted when learning was difficult. But I could write far more pages about the number of times that I didn't take the opportunity or get back up and, as a result, failed to learn. As my husband often reminds me, "You do tend to quit things." (*But this book is self-deprecating enough, so let's move on.*)

Despite all the tears and the butt pain, I enjoyed the experience more than I hated it. As difficult as any learning experience can be, it can also be rewarding and at times even fun.

My snowboard instructor, a wonderful Danish woman, quoted *Titanic* with me as she held my hands down the bunny slope: "Don't let go, Jack." My colleagues, all of whom are far smarter than I, send me memes as we struggle to develop a new idea or wrestle with interpreting our data. Working with them makes learning fun—even in its hardest moments.

And of course, the outcomes of learning—finishing that paper after years of grappling with an idea, not making the same mistakes in your personal life again, or making it down the piste for the first time—act as positive rewards in themselves. The outcomes often justify the painful pursuit.

However hard or fun it may be, learning is essential for improvement. I won't sit here in my ivory coffee shop and tell you that it is essential for success, because, to put it plainly—it isn't. Our society and the associated systems were not designed to reward learning. They were designed to reward looking like you are learning. Two very different things.

Many of these systems can be cheated. For instance, you could graduate school by taking all online classes and asking someone else to complete your assignments. When it comes to self-development, you could never learn from your mistakes and simply change your friends every time one set gives up on you. You could ascend to leadership positions by acting like you know things that you have no clue about.

So no, I won't tell you that you *need* to learn to be *perceived* as successful in this world.

There is a difference between perceived and actual effectiveness. What we perceive to be effective is heavily influenced by our biases and stereotype—what we think a leader should do or say. In contrast, actual leader effectiveness is measured by metrics of success such as how much profit was made, high levels of engagement from employees, or the development of sustainable solutions to difficult problems. We see this dichotomy clearly in the peacock vs bower bird debate. We are often blinded by a leader's confidence, failing to appropriately assess their competence. When it comes to learning, leaders can fool us with their confidence and avoid learning anything at all. Although I'd like to believe that this will catch up with them over time, the number of leaders wielding power who appear to have learned nothing (or very little) suggests otherwise.

To be an *effective* leader, however, you must learn.

During the COVID-19 pandemic, leaders learning became an intriguing topic of everyday discussion. I remember riding in friends' cars and hearing them make statements such as, "At least we know how to handle it next time." Media outlets noted that successful countries were writing the playbook for more effective responses to future pandemics.

For the general public who lack expertise in epidemiology and pandemic response, these are logical statements. However, if we simply scratch the surface of world history, we quickly realize that COVID-19 was not the first pandemic. In modern history alone, we could consider Ebola, the swine flu, the Spanish flu, polio, and HIV/AIDS. All of them occurred within the last century(ish). Prior to the 1900s, we find the Black Death (bubonic plague), smallpox, cholera . . . you get the point:

COVID-19 wasn't the first pandemic.

For years, scientists had been signaling that a catastrophic, global pandemic was on the horizon. In 2017, Bill Gates noted,

> Whether it occurs by a quirk of nature or at the hand of a terrorist, epidemiologists say a fast-moving airborne pathogen could kill more than 30 million people in less than a year. And they say there is a reasonable probability the world will experience such an outbreak in the next 10 to 15 years.[1]

In the months leading up to the first case of COVID-19 in Wuhan, Netflix released a documentary on the potential for a catastrophic pandemic that could change life as we know it. In the film, the director of USAID's Emerging Threats Unit states, "When we talk about another flu pandemic happening, it's not a matter of if, but when."[2]

The experts predicted a virus similar to COVID-19, and for years before the pandemic began, they had warned governments and leaders about the risk.

In response to the looming threat, scientists and government experts wrote playbooks. They disseminated these playbooks. They even practiced executing these playbooks! For example, the US previously published a 69-page document explaining exactly how government leaders should respond if a "high-consequence emerging disease threat" materialized. This playbook referenced several potential threats, including . . . wait for it . . . a novel coronavirus![3] In addition, the Trump administration had conducted a dry run exercise in 2019 focused on how they would respond to a pandemic crisis.

Despite these playbooks and opportunities to learn from practice, many leaders appeared to repeat mistakes of the past. They failed to learn. Imaginary Living Room Olympian Jonathan Van Ness (JVN) of *Queer Eye* fame talks about leaders' general failure to learn from previous pandemics in their stand-up act. As someone living with HIV/AIDs, JVN has been living through a failed government pandemic response for years. "You are surprised [by the response]?" JVN jokingly asks the audience.[4]

If we reflect on the global response to AIDS, we can see an example of both failed leadership, as well as a missed opportunity to learn. From a scientific perspective, the French government identified the cause of AIDS

relatively quickly, an accomplishment that would later win the team a
Nobel Prize.

From a leadership perspective, the Reagan administration severely
underestimated the impact and failed to provide the necessary resources
and support to combat the disease. Donald Francis, a member of the CDC
team working to combat HIV/AIDS in the United States during its emergence, recounts the Reagan administration's response.[5] He points to the
direct impact of deficient policy and financial support on the spread of
the disease both within the country and around the world, attributing the
failed response directly to Reagan.

In the development of the United States' response, Francis notes the
lessons learned from previous pandemics and the messaging used to combat the spread of these diseases. With Ebola and smallpox, for instance,
straightforward messaging worked well, as the consequences and sever-
ity of the diseases emerged quickly and obviously. With AIDS, a new
approach was needed due to the disease's 10-year incubation period and
the long-term nature of the necessary behavioral changes. Learning from
previous efforts and applying their knowledge to the unique characteristics of AIDS, the CDC proposed its plan:[5]

> So with the usual CDC zeal, I met with behavior change experts
> to come up with a plan and a budget of what it would take
> to decrease the risk of AIDS in both gay and straight people
> at risk. In the absence of a vaccine to prevent HIV infection,
> the approach to prevention was rather straightforward—teach
> uninfected people how to remain uninfected and teach infected
> people how not to infect others.

Unfortunately, the Reagan administration rejected the CDC's plan. As
Francis recalls, Reagan told the CDC to "look pretty and do as little as
you can."

It's important to note that at the time, the CDC estimated an 80 percent
mortality rate. As the AIDS pandemic continued, however, it became apparent that nearly everyone who contracted AIDS would die from the disease.
Nearly everyone.

Although AIDS is no longer a death sentence thanks to continued investment and research, the mortality rate at the time suggested that urgent action was required. Scientists and government officials were acutely aware of the consequences of this disease and of letting it spread. But they let it spread anyway.

In his conclusion, Francis falls just short of damning the Reagan administration to hell:

> So much of our early response to AIDS was mishandled and misdirected in the United States. As much of the world turns to the CDC for leadership in cases of new epidemics, the resulting vacuum had much wider ramifications. But with AIDS, it was not just an absence of leadership. It was often active obstruction of logical responses. These people caused immense preventable suffering and death—and it is likely that no one in the Reagan Administration will ever be held accountable.[5]

Published in 2012, 8 years before the emergence of COVID-19, this article provides a perfect opportunity for leaders to reflect on the failings of previous administrations and to prepare a more robust response. While not all leaders learned from past mistakes and missteps, some leaders did. Singapore and Halinah Yacob provide on such example.

Singapore's success at managing COVID-19 has been directly associated with its preparation and learning from previous crises. One analysis stated, "Singapore's crisis management capability is the result of continual learning from past crises."[6]

Singapore's President, Halimah Yacob, is the first woman to lead the nation. Although she was technically "elected," changes in governmental rules on candidate eligibility left her the only candidate standing in the race. In contrast to a popularly elected leader, her ascent to power suggests that she may not be universally loved or respected, creating challenges for her when needing to assert her power and ask Singaporeans to follow her direction.

Also important to Halimah's presidency is an understanding of the largely ceremonial role of Singapore's president. She appoints the prime minister, who then leads the government. However, she maintains veto power. As such, her role in the execution of Singapore's response was rather limited. And while we likely cannot directly attribute all of the country's successes to her, we also cannot rule out her influence.

Throughout COVID-19, Halimah was seen supporting the country's previously established efforts to combat a pandemic and existing institutions and processes aimed at navigating a crisis. For instance, previous Singaporean governments established the Homefront Crisis Ministerial Executive Group Committee (HCMEG) to help the country effectively respond to crises. The HCMCEG was formed after the *Laju* ferry hijack in 1974 and later played a critical leadership role in response to crises such as the 1986 Hotel New World collapse, the 1991 SQ117 hijacking, and the 2003 SARS outbreak. Based on lessons from the impact of SARS, the HCMCEG was later restructured to be part of the larger Homefront Crisis Ministerial Committee (HCMC). Included in the HCMC are components such as a coordination center, a crisis management group, an operations committee, and incident managers.

Drawing on previous crisis experiences, the HCMC was intentionally structured to communicate effectively across all government bodies. The Singaporean government historically emphasized a "whole-of-government" or collective mindset that highlights the need for interdepartment, multidisciplinary responses to crises.[6] This approach reflects the "oneness" of the country, suggesting that government agents should work with its citizens to develop effective solutions that work for the whole country. It underscores the presence of the Singaporean government on a daily basis. When crisis comes knocking on their door, the idea of working together comes easily to Singaporeans.

The Singaporean government also developed specific protocols on how to respond should a threat similar to SARS emerge. These include practices such as contact tracing and quarantine. The protocols led Singaporean leaders to implement travel restrictions early on and to begin contact tracing within days of the announcement from China about a dangerous new virus.

In April, the Singapore Parliament passed the COVID-19 Temporary Measures Act 2020, which introduced policies and practices related to human movement as well as to social and economic activities such as remote marriages and property tax remission. In a later act in the same year, the government addressed how voting and candidate procedures for elections would be altered to account for the changing circumstances and restrictions. Later, parliament would extend its actions to stimulus packages and other actions aimed at providing sufficient support to their citizens.

In contrast to the United States where governmental action spurred debates around civil liberties and individual rights, Singaporeans were largely supportive of measures taken. Some of this response is attributable to Singapore's regular interventionist style of government. Singaporeans are used to government intervention. But the government also clearly communicated the temporary nature of its measures—a communication strategy that undoubtably helped with policy adoption and compliance.[7]

Rounding out its arsenal, Singapore also took a zero-COVID approach and encouraged vaccination hard and early.[8] This approach helped the country keep COVID-19 at bay until vaccinations created a safer environment for Singaporeans to move about. Messaging around vaccines focused on the scientific benefits and evidence-driven decision making. Once again, the government's messaging was clear.

Singapore learned. And its leaders, in particular, Halimah, followed the lessons from previous crises and the systems put in place by previous leaders to ensure such crises were effectively managed. Halimah could have thrown out the playbook. She could have let arrogance take the reins and manage it how she saw fit. But she didn't. She and the rest of the government took rational, evidence-based actions that were largely based on lessons from the past—lessons that help Singapore effectively combat COVID-19.

There are several examples of men, particularly in Asian countries, who similarly learned from past crises and experiences.[9] However, as noted at the outset of this book, there have been enough pages dedicated to men's successes to last a lifetime. As this book is about women, the focus is on *their* successes.

If we move away from the COVID-19 crisis, we see another great example of learning from Germany's Angela Merkel.

It is perhaps easy to believe that Merkel was always the stoic, politically cunning woman she is today. As told in her biography by Qvortrup, however, much of Merkel's success was due to teachings from her mentor and the quick pace with which she learned and adapted to the political environment.[10]

Entering the political scene at age 35, Merkel immediately shot to the top of the field. Ambitious and determined, she networked with the best of the best, even finding a way to connect with then-chancellor, Helmut Kohl, while she was still merely a candidate for political office. Kohl, already aware of Merkel and her talent, took a meeting with her, setting in motion the launch of Angela Merkel as a political icon.

After Merkel won her constituency by impressive numbers in 1990, Kohl appointed her to his cabinet as the federal minister for women and young people. This move put Merkel on the political map. Their relationship and the influence Kohl had on her career was well known, with the press even nicknaming her "Kohl's girl."

In her early days, Merkel was not known as the politically cunning leader she is today. As Qvortrup recounts, Merkel regularly cried in the face of conflict with other political leaders. She knew, however, that crying in the office, particularly in an office dominated by men, would not set her up for a successful career—she quickly recognized the need to change.

As a leader, Merkel made both brilliant decisions and misguided missteps. As minister of the environment, for instance, Merkel and her office miscalculated the radiation levels important for a particular deal on banning cars. In response, one of her harshest critics, Gerhard Schroder, publicly referred to her as pitiful and incompetent. Others believed her to be the weakest of Kohl's cabinet.

It was at this time that the men truly underestimated Merkel and her ability to adapt. Other leaders in her party who showed ambitions for the top job discounted her as a political rival. Because others underestimated her, she was offered jobs and positions that no one would dream of offering their political rivals—positions that placed her in the public limelight and inches from the most powerful position in the country.

This criticism and doubt only fueled Merkel and her ambition. Over the next few years, she watched and learned how to play the game. She took copious notes and transformed herself into a political powerhouse.

This is perhaps best demonstrated by her 1999 takedown of Chancellor Kohl and the Christian Democrat Party leader Wolfgang Schäuble. Drama over illegal party donations was sending the Christian Democrat Party plummeting in the polls. At the time, Merkel held a party leadership position and used her media contacts to reach out to the political correspondent at a prominent newspaper. Rather than play the expected hand, defending the former and current party leaders' behavior (not to mention the man who was highly regarded as her political mentor), Merkel threw them under the bus—*Mean Girls* style. She wrote a scathing article about their behavior and the damage it was doing to the party.

Merkel had changed. She was no longer the woman who cried at conflict but the woman who approached it head on.

The stories of Halimah and Merkel highlight several key points about the learning process. First, there are multiple pathways to learning. Although academic learning may be first to mind, we also learn by doing and by watching what others do. When it comes to learning by doing, practice is essential. We need opportunities to continuously practice learned attitudes and skills. In learning to snowboard, for example, I practiced on the bunny hill a thousand and one times before advancing up the slopes. Similarly, if you've taken a training course in which the trainer made you role-play or discuss a case with your coworkers, you've engaged in practice. With COVID-19, we listened to the expert guidance from governing bodies, scientists, and leaders on the appropriate response to becoming ill.

Second, feedback is queen. Feedback can come from multiple sources. We receive direct feedback from our performance itself. Falling down in the middle of the piste, for instance, is feedback telling me that I'm not quite ready for my Olympic debut. When we fail an exam, that's feedback. When leaders make a financial decision that tanks their company's stock market performance, that's feedback. When leaders made decisions about how to manage COVID-19, they received feedback in the form of case counts and death rates.

We also receive immediate feedback from others who judge our performance. In training, for example, a trainer will comment on a role-play or a team's case analysis. In my snowboard lesson, my instructor yelled, "You're doing it! Keep going!" When it came to COVID-19, scientific experts provided feedback to leaders regarding the execution of their advice and to the public regarding their opinions of the leaders' decisions and actions.

What we do with feedback influences whether or not we learn. We can ignore feedback, or we can reflect on it and use it to improve our future actions, as the Singaporean government did with lessons from previous pandemics.

Third, we learn not only by doing but also by watching. Albert Bandura, a famous psychologist, termed learning by watching the "social learning theory." If you've ever taken an introductory psychology course, you've likely heard about him and his bobo dolls. In his experiments, Bandura was interested in whether or not children learned by simply watching others—a view that directly challenged the in-vogue theories of his time. To test his hypotheses, he set up a traditional experimental protocol in his laboratory in which participants were assigned to one of three conditions. In the aggressive condition, children watched as an adult beat up the doll. The remaining children either saw an adult interact non-aggressively with the doll or did not see anyone interact with the doll at all. The children then entered the laboratory and Bandura observed their behavior.

As he watched, he noted that children who witnessed an adult interact with the bobo doll aggressively were far more likely to beat up the doll than were children in other conditions. He even noted that these children developed new ways of harming the doll! In contrast, children who witnessed nonaggressive actions toward the doll or no interactions at all were less likely to interact with the doll aggressively.

What might seem an obvious conclusion now was then a radical departure from the predominant view of human behavior and learning. At the time, popular theories argued that learning required either reward or punishment. Bandura's bobo dolls, however, offered an alternative: humans learn by observing others even when no rewards or punishment are present. In the conclusion of his famous paper describing his experiments, he notes:

> Traditional theories of learning generally depict behavior as the product of directly experienced response consequences. In actuality, virtually all learning phenomena resulting from direct experiences can occur on a vicarious basis through observation of other people's behavior and its consequences for them. Man's capacity to learn by observation enables him to acquire large, integrated units of behavior by example without having to build up the patterns gradually by tedious trial and error.[11]

We learn by watching others. In observing how others behave or respond to a tricky situation, we can also observe the feedback they receive. Just as we might learn from a training exercise and a trainer's feedback on our performance, we can similarly learn from how others respond to an exercise or a crisis. With COVID-19, for instance, Halimah and her government observed previous leaders' responses to disease outbreaks and the effectiveness of these responses in controlling the disease. She could then act on the current threat on the basis of lessons gleaned from past leaders.

Cumulatively, when we practice or when we learn from others, we are building up our case-based knowledge. We can then use this knowledge to solve future problems that are similar to those we or others have encountered in the past. When we face similar challenges, for instance, the previous case or cases will come to mind and suggest to us a response.

The more case-based knowledge we have, the more expertise we have and therefore the easier it becomes to respond quickly *and* accurately. When leaders build up enough case-based knowledge, they possess the expertise that allows them to act intuitively.

For instance, consider the following scenario: you are setting out on your first international vacation and need to book restaurants for dinner out each evening. As this is your first time, you scour the Internet for places to eat—looking at Google reviews, Trip Advisor, Open Table, and every personal blog ever written about restaurants in that area. Based on your search, you book a range of restaurants. Some are absolute hits, and some fail to satiate.

The next time you go on a trip, you consider what those hits had in common. Was it the vibe? Did they have similar reviews on a particular website? Were they recommended by a certain blogger? You return to the websites where you found the most success and refine your search process.

You now repeat and continue to refine this process before each trip. By your tenth international trip, you know what you want and what to look for, so you head straight to those resources. Through experience, you've built up your expertise on how to search for restaurants you'll love. And the process is now so familiar, it is nearly automated.

The more case-based knowledge you accumulate and the more you integrate this knowledge into your overarching narrative and worldview, the more effective you will be as a leader. Doing so is far more complex and takes significantly more energy than clicking through an online slide deck on the six essential skills for leadership or even reading this book. Learning is an active process, and case-based learning requires reflection, integration, and action.

WHY DON'T WE LEARN?

I mentioned at the start of this chapter that not everyone learns even when presented with the same opportunity. The reason is not quite as simple as failing to take the opportunity. Learning also requires that we recognize a gap, we seek out, receive, and process accurate feedback, and that we choose to make a change.

This is a particularly difficult set of steps for those in leadership positions. As leaders climb the ladder, they receive less and less feedback with each step.[12] As you are likely not shocked to hear, many of us hesitate to express our feedback to leaders in positions of substantial power. This is particularly true in hierarchal organizations and societies where leaders frown upon being challenged or when we go over a leader's head to speak with their immediate supervisor. Even when leaders at high levels *elicit* feedback from their followers, we still might feel uncomfortable sharing our honest opinion. These leaders wield consequential power, such as authority over whether we keep our job, get promoted, or can access resources. It is understandable that we might not be willing to walk up to a senior leader or the president of a country and say, "Hey, you screwed up." (Although the internet has created new pathways that embolden some to do so behind the safety of their keyboards.)

Leaders, then, receive less feedback and may receive less *accurate* feedback the higher up they progress.

The implication for learning is that leaders may have a more difficult time learning in the same way that those of us lower down the ladder might. However, we often see leaders with coaches and teams around them who, if well cultivated, can provide direct feedback. Seeking feedback in this way is much more intentional. To learn and continue improving, leaders must elicit feedback, create an environment where people feel safe providing it, and take time to reflect and act on the input they receive. They also must be discerning about who is providing honest feedback and who might be acting in their own self-interest.

PRACTICAL LEARNING STEPS

To avoid leaving you with an abstract idea, here is my recommended action-oriented plan for building up your learning muscles:

1. *Make time for daily reflection:* I'm as guilty as the next person of filling my days to the brim and leaving no space to reflect on the day. Make time, even just 10 minutes a day, to sit with your thoughts and reflect on your own actions and the actions of others around you.

2. *Draw a mind map:* Even if you lack doodling skills, drawing out your thoughts can help you make connections in a new way. This is partly because we can hold only so much information in our head at one time. By sketching a mind map, we can offload some of the information to focus on other cases or ideas related to it.

3. *Ask for feedback:* If you don't receive feedback on a decision or your actions, ask someone who can appropriately judge your actions. In work cases, this might be your peers, your supervisor,

or even those working for you. Gaining a 360-degree perspective on your performance provides insight into how different groups view you and your choices. It's up to you, in your reflection time, to choose how to act on this feedback.

4. *Start a conversation:* Although we might observe others' actions, we might not see all the feedback they receive or know the personal impact of their choices. Asking others about their experiences can provide us with a more holistic perspective on a case or situation, allowing us to fuse better connections in our mind maps.

Resilience

The difficulty of learning necessitates that learners possess a certain amount of resilience, or grit, to persist through the process. When learning, we metaphorically and sometimes physically get knocked to the ground. It smacks us in the face with the recognition that we don't know how to do something, what something means, or where to go from here. To keep going, we must pick ourselves up, dust the dirt from our pants, and try again.

Bearing this in mind, individual resilience, or the act of bouncing back after being knocked down, is essential to learning and to growth.

However, resilience is not an excuse to be a jerk. We often see resilience used as a crutch for bad behavior. Bullies, for example, might argue that their prey just need to be more resilient. We see whole companies offer resilience training to help employees overcome a toxic work environment, outrageous hours, and bad leadership—rather than address the heart of the problem.

I see headlines about women needing more grit or more resilience to make it in male-dominated fields. If only women were just a bit more resilient and toughed it out a little longer, then they would grow into leadership positions.

A recent trend has even focused on offering "ladies-only" resilience training: Be more resilient, ladies! Suck it up a little more, ladies! Only a little more abuse, and then you'll be there, ladies!

With all due respect, *hell no*.

Yes, learning and growth require resilience. But women should not need to resilience their way out of a toxic and abusive work culture that was not built to include them.

Women *are*—permanently and indispensably—a part of the work culture, and it's therefore the culture that must be resilient enough to respect their presence.

Thanks for coming to my Ted Talk.

Emotion Management

It's the summer of 2010, and your plane lands at New York's JFK airport. As the plane hits the runway, you gaze up from the pages of your tantalizing beach read and daydream out the window. As you are caught somewhere between your dream beach vacation and the bustling noise of the other passengers, the plane idles on the taxiway. The pilot announces you will be waiting a few more minutes for a gate to open.

You hear commotion between a flight attendant and passenger coming from a few rows ahead but can't quite hear what they are saying. Your attention returns to your book as you try to pass the time before you deplane and stretch your legs.

After a few minutes, the plane intercom crackles, and you listen for an update on the gate situation. Instead, much to your surprise, the flight attendant says, "I've been in this business for twenty years, and that's it. I've had it. I'm done."

With that, he grabs two cans of beer, opens the emergency exit door, activates the emergency slide, and jumps out of the plane.

Several passengers gasp in horror, while others laugh at the stunt. You think, *What the hell?* before noticing the flight attendant struggling to climb back up the slide. Slipping back down with every inch up, he claws his way to the top of the slide only to grab his forgotten bag and jump back down the slide.

He struts down the runway and off into the sunset as he tosses his airline assigned tie to the wind.[1]

Steven Slater's real-life exit from Jet Blue flight 1052 caused a stir in the airline industry. The public, too, was caught up in the story, not only because Slater was arrested for his actions (he abandoned the plane on an active taxiway, endangering passengers on his flight and others) but also because he brought attention to the known, but not often discussed, emotional labor of flight crews.

Emotional labor, or the emotion management required on the job, is largely synonymous with our view of customer-facing roles—restaurant servers, customer service representatives, Disneyland workers, and of course, flight attendants. Each of these positions requires a significant amount of emotion regulation. The job holders must display emotions appropriate for the setting (usually a friendly smile), manage their own emotional responses, and influence the emotions of those with whom they interact. Mantras such as "service with a smile" highlight the codified nature of emotional labor in these roles—regardless of how you personally feel, you *must* look and act happy.

For many roles, this emotional component is a make-it-or-break-it requirement. Imagine, for example, arriving at Disneyland, the *happiest* place on earth, and being greeted by a frowning gate attendant who, angrily greets you with, "Hey. Hope your day doesn't suck." Doesn't quite match the magic kingdom vibe, does it?

Or maybe you pull up to Chick-fil-A drive-thru or check in for a stay at the Ritz Carlton, two companies renowned for their customer service, and as the employee hands your chicken sandwich through the window or passes you your room key card, they smirk at you, roll their eyes, and say, "Just take it."

Such behavior doesn't conform with the friendly, welcoming environment you expect, nor does it promote the environment that keeps customers coming back to these businesses. As the day-to-day faces of the company, employees communicate the values of an organization through their actions. Their emotional expressions signal the vibe of the company to customers and influence how a customer feels about the company (and what kind of Google review they will leave).

But emotional labor is more than just smiling at customers. Emotional labor also requires the execution of complex emotions in high-stakes, emotional events. Take Slater, our dramatic-exit flight attendant, as an example. Slater reported that two passengers had quibbled about overhead bin space during boarding, setting a negative tone between the passengers and Slater from the start. In his statement (which was later *not* corroborated by others who witnessed the situation), he reported that the two passengers stood up to collect their bags while the plane was still taxiing. When he confronted them, the passengers bumped him in the head with their bag.

In the world of emotional labor, this is the moment you train for. Emotions loom heavy in the air, the environment heats up, and your responsibility is to remain calm, smile, and bring everyone's temperature down.

"Peacing out" of the plane while on an active taxiway does not classify as successful emotion management.

In contrast, I am currently sitting in a coffee shop window, facing a local pub along the River Thames in London. I hear chatter behind me and turn to see the manager, Rebekah, engaging in some emotional labor of her own. A customer with curly, gray hair, wearing a flowy pink floral dress and a denim jacket, explains that she booked a table for 12 people for lunch—but the café has no record of such a booking. The woman and Rebekah step outside the café to discuss the situation, to which I have a front row view out my window. The woman looks flustered and a bit angry. This is England, however, so she doesn't ask for Rebekah's supervisor, she doesn't yell, and she certainty doesn't say anything rude. She simply tuts (a small click of the tongue to signal one's irritation) and sighs heavily. Rebekah calmly explains that she will do her best to accommodate the group. She remains calm, subtly smiling as she helps the customer fix her reservation problem. The conversation appears to resolve calmly as Rebekah introduces the woman to the manager at the pub across the street. The woman in the pink dress enters the pub and, I assume, enjoys a lovely lunch with her 11 friends.

Unlike Slater, Rebekah has managed her emotional response to the customer and helped shift the tone of the conversation and the woman's emotions to effectively resolve the situation. *You go, girl.*

As demonstrated, it is the emotional laborer's role to manage the emotions of the situation. That is not to say that the customer's behavior is morally right and justified and that the person engaging in the emotional labor should *have to* manage their emotions. That is far from the point. In fact, I'd be hard pressed not to mention the dangers that the "customer is king" (or queen) mentality wreaks on people who hold these positions. We know that people who regularly engage in emotional labor experience high levels of burnout and, as a consequence, frequently leave these positions. We, as customers, certainly bear responsibility for treating individuals in these roles humanely.

While true, it is also true that, until people become perfect, emotional labor will be a mainstay of any job that requires human-to-human interaction.

And, just as human-to-human interaction is a definitional component of leadership (remember: you can't be a leader without followers), so too is emotional labor. Although perhaps not as obvious an example as a call center representative or coffee shop manager, leadership also requires regulating our own emotions as well as managing the emotions of others.

Consider influence—the fundamental goal of leadership. To influence another person, we often must adopt a particular emotional tone or response with the goal of eliciting a desired emotion or response in that person. Throughout the COVID-19 pandemic, for instance, world leaders had to manage our fears, our anxieties, our anger. They did so with the goal of managing our behavior, attempting to influence us to help slow the spread of the virus and keep us safe.

While managing our emotions, these leaders had to simultaneously manage their own emotional response to the virus. After all, leaders are people too. They experienced their own fears and anxieties as the virus took hold of the world. And while expressing some of their own authentic emotions may have been desirable in theory, leaders couldn't publicly express their fears in the same way that the rest of us could at that time.

Like many, my partner, family, friends, and I spoke in the early months of COVID-19 about how scared we were, the uncertainty of what was to come, and the anger that our lives had been completely disrupted. As private citizens, these conversations were normal and quite appropriate. But imagine if Angela Merkel had held a press conference to say she was scared witless and had no idea what was going on. Or if Tsai Ing-Wen had announced to Taiwan that she thought the End of Days had come. We wouldn't classify such comments as effective leadership. Instead, they and other world leaders had to process their own emotions first and then craft a plan for helping the rest of us work through these scary times. We look to leaders to guide us through difficult situations and help us make sense of issues. Leaders serve as signposts for how we should feel about a situation.

Emotional contagion refers to when we "catch" others' emotions. If I smile at you, you are then likely to smile at me. And when you smile, you are likely to feel happy! We know this "smile contagion" happens in person, and research in the early 2000s demonstrated that it also happens online. A study using Facebook status updates showed that when Facebook users saw more positive posts in their feed, they were less likely to make posts themselves that contained negative emotions, and vice versa.[2]

In the context of leadership, emotions trickle down from leaders to impact how their followers feel about a situation. Emotion management is therefore a key skill required for successful leadership.

Although the importance of emotion management in leadership may seem obvious, our conversations on emotions and leadership are typically emotion-management adjacent—we comment on a leader's emotionality but not necessarily on the underlying management of their own and of our emotions. We talk about how leaders are too emotional or not emotional enough. We don't talk about the effort it took to regulate their emotions or to make us feel a particular way.

Further, our conversations of emotions and leadership are heavily biased by our stereotypes, particularly our stereotype of women as emotional disasters who follow their hearts rather than their heads. This belief sounds something like, "Leadership isn't for the ladies—they are far too emotional." At least once every semester I read a student paper that explicitly states this claim as a reason women are not suited for leadership positions.

While many of our stereotypes are implicit, meaning they influence our thinking but we might not blurt them out in public, the belief that women are too emotional for leadership is an explicit stereotype that has been famously stated, out loud, in front of other people, by many.

For example, when faced with a Supreme Court nomination, US President Nixon stated:

I don't think a woman should be in any government job what-
ever. I mean, I really don't. The reason why I do is mainly
because they are erratic. And emotional. Men are erratic and
emotional, too, but the point is a woman is more likely to be.[3]

Of course, that was the 1970s. Things have totally changed
since then, right? *Right?*

Let's look at the 2016 US presidential race. A regularly touted reason
for opposing Hilary Clinton was that her emotions made her "dangerous."
And some expressed concerns about being unable to trust a woman during
her period to make sound decisions—she'd go for the nuclear option!
Clinton herself recognized this while speaking with Amanda de Cadenet:[4]

Here is my dilemma . . . as a woman in a high public position
or seeking the presidency as I am, you have to be aware of how
people will judge you for being, quote 'emotional.' And so it's a
really delicate balancing act—how you navigate what is still a
relatively narrow path—to be yourself, to express yourself, to
let your feelings show, but not in a way that triggers all of the
negative stereotypes.

The good news is that the view of women as "too emotional for leadership" is lessening. A 2019 report from Georgetown University's Center on
Education and the Workforce found that one in eight Americans (13 percent) believe that women are too emotional for leadership positions.[5]
Although a far cry from the 50 percent in the 1970s and certainly a mark
of progress in our views of women, this view remains a substantial barrier
to women's advancement.

Research finds that women and men demonstrate similar fluctuations
in their emotions. In fact, men and women respond with similar levels
of emotion to the same situations.[6] In a study published in the journal
Nature,[7] for example, researchers asked men and women to track their

emotional responses for 75 days. Each night, participants received a survey in which they reported the extent to which they felt positive and negative emotions within the previous 24-hour period. Analyzing the emotions across the 75 days, the researchers found that women and men experienced similar shifts in their emotions. When small differences in emotions that did exist, the data suggested that men may have more variability in their emotions compared to women!

Although previous studies have shown gender differences in emotional responses, these studies have been heavily criticized for their reliance on self-report assessments, asking participants to report their own levels of emotions. A major critique of these measures is that they are subject to the same biases and stereotypes as those that influence others' perceptions of our emotions. Women, for instance, may feel socially pressured to respond in a particular way because they know society expects them to have "all the feels." Happening at an implicit, rather than explicit, level, these expectations influence how each of us responds about our emotions. When researchers account for this potential bias in the data using fancy statistical procedures, emotional responses between men and women appear quite similar.

Additional support for the lack of gender differences in emotional responses comes from studies of brain activity. For example, a meta-analysis of brain activity related to emotional reactions showed no gender differences in activity in the amygdala—the part of the brain responsible for processing emotions.

If you need an example to challenge your notion that women are too emotional for leadership, look no further than Angela Merkel. Crowned Europe's Great Pragmatist, Merkel was known for her *lack of* emotion and her steady hand. Her *un*emotional nature was often celebrated as a strength, demonstrating her ability to approach problems logically and calmly.

However, the press also regularly criticized Merkel for the same characteristic—a catch-22 faced by many women. Some argued that she lacked the rallying pizzaz of a charismatic leader and left some followers uninspired. From a gender perspective, we could also argue that she didn't demonstrate the overly positive emotions we expect of women. She was not warm, positive, and uplifting enough.

Regardless of your take, Merkel's leadership and empirical research demonstrate a key point:

> Women in power are not more likely to make *emotional* decisions than are men in power.

Period. Full stop.

Instead of the emotional, cry-on-the-couch-in-our-pajamas-eating-ice-cream-while-the-world-burns leaders that stereotypes suggest women will be, society's expectations of women make them masters of emotion management. From a young age, women are conditioned to express warm, positive emotions. We explicitly and implicitly teach women to focus on being positive, to smile, and to never show anger. And there are serious consequences for violating these emotional expectations.

For example, a 2018 study compared reactions to male and female lawyers using anger in their closing arguments.[8] Participants viewed recorded closing arguments from a murder case from either a male or female lawyer. Importantly, as this was a controlled experiment, the script used in each recording was identical—meaning that the words were the same regardless of the gender. The only aspects of the argument that differed were the gender of the lawyer delivering the argument and the tone of the argument (angry or calm). Researchers asked participants to rate the lawyer on a series of negative traits (e.g., shrill, hysterical, dramatic) and positive traits (e.g., competent, powerful, confident). The participants then reported how likely they were to hire that lawyer should they find themselves in need of one.

Ready for the results?

Participants were more likely to report wanting to hire the male lawyer when he delivered his closing statement in an angry tone compared to in a calm tone. For female lawyers, however, the trend was reversed: participants reported wanting to hire the female lawyer when she delivered her closing statement in a calm tone rather than an angry tone.

Looking closer at the data, the researchers found that the likelihood of hiring the lawyer was significantly impacted by reported perceptions. For the male lawyer, strong, positive perceptions such as "confident" and "competent" when using an angry tone compared to a calm tone were associated with higher likelihood of wanting to hire that lawyer. For the female lawyer, however, it was stronger negative perceptions such as "shrill" and "hysterical" that led to participants preferring a calm tone over an angry tone.

Men in the courtroom were judged as more competent when they expressed anger over calmness, and this attitude predicted whether a potential client would want to hire them. The opposite was true for women— women in the courtroom were penalized for expressing anger. As a result, participants stated a preference for hiring a calm rather than angry woman. In this instance, men's emotionality (remember that anger is, in fact, an emotion) was viewed positively, whereas the same emotionality was viewed negatively for women.

This effect worsens when taking into account race. For example, research has found support for an "angry black woman" stereotype, which views black women as unfeminine, aggressive, and intent on weakening their partners. In one study, this stereotype led students to rate black female speakers as ruder than white female speakers.[9] In another study, black women in managerial and executive roles reported that this stereotype negatively impacted their work.[10] Other researchers asked participants to select traits that represented black and white women. While traits such as "strong" and "loud" were selected for black women, traits such as "sensitive" and "family-oriented" were selected for white women. In the workplace, negative attributions of black women who express anger have been linked to lower performance evaluations and leadership capability.[11]

In addition to showing warm and fuzzy emotions, women are expected to be more empathetic, focusing on others' emotions and experiences.[12] Empathy is commonly defined as putting yourself in someone else's shoes. Scientifically, empathy's definition is less compact. First introduced in the 1950s by Carl Rogers, an American psychotherapist, the term focused on a therapist's ability to perceive the emotions of their client and to communicate their understanding of those emotions back to the client.[13] Looking closely at this definition, we see that empathy involves more than emotions—it also includes cognitive (e.g., perceiving) and behavioral (e.g., communicating) components. For example, when you feel empathy for another person, the cognitive component represents when you "feel" their pain. In contrast, taking flowers to that person or calling them to let them vent demonstrates the behavioral component of empathy. Although scientists do not fully agree on a single definition, extensions of Roger's definition over time have led to the general view that empathy is a multi-dimensional skill that can be learned and practiced.[14]

As stereotypical gender roles suggest that women should focus on others, women tend to demonstrate more empathy than do men. Although some gender differences in empathy may be attributed to hormonal and neurological differences, substantial evidence suggests that empathy is learned and reinforced as girls develop. In fact, the empathy gap between boys and girls increases later in childhood, suggesting hormonal, neurological, and learned explanations for this difference.[15]

The demanding expectations of women to show empathy and to display positive emotions results in women practicing emotion management and the consideration of others' emotions more than men. This makes women particularly skilled at managing their own emotional expressions as well as considering how others may be feeling.

A leader who can manage their own emotions and who considers how others may be feeling about a situation sounds pretty great, right? Unfortunately, much of the discourse around gender differences in emotions to date has focused on how women must change if they want to be successful leaders. Women must become less warm. Women must become less empathetic. Women must be assertive, selfish, and cunning. Or as the cheerleaders in *Jumanji* say, "Be aggressive. Be, be aggressive!"

If women want to be leaders, they need to be less emotional and more like men.

Unfortunately, the view of leadership as a tough, unemotional man's sport often leads us to downplay the role of emotion management in leadership. If managing emotions is a key component of effective leadership, why should we ask women to do it less? Should we not ask men to manage their emotions more?

What if our expectation that women respond with gentleness rather than anger, that they consider the experiences of others rather than the pursuit of their own goals, results in more effective conflict resolution, communication, and solutions that work for a larger number of people?

Spoiler alert: they do.

In a review of the academic literature on empathy and leadership, researchers found that empathetic leaders increased self-awareness, listening skills, and mentoring success. In addition, empathy led to better relationships between leaders and followers. Together, these improvements contributed to enhanced leadership effectiveness. A 2021 survey of 900 US employees conducted by Catalyst, a nonprofit focused on creating more inclusive workplaces for women, found that a manager's empathy was associated with higher levels of innovation, engagement, and feelings of inclusivity; decreased burnout; and lower intentions to leave an organization.[16]

What if, instead of asking women to be more like men, we developed boys and men who weren't afraid to process their own emotions, to act softly, and who could empathize with others?

I've avoided discussing men's emotions thus far, as men are not the focus of this book. But it bears mentioning that our stereotypes similarly force men into emotional boxes. Although they experience slightly more freedom than women in what emotions they express, they still experience pressure to avoid expressing particular "lady" emotions.

If we opened our views on emotions to consider how developing our empathy and emotion management skills may be useful tools for everyone, perhaps women and men would both benefit. And if leaders—both men and women—develop these skills, then we will see a more effective approach to leadership that prioritizes the views, feelings, and experiences of others.

One leader who has been highly praised for her emotion management and empathetic leadership is Jacinda Ardern. As prime minister of New Zealand, Ardern faced multiple crises. In 2019, she led her country through the Christchurch massacre, where a white supremacist killed 51 people at two local mosques. Later that same year, a volcano on White Island erupted, killing 22 people. And in the months thereafter, New Zealand was faced with the rapid spread of COVID-19.

Ardern's response to each of these crises was largely praised around the world both for the pragmatism of her actions and for her expression of empathy. In response to the 2019 Christchurch shooting, for instance, she visited the community impacted, wearing the traditional headscarf, a hijab. As she pledged to reform her country's gun laws (which she did in the weeks to follow), she also offered to cover the funeral costs of all who were deceased and vowed to never repeat the name of the gunman but to say the names of those who had lost their lives. News outlets from the *Washington Post* to the BBC to France24 praised her for her empathy, love, compassion, *and* strength—a rare combination for leaders.[17-19]

A similar line of praise was echoed for her response to the COVID-19 outbreak. While acting decisively, Ardern emphasized kindness and reminded the people of New Zealand to check in on one another. As reported by *The Atlantic*, "her leadership style is one of empathy in a crisis that tempts people to fend for themselves. Her messages are clear, consistent, and somehow simultaneously sobering and soothing."[20]

Although not without criticism, she has largely received international praise for her empathetic leadership approach. And her empathy has not been at the expense of other important leadership characteristics, such as pragmatism and decisiveness. Ardern's brand of leadership combines these characteristics masterfully, leaving many wishing they had this kind of leadership in their own country.

In an interview with *The Guardian*,[21] Ardern summarized her leadership, emphasizing that empathy does not come at the expensive of strength. Rather, it *is* a strength:

> Kindness, and not being afraid to be kind, or to focus on, or be really driven by empathy. I think one of the sad things that I've seen in political leadership is—because we've placed over time so much emphasis on notions of assertiveness and strength—that we probably have assumed that it means you can't have those other qualities of kindness and empathy. And yet, when you think about all the big challenges that we face in the world, that's probably the quality we need the most. We need our leaders to be able to empathise with the circumstances

of others; to empathise with the next generation that we're making decisions on behalf of. And if we focus only on being seen to be the strongest, most powerful person in the room, then I think we lose what we're meant to be here for. So I'm proudly focused on empathy, because you can be both empathetic and strong.[21]

As empathy focuses on the consideration of others, those who are more skilled in empathy may have a more well-rounded view of how others see or feel in a particular situation. As such, empathetic leaders may be better able to recognize the needs of multiple relevant stakeholders. Extending this further, these leaders may also be better positioned to influence a larger range of stakeholders, thereby widening their impact.

For example, at the height of the COVID-19 pandemic, both Ardern and Erna Solberg, prime minister of Norway, held press conferences specifically for children. Recognizing that children's lives were turned upside-down by school closures and limited social interactions, both leaders understood that children represented a distinct stakeholder group with their own fears and concerns. Similarly, as it was unclear the impact on children and the ways in which COVID-19 spread among them, children's cooperation and participation in the fight against COVID-19 was essential.

By holding a press conference specifically for children in their countries, these leaders showed the children that they were valued and an important part of the country's response to the virus. Further, they were able to directly address the specific concerns of children—concerns that differed from those of their parents. For instance, Solberg answered questions such as: "Can I have a birthday party?" and "Can I visit my grandparents after I went to a shopping center?"[22]

In her children-focused press conference, Ardern, along with two scientists, addressed questions and concerns from her child constituents. Together, the three women tackled New Zealand children's questions about safety, transmission, and the importance of washing your hands. Although kids' questions may have followed similar themes to those of their parents, addressing their questions specifically allowed Solberg and Ardern to put on their "kid gloves" to address children where they were at—adjusting tone, expressions, and language as needed. In doing so, they spoke directly to a specific stakeholder group that was important in fighting the virus.

The good news is that holding children's press conferences and responding empathetically to a mass shooting, pandemic, or volcanic eruption is not some innate trait—women learn and practice the underlying skills that lead to these outcomes their whole lives.

The fact that emotion management and empathy are both learned suggests that all of us can become better at managing emotions and responding empathetically.

But how?

I'm so glad you asked.

IMPROVING YOUR EMPATHY AND EMOTION MANAGEMENT

Research from the health sciences shows us that training improves health practitioners' empathy. For example, a 2016 meta-analysis examined 18 randomized controlled studies of empathy training.[23] Typically associated with drug trials, randomized controlled studies assign participants to either a treatment or control group. In the treatment group, participants receive the experimental drug in question, or in this case, the empathy training. In the control group, participants receive the placebo drug (usually a sugar pill) or in a training context, a training focused on an alternative topic. This meta-analysis compared 18 gold standard studies in which researchers compared the results of empathy training to receiving an alternative "placebo" training. Results across all 18 studies showed that empathy training works.

If you don't have easy access to an empathy training course, here are a few steps you can practice in your own work life to improve your empathy:

- *Practice active listening:* Western culture typically emphasizes speaking, usually loudly. And while making your voice heard is important, it should not come at the expense of listening to others. Active listening, which requires focused attention on the words, tone, and body language of the speaker, goes a long way in making that person feel seen or heard. To practice, consciously focus on the words of others in your conversations. If you find your mind wandering, try to catch yourself and bring your focus back to the speaker. In my training courses, I have often used an active listening game in which one partner describes their dream vacation without stating the destination while the other partner listens. At the end of the game, the listening partner must guess where the speaking partner wants to travel to. The trainees often report how "different" it feels to be so engaged in a conversation. Next time you engage in active listening, notice the effort, the feeling, and your ability to better recall the details that person shares with you.

- *Pay attention:* I love my Apple watch. It reminds me how lazy I am while simultaneously keeping me connected with my friends. But that information comes at an expense—it distracts me from the conversations and other activities I'm engaged in. For example, I am sitting with my best friend who is baring her soul about problems with her husband when my wrist buzzes. I look down to see that my watch is telling me to stand. I focus back on my friend, but it is too late. I'm already distracted and have to ask my friend to go back a point. Apple watches aren't the only things that pull us out of conversation—dogs barking, our own thoughts, other people—all distract us. When talking about online or phone conversations, technology issues also distract us. In communications research, these types of distractions are referred to as "noise," and they disrupt our ability to hear and, ultimately, understand what the other person is saying. So, if you want to practice your empathy, focus your attention on the person in the moment. Limit distractions. Outside of conversations, you can do this on a daily basis. By paying attention to others and recognizing patterns of behavior, you will recognize when people deviate from their patterns. When their behavior changes, it is your opportunity to show you have been paying attention and to follow up with them.

- *Be curious:* Have you ever had someone show genuine interest in you? Do you remember what it felt like when they asked you questions about your life and followed up with meaningful questions that demonstrated they were listening to you? Alternatively, have you ever had someone talk at you for 30 minutes about their new beach life and not once ask you about how things are going for you? Those two conversations leave you feeling differently, don't they? The first shows someone cares about you, whereas the second shows they care about themselves. When demonstrating empathy, we want to show our interest in others by asking questions. Just be careful, as not everyone may want to share details with you. While curiosity can be beneficial for demonstrating empathy, so too can recognizing others' boundaries.

A small caveat: Although empathy has many positive outcomes, it can also have downsides for the empathizer. Just like managing emotions in emotional labor, being empathetic is tiring. It takes cognitive, emotional, and behavioral effort. And unlike mimosas at a Sunday brunch, this effort is not bottomless. The more effort we expend feeling empathetic toward one person, the less effort we may have to be empathetic toward another person. Potential methods for reducing the negative outcomes of expending too much empathy, includ looking for common ground with the other person, making it a team effort, and encouraging breaks.[24]

In addition, the emotional labor literature differentiates between surface and deep acting, where surface acting refers to "faking" the emotions and actions, and deep acting refers to believing in them. Those who engage in surface acting are more likely to experience burnout than are those who engage in deep acting. In other words, those who fake it experience worse outcomes than those who actually feel it.

But as beneficial as it may be to genuinely feel particular emotions, expressing them may not always work to our advantage. Remember, world leaders may have genuinely felt frightened by COVID-19, but telling us how frightened they were would not have been beneficial to managing global panic (not to mention global stock markets).

This is when emotion management becomes important.

To successfully manage an emotional response, leaders must engage in a skill called emotion regulation—the strategies we use to manage, respond to, and influence our own emotions (internal regulation) and the emotions of others (external regulation). These strategies disrupt our emotional processing cycle to help us take control of how we feel.

When left to play out, our emotional processing looks something like this: we experience an event, and certain parts of that event catch our attention. As we focus our attention on these elements, we begin to appraise the situation in relation to our own goals—Is this how I expected to feel? Is this what I wanted to happen? In response to this appraisal, we react and experience an emotion. This emotion, in turn, influences how we view the situation and the process repeats.[25]

To put this process in context, a leader may be delivering an important speech intended to rally a crowd behind her viewpoint. As she (let's call her Amanda) begins her speech, she gazes into the crowd at a sea of blank stares and frowns. Amanda focuses her attention on a few key faces toward the front of the crowd who appear upset with what she has to say. As this is intended to be an uplifting and charismatic speech that sparks positive emotions and actions, the frowning faces do not meet her expectations for how the crowd should be responding. This makes Amanda anxious, leading her to begin sweating and shifting her weight from foot to foot as she continues to speak. As the sweat slowly begins soaking her blouse, the situation grows increasingly dire—frowny faces and sweat stains with no cute blazer to hide them! Not only is the crowd not feeling Amanda's speech, but now, not even Amanda is feeling inspired. She then begins to sweat more, increase her "ums," and twirl her hair between her fingers. And the cycle continues.

But of course, we've all seen the movie where the cycle is disrupted, dramatically altering the plot trajectory. The speech starts off poorly and then something clicks in the speaker, the inspirational music swells, and the speech takes a dramatic turn for the better—ending in cheers and a standing ovation from the crowd.

To see this in action, let's look at the film *Legally Blonde*. Dumped by her boyfriend Warner, Elle Woods finds herself completely dejected—spending days in bed with chocolates and her dog, Bruiser. Soon thereafter,

Elle develops a "completely brilliant plan" to get her ex back. The music and her emotions dramatically change, and the motivational montage begins. No longer is Elle depressed; she is now energized and committed to gaining entrance into Harvard Law and winning over her ex.

Aside from excellent writing and acting, what is it that shifts in Elle Woods to turn her trajectory around from a state of despair to an inspired mission?

Elle realizes that being depressed isn't achieving what she wants. What she wants requires action. It requires a near perfect score on LSAT. And it requires a transformation. She needs to make a change. It is in the shift in her emotions from depression to hope that she responds to the negative appraisal of the breakup by recognizing that a change is needed to align reality with her goals.

If we apply the emotion cycle to this scenario, we see Elle on a date (the situation), get dumped (attention), evaluate that this is not how she thought her evening or life would go (analysis), and sink into debilitating sadness (response). Disrupting this process is her ability to manage her sadness and change her appraisal of the situation to ultimately change her emotional response. How did Elle do this?

Only Reese Witherspoon and the directors could tell us for sure, but research on emotion regulation argues that there are five options:[26]

1. Situational selection
2. Situation modification
3. Attentional deployment
4. Cognitive change
5. Response modulation

The first two strategies, situational selection and situational modification, focus on managing the environment itself by either declining to participate (selection) or suggesting a specific environment conducive for you (modification). If Elle were engaging in situational selection, she could have dumped Warner first, or chosen not to date him at all. In doing so, she could have avoided the potential outcomes of being dumped (but also those of being in love!). Instead, she likely engaged in situation modification. Rather than regulate her own emotions, she chose to change the situation by plotting to get Warner back.

Attentional deployment refers to how we focus our attention when faced with emotions. We can either distract ourselves by focusing on other elements of the situation or we can ruminate, sustaining our attention on the impetus of our emotion. In Elle's case, she is depicted ruminating on the situation while she lies in bed eating chocolates, which ultimately keeps her temporarily in a cycle of depression. Because she manages to emerge from her bed-ridden state, however, this strategy fails to explain her transformation. If Elle were to have used distraction, she likely would have focused on her current studies, a job, or perhaps jumping back into the dating pool. She chooses none of these options, however, and instead, keeps her attention steadfast on Warner and the breakup.

The most popularly discussed and generally well-regarded emotion regulation tactics fall into the next category: cognitive change. In this category, the focus is on changing or evaluating our emotional response. With cognitive reappraisal, the goal is to reinterpret the stimuli. A common rendition of this strategy is to turn a challenge into an opportunity, applying the old adage, when one door closes, another door opens. These ideas are rooted in cognitive reappraisal and the philosophy that to change our emotions, we simply need to change the way we see the situation. In Elle's case, she may have looked at the breakup as an opportunity to refocus on herself, or perhaps recognize that Warner was a bad boyfriend and she now has the opportunity to pursue new romantic and platonic relationships. (*Of course, she doesn't recognize this until much later in the film.*)

The second strategy in this category is acceptance. With acceptance, we recognize our emotions and consider why they may be occurring. For instance, the night before I wrote this chapter, I woke up in the middle of the night feeling anxious—existential-dread-level anxious. As I lay there, attempting to control my overly exerted breathing (a strategy we talk about next), I began to consider why I was feeling this way. First, I acknowledged that I was having some form of a panic attack. Second, I asked myself whether this was a random heart palpitation that would lead to my death, or was it brought on by falling asleep reading BBC news and stories of the US capitol insurrection, the war in Ukraine, and the Uvalde school massacre? I then considered whether those two things could be linked. All of those stories are terrifying, and perhaps falling asleep while thinking about them led to my waking up an hour later filled with existential dread that made my heart race.

Recognizing that the bedtime stories I chose were those of nightmares, I validated my anxiety and, in doing so, gave my anxiety a cause. This moved my anxiety from a scary random event to an explainable one. Within minutes, my breathing slowed and I was able to fall back to sleep. For Elle, she may have processed her emotions by recognizing that her negative emotions were warranted—heartbreak hurts. Perhaps then, she could have begun a healthy recovery process (although this would make for a much less interesting plot line).

The last category of emotion regulation tactics focuses on managing the response itself. For example, we might suppress our anger in situations where an emotional outburst would be inappropriate, or we might contain our excitement if we are trying to conceal good news. In Elle's case, this means pushing down her feelings of heartbreak and ignoring them so she can move on with her sorority commitments. Another means of emotion regulation is to alter our physiological responses using, for example, breathing exercises or meditation. Elle could have signed up for a meditation session to help reduce her negative thoughts. Instead, she sought therapy at the nail salon (arguably, an equally valid approach).

Of the various strategies available, which one works the best? Research examining the effectiveness of these strategies generally finds cognitive reappraisal to be the most beneficial in shifting emotions and physiological responses as well as in effecting long-term changes.[27] However, contextual variations can influence its effectiveness. Those who engage in cognitive reappraisal frequently may be better equipped to successfully manage their emotions in future situations.

Although studies on gender differences in emotion regulation outside of a clinical setting is limited, the research that has been conducted suggests that women may be more likely than men to positively reappraise negative situations.[28]

If you want to improve your cognitive reappraisal skills, here are a few tips:

1. *Take a beat:* To the extent possible, give yourself space to cognitively process the emotion rather than simply react to it. During a difficult meeting, for example, be prepared with filler words that allow you time to process. Filler words can include repeating the question or statement or saying, "that's a good point." Remind yourself that it is acceptable—and even respectful—to ask for a minute to consider what was said before you respond. You can also ask for a minute to note, on your computer or notepad, the concerns or opinions under discussion so you can reflect further on them later. While those notes may be useful later, what you are really doing is giving yourself space to think rather than immediately react.

2. *Recognize reality:* Every individual is the most important person in their own world. But that doesn't mean that every event in an individual's life has earth-shattering consequences. In fact, most things probably aren't that important in the grand scheme of things. Gaining perspective and allowing yourself to see the situation for what it is (rather than as the end of the world) can help you reappraise how you feel about it.

3. *Find the positive:* It is often hard to find the positives in every situation. Some things are just plain bad. But most events offer complexities you can explore after the crisis is over. Even the worst event can be a learning experience in time. When appropriate, look for the good in a situation. Can you learn something about yourself or the others involved in the experience? Is there a good outcome hiding behind the bad? Is this situation better in the long term even if painful in the short-term? Focus on the positive elements that you identify and cling to those.

Cognitively reappraising events isn't always possible or easy. To the extent possible, allow yourself to feel the emotions and accept them before moving on. If you can't do so in the moment, be sure to revisit how you were feeling and to retroactively process your emotions through journaling, conversations, or formal therapy when needed.

A BRIEF NOTE ON EMOTIONAL INTELLIGENCE

Emotional intelligence theory (sometimes called *emotional quotient* [EQ]) was introduced by researchers Peter Salovey and John Mayer in 1990. The term was later popularized by journalist Daniel Goleman.[29] The original conceptualization of emotional intelligence focused on the skills that contribute to "the accurate appraisal and expression of emotion in oneself and in others, the effective regulation of emotion in self and others, and the use of feelings to motivate, plan, and achieve in one's life." Researchers have since clarified the concept to focus on four main principles:[30]

1. Perceiving emotions
2. Using emotions to facilitate thought
3. Understanding emotions
4. Managing emotions

Emotional intelligence's popularity skyrocketed in recent years and unsurprisingly so. Intuitively, the idea that we can be intelligent in other ways than bookish appeals to us. We've all met people who seem to understand others or who "get" people. On the surface, the idea of emotional intelligence makes sense and to some may even seem obvious.

Unfortunately, scientists hotly dispute the scientific evidence around the validity of emotional intelligence. From a scientific perspective, there is a relatively high bar for demonstrating that an idea in a scientist's mind exists in reality. Scientists must go to great lengths to show that a concept exists outside of their imagination and that the concept differs substantially from existing ideas. For instance, from a theoretical perspective, when suggesting a new idea, scientists must first argue for its importance and necessity. They must present a clear definition of and framework for the concept. With emotional intelligence, for example, Mayer and Salovey identified four primary components, noted earlier.[31]

After putting forward a definition, scientists must then argue how the idea differs from and is similar to other popular ideas. For instance, how does EQ differ from IQ? Or, how does emotional intelligence differ from social skills? Next, scientists must empirically demonstrate that the ideas they claim to be true are in fact true. They commonly do this by developing a way to measure their concept (e.g., a rating scale) and asking a large number of people to participate in a survey. In this process, scientists typically ask respondents to also complete surveys of the existing concepts to which they are comparing their own work. If we were developing empirical evidence for emotional intelligence, we would ask participants to take our surveys of emotional intelligence, IQ, and social skills. Statistical procedures can then be used to assess whether the measure represents the concept accurately and, if so, how the new concept relates to existing concepts. In addition, to help demonstrate the importance of the new concept, scientists must show that their new concept predicts meaningful actions or behaviors. With emotional intelligence, we might expect that higher emotional intelligence scores are related to higher customer service scores.

The research on emotional intelligence doesn't pass the empirical test. When comparing how well it predicts who best to hire, promote, or retain to other well-known and well-established predictors of success at work such as IQ and personality traits, current measures of emotional intelligence fail to add any additional unique information. In other words, there isn't sufficient evidence that EQ offers us any new, valid information beyond what IQ and personality tell us.[32]

Given its popularity, practitioners were quick to develop tools for assessing and developing emotional intelligence in the workplace. As these tools were developed for industry settings, the data is often proprietary, making them inaccessible to the public and scientists. The rapid increase in popularity also led to the quick development and implementation of emotional intelligence in the workplace—arguably before it was fully understood. As a result, emotional intelligence has outpaced itself in scientific validity, leading to the adoption of a popular, but not necessarily sound, idea.

Emotional intelligence has important downsides to consider, perhaps the biggest of which is its use to manipulate others' emotions. Elizabeth

Holmes, the founder of Theranos, clearly demonstrated this darker side when she pulled on the emotional heartstrings of investors and the public to garner support for her rising company. Holmes was determined to develop technology that would allow users to detect diseases and other illnesses—a technology that, she argued, would revolutionize healthcare. As detailed by John Carreyrou in *Bad Blood*, Holmes regularly cited her "beloved" uncle's death from skin cancer as a motivation for her starting the company.[33] If only he had known sooner, her argument went, then he could have been saved.

What's wrong with this story, you ask? In theory, her dream is lovely. In reality, not only was this technology not feasible (at least not at the time this chapter was written), but she also barely knew her uncle! Holmes and her team could never get the technology to work, and she would go on to lie and defraud investors in her attempts to raise capital for her fledgling startup. Central to the point is that Holmes was (and still is) a master of emotional manipulation. She used her understanding of others' emotions to her advantage. While most of us may do this from time to time to get what we want from our kids, parent, or spouse with little consequence, Holmes's behavior demonstrates the dangers of taking emotional manipulation to the extreme. She not only defrauded investors in amounts in the high millions, she also misled the public and gave many false hope (and false results!).

This doesn't inherently mean that emotional intelligence is a waste of our time and we should abandon the concept altogether. Many aspects of emotional intelligence, including emotional awareness and management, show the difference between more and less effective leaders. But our obsession with emotional intelligence as a popular concept, rather than the science of managing our emotions, can distract us from learning the underlying and critical skills that can help us lead effectively.

Risk Taking

In between advertisements for colorful dresses and vegan meat alternatives, my Instagram feed scrolls through the lives of my high school theater friends who are navigating parenthood, another friend's Monday afternoon lunch, and my colleague's latest work conference. The body positivity influencers jiggle their tummies to make me feel less bad about mine, all while the BBC breaks the latest news about Europe's heatwave. Hiding amid these posts, I see Jacinda Ardern snapping a selfie on her flight to Japan. It catches my attention (#fangirl), and I swipe through her "hard" posts where she sprinkles selfies amid official pictures of herself meeting with world leaders from her most recent trip.

Although Ardern is not the first world leader to document her duties on social media, she is one of the first to do so in such a personal manner. A quick flick through her page reveals a mix of work-related and personal activities. She documents her experience with COVID and her family's Boxing Day antics alongside photos of her typical workday and areas of the Beehive (the executive wing of the New Zealand Parliament Buildings where Ardern's office is located) usually hidden from the public. In widely sharing a more personal side of leadership through social media, she opens herself to New Zealanders in a unique way, building a different kind of connection with her followers than did her predecessors.

Ardern is certainly not the only world leader with an Instagram account, and you likely won't be surprised to learn that, as the leader of a small nation, she also isn't the most followed leader on Instagram. Joe Biden (current president of United States), Narendra Modi (current prime minister of India), Jair Bolsonero (former president of Brazil), and Joko Widodo (current president of Indonesia) all have more followers than does Ardern.[1] But what makes her different is *how* she uses social media. While other leaders post only formal press pictures and clips of their speeches, Ardern shares her personal photos from her political engagements and even goes live on Facebook to answer questions in real time.

Perhaps her most relatable moment came during a 2021 Facebook livestream when she faced a work-from-home disruption similar to that experienced by many parents. While Ardern was updating her country on the current state of COVID-19, her daughter made an unexpected appearance.[2]

"Mummy?" Neave, her daughter, said.

Not missing a beat, Ardern turned to her daughter and gently instructed her to go back to bed, assuring Neave that she would be with her when she finished. Turning back to her viewers, Ardern said, "Well, that was a bedtime fail, wasn't it?"

In that moment, the world saw Ardern as a mom. As a woman. As a human. In that moment, she was not a statue leading their people into battle or a perfectly polished debater. She was simply a person.

Similarly, Finland's Sanna Marin has been praised for her authentic approach to social media. Like many of us, she too posts about pasta sauce recipes and motherhood. She even posted a breastfeeding selfie to her Instagram—a move many called a "breath of fresh air" from the typical stuffy approach to leadership.[3]

With their more personalized approach to Instagram posts and the way these leaders connect with New Zealanders and Finns through other social media platforms, Ardern and Marin stand out from other world leaders. They use approaches to leadership and communication that are fundamentally different, forming unique relationships with the people of their respective countries.

Ardern's and Marin's approaches violate many rules in the traditional leadership book. They let people in, show their vulnerabilities, and remove themselves from the pedestal that many leaders cling to. Some might argue that their actions will contribute to a loss of power. After all, information is power, and if you share all (or a lot) of your information with others, you also share your power.

However, Ardern's and Marin's leadership styles have generated positive responses from people around the world. Their approaches gain them followers, attract wider audiences, and show new ways of leading. And as women who directly contradict our stereotypes of leaders (i.e., they aren't men), Ardern and Marin may be uniquely positioned to do so.

To see why this might be the case, let's look at the recent wedding of two of my friends. These two were planning their wedding at around the same time my (now) husband and I were and we would regularly chat over dinner about who was wearing what, the music, the dancing, the food, and most important, the wine. In one of these conversations over a dinner in Soho, they shared that they felt they had leeway to do things differently. Not being a heterosexual couple, they didn't feel obligated to follow the same traditions: Did someone really need to walk down the aisle? Was an aisle even needed?

Because their relationship didn't align with the traditional requirements of a heterosexual wedding, they did not feel beholden to the norms and expectations of what is now seen as a traditional wedding. They felt they could start from scratch. They could do something different.

In the same way that my friends' love fails to align with our traditionalist views of wedding ceremonies, so too does Ardern fail to align with our traditionalist requirements of white-male leadership. This chasm between reality and tradition creates an opportunity. My friends can reimagine their wedding day because we don't yet have a script for what a homosexual wedding should involve. Ardern can lead differently because we don't yet have a script for what a woman leading should look like.

As the number of women in leadership positions continues to grow, women will continue to shape our views of what leadership can and should like.

Of course, men in leadership can do the same. They have the platform and the power to reshape our views, but they are likely fighting against stronger forces. Centuries of male leadership have led to an ideal image of men in power, and even today, men are expected to uphold that image.

Consider Play-Doh as an example. We can bend and shape it every which way for hours as long as we continue to move it, but once the Play-Doh sets, we can't easily reshape it. To reuse it, we have to add drops of water and work that water into the shape, loosening the dough by kneading, pushing our fingers and palms into the dough until it becomes soft again. Once it's soft, we can remold it into a new shape.

In this analogy, women act as the water in our reshaping of leadership. They introduce a new substance to our old, hardened dough, and with work, they reshape our views of leadership.

The problem is, people aren't Play-Doh, and this stuff is rock solid.

The psychology literature refers to the concept that our views are bound to earlier or existing conceptualizations as the "anchoring effect."[4] First introduced by Amos Tversky and Daniel Kahneman (1974) in their now famous work on heuristics (mental shortcuts), the researchers examined how an estimated value of an object influenced later guesses about the value of that same object. In their classic study, they asked participants to estimate percentages for different questions (e.g., How many African countries are in the United Nations?).[5] Before participants responded, the researchers spun a wheel to reveal a random number between 0 and 100. The wheel was totally random and unrelated to the question at hand. Despite its irrelevancy, the value displayed on the wheel influenced participants' guesses. Participants who saw a 10 on the wheel, for instance, were more likely to guess 25 percent, whereas participants who saw 65 on the wheel were more likely to estimate 45 percent. Even when providing incentives for correct answers, participants were still anchored to the unrelated number from the wheel.

Anchors can come from random wheels, others' statements, and our own beliefs. The research on the anchoring effect suggests that we are susceptible to its influence in nearly all of our decisions. For example, we see the anchoring effect in salary negotiations,[6] investment decisions,[7] and creativity.[8]

When it comes to stereotypes of leadership, our expectations of a leader are anchored to the men, predominantly *white* men, we have previously seen. Intriguingly, research integrating the anchoring effect and attitude change theories suggests that the more different or extreme an initial estimate is from the "true value," the less likely it is that anchoring effects will take hold. For example, a 2001 study examined participant estimates in response to eight questions (e.g., What is the record high [hottest] temperature for a day in Seattle, Washington?).[9] All participants were shown random values prior to providing their own estimate. The values of these estimates varied from moderate to extreme. The moderate estimates were within a realistic range of temperature, while the extreme values varied from unrealistic to impossible. Results from this study showed that anchoring took place but that as the extremity of the value increased, the likelihood of anchoring decreased. In other words, the more extreme the estimate, the less anchoring occurred.

The authors argued that this was due, in part, to the way anchoring unfolds. If we think about our anchors as a range of potential solutions, then this range will have boundaries.

For example, take the classic "How many jellybeans are in this jar?" challenge at your local insurance office.

You might look at that jar and have no idea of the exact jellybean count, but, depending on the size of the jar, you will have a range of potential values. In a small 16-ounce Mason jar, for instance, you might believe the count to be at least 100 jellybeans but no more than 500. Anything below 100 or above 500 would therefore seem implausible.

If I were to suggest to you that there are 390 jellybeans in that jar (the likely number of jellybeans in a 16-ounce Mason jar according to calculate-this.com) and then ask you to share your guess, you are likely to stick around 390. The same would be true if I suggested that there may be 250 jellybeans in the jar. These values are within your reasonable range, and therefore, anchoring is likely to occur.

If, however, I told you I thought there were 75 jellybeans in the jar, or 1,000 jellybeans in the jar, you'd probably roll your eyes at me. However, you might still be slightly anchored to those values. If I told you 75, you would likely guess within the lower range of your boundaries (e.g., 100), and if I suggested 1,000, you would likely guess at the upper range (e.g., 500), but you wouldn't be as closely tied to those values as when I suggested numbers within your range.

Taken even further, if I suggested that there are only two jellybeans in that jar, or that there are 1 million jellybeans in that jar, you would probably tell me to get lost and then make an entirely new guess.

If we apply our jellybean analogy to women in leadership, we can see an explanation emerge as to why women like Ardern, women very far from our existing archetypes of male-dominated leadership, may not be as influenced by our stereotypes as women who more closely align with our traditional views of leadership.

If we imagine our views of leadership as a box, we can see that there is some space for what is to be considered leadership. Currently occupying that box is our male-dominated view of leadership (please excuse my stick figures).

A woman who demonstrates a similar approach to leadership as these men will likely activate our tendency to anchor and increase the probability that we will compare her to our extant view of leadership.

If a woman, however, comes along and is *very* different from our views of what it means to be a leader existing outside of our boxes, then we may simply compare her to the boundaries of our beliefs rather than attempt to force her into the box completely.

If this is true, then this out-of-the-box woman may have more flexibility to behave differently than our anchors or stereotypes suggest. But keep in mind that we are still comparing her to our boundaries—meaning we will accept Ardern leading from Facebook Live or in a cute dress and heels, but we probably won't accept a Martian espousing their views on intergalactic harmony.

At least not in 2023.

As more women take on these outside-of-the-box approaches to leadership, they are slowly but surely chipping away at what it means to be a leader and expanding our leadership definition box.

This is not to say that everyone will be accepting of new ideas of leadership. On the first point, research repeatedly shows us that individual differences—characteristics such as gender, religious and political beliefs, and personalities—influence how open we are to new ideas and people. The research on anchoring effects shows us the same. The anchoring effects discussed here are averages, representing the general pattern that we see. As with any average, there will be people on either side as well as at the extremes: some people may be more open to accepting new ways of leading, particularly by women, while others are more closed off to change.

That being said, the women who lead differently and who go against the grain of our leadership archetypes, face a unique opportunity to innovate, to be creative in the way they lead. At times, this can even mean innovating the role of leadership itself.

Research on creativity and innovation tells us that many of the skills important for creativity are similarly important for leadership.[10] In fact, several researchers have positioned creative thinking as an essential skill for leaders. Leaders are regularly faced with complex problems, some of which may have obvious answers. Other problems, however, may be new. These types of problems often require creative solutions that rely on a leader's ability to think differently. When it comes to women in leadership, they face an especially novel landscape that may further emphasize the need for these skills.

When talking about creativity, we typically discuss activities like brainstorming and aha! moments. But creativity involves several other complex processes. While some debate still exists, research generally supports at least four key activities—problem definition, information gathering, idea generation, and idea evaluation.[11]

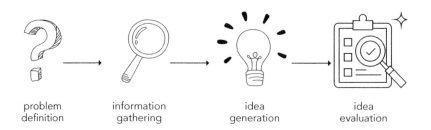

problem definition   information gathering   idea generation   idea evaluation

These processes require significant investment. It takes time, energy, and resources to develop an idea, and additional time, energy, and resources to implement that idea. These activities are costly in several ways. However, creativity and innovation are still possible in efforts with a smaller set of resources. New research tells us that limited resources, or what organizational scientists call "constraints," can facilitate creativity.[12] "The Green Eggs and Ham Hypothesis" first argued for this effect using the example of Dr. Seuss' limited word count when writing Green Eggs and Ham.[13] By limiting himself to only the same 50 words (or less), the hypothesis suggested that Seuss was forced to develop a novel story that might not have otherwise been possible should there have been more options available. In the same way that being faced with too many options at your local bakery can paralyze your decision making (*or is this just me?*), so too can too many options paralyze our creativity. This idea that constraints can positively impact creativity has been recognized by business leaders for years with the likes of Marissa Mayer (former CEO of Yahoo!)[14] and Biz Stone (co-founder of Twitter) touting their benefits.[15]

During COVID-19, Ethiopia worked within their unique constraints to develop effective, and often novel, solutions to combatting the virus. Because Ethiopia is one of the poorest countries in Africa, many expected COVID-19 to wreak havoc across the country. Despite advances in its economy, it remains a poor country with a per capita gross national income of only $890. For context, the current per capita gross national income of the United States is around $60,000; of Australia, $51,000; and of South Africa, $12,000.

When COVID-19 first emerged, most people expected Ethiopia to experience significant suffering and difficulty. The country was already battling a number of healthcare crises, including the AIDS epidemic and issues of maternal mortality.[16] In addition, Ethiopia's capital city, Addis Ababa, serves as an East African travel hub. The Addis Ababa Bole International Airport, for example, on its peak day in July 2019, hosted 310 flights and nearly 30,000 passengers.[17] While these numbers aren't on par with the world's busiest airports (for comparison, London Heathrow, which is consistently ranked the busiest airport in the world, welcomed more than 100,000 passengers daily in 2019), 30,000 mingling travelers, indoors, in the middle of a pandemic, is certainly less than ideal.

To put it lightly, Ethiopia was in trouble and had limited financial resources to manage the impending crisis.

And they knew it.

In many reports, the Ethiopian government recognized that the "popular" response to COVID-19 of shutting down the country and stopping nearly all air traffic would not work. Ethiopia's problem was different from that of richer countries: the parameters of the problem and the resources available to solve the problem were unique.

Perhaps because Ethiopia's leaders understood the uniqueness of their country's problem so well and were subsequently able to leverage their resources effectively, Ethiopia managed to keep the virus relatively under control.[18]

As the first woman to serve as president of Ethiopia, and as of 2020, the only woman serving in the head-of-state position for an African country (*you go, girl!*), Sahle-Work Zewde received significant press attention in 2018 and 2019. She was appointed unanimously by parliament and clearly represented progress for women in Africa.

Similer to Singapore, however, her role as Ethiopian president is largely ceremonial. The *Africa Report* even referred to her as a "pointless president" due to recent constitutional reductions in her role.[19] Although her appointment is undoubtably historic and provides a light for women in Ethiopia and globally, she likely had little, if any, influence over governmental policies in response to COVID-19. Perhaps the only exception is her informal influence through her public presence and speeches.

Many have attributed Ethiopia's response not to Zewde but to the minister of health—Dr. Lia Tadesse—who was heralded by the Ellen Johnson Sirleaf Presidential Center for Women and Development as a "Covid-19 Heroine."[20]

Tadesse was serving as the acting minister of health in early 2020 before being officially given the role just one day before Ethiopia reported its first case of COVID-19. As a new minister, she needed to manage multiple ongoing health crises while limiting the spread of COVID-19 in her country. Recognizing the challenge early, she quickly activated the country's emergency response system in January 2020—approximately two months before the first case of COVID-19 was detected in her country. One of her first acts was to form the National COVID-19 Advisory Committee, a formal committee of experts to advise on the country's response. Subcommittees within the group focus on issues; for example, a psychosocial team supports patients and a resource allocation team helps to mobilize available resources.

Tadesse's resource allocation focus sets her response apart from the rest. As the country lacked the resources of richer countries to erect new hospitals from thin air within days (looking at you, China) or pump large sums of money to vaccine development (the United Kingdom contributed more than £88 million to the development of the Oxford/AstraZeneca vaccine[21]), Ethiopia leveraged and exploited existing resources to its advantage. For example, UN Women's report on women's leadership during COVID-19 noted Tadesse's use of existing health promotor net-works to share critical information.[22] In this way, she garnered citizen support for government policies and practical mitigation steps using estab-lished, trusted sources. In addition, she asked private sector businesses to shift their production to critical infrastructure components such as hand sanitizer and masks—a call she argued was a part of, and yet beyond, their corporate social responsibility.

Ethiopia could not afford to take the same actions that richer nations were implementing, actions such as countrywide lockdowns and a com-plete halt to flights entering the country. Instead, the leaders focused their approach on public messaging. In addition to the measures previously noted, the government infused the messaging into day-to-day life. If, for example, you made a call in Ethiopia during the early months of the pan-demic, instead of hearing a ringtone (*ring ring* or *beep beep*), you heard a reminder to wash your hands, social distance, and wear your face masks.[23]

Tadesse also directed available resources to vaccination messaging, encouraging the public to get the shot through multiple communication challenges—phone calls, radio advertisements, and TV placements.

Tadesse worked with what she had. She exploited the resources avail-able to her to create a successful strategy that, to a large extent, reduced the negative impact of COVID-19 in Ethiopia—particularly in the early months.[7] For comparison, in the first 6 months of COVID-19, the United Kingdom, with approximately half the population of Ethiopia, reported 6,000 times the number of cases reported by the East African country.[23]

Many have remained skeptical about the case numbers stemming from a country with a largely authoritarian rule. However, as the pandemic continued, the World Health Organization noted a different pattern of infection within African countries—suggesting that perhaps, these numbers were accurate (or close to it) after all.

Unfortunately, in the time following the COVID-19 pandemic, Ethiopia became embroiled in political turmoil and an all-out civil war. This conflict significantly damaged the available health facilities and led to famine and further health crises throughout the country. Still, even in the face of massive political upheaval that further constrained the range of possible solutions to fighting COVID-19 in Ethiopia, Tadesse continued to use the country's unique resources to her advantage. She leveraged outside resources by partnering with the World Bank to finance vaccination efforts in hard-to-reach rural communities. This partnership also focused on rebuilding critical health infrastructure, such as hospital buildings, that have been damaged in the recent conflict. In taking these actions, Tadesse shows us the importance of clearly identifying the problem at hand and subsequently leveraging available resources and capabilities to find creative solutions to said problem.

However valuable it may be, it's important to remember that creativity comes with risk. We so often hear about successes of creativity, singing the praises of creative leaders on my student's biography top choice lists (e.g., Steve Jobs, Elon Musk, Jeff Bezos) that we can easily forget about survivorship bias. Survivorship bias reminds us that we typically only hear about those who succeed and we rarely hear news of those who fail. As a result, we assume that those leaders who we can see accurately represent a sample of leaders. But do they? What about those who flamed out on their way? What about those who persisted only to give up after the 100th try. What about those who were forced out because of their gender or their skin color? In focusing so much on success, we can forget that leadership and in particular, being creative comes with personal, financial, and social risk.

Leaders must invest their resources—however large or small—wisely and make judgment calls as to which creative solutions warrant the investment. In Tadesse's case, Ethiopia made the call to take an approach that differed from the predominant response of richer countries. This approach was more closely aligned to Ethiopia's unique problem and context. The leaders chose to leverage their available resources to respond creatively to the unique threat they identified. As many of these tactics were untested and the impact of these interventions were unknown, adopting them was inherently risky.

In addition to the risk associated with trying a novel approach, judging the potential success of new ideas is notoriously difficult—further increasing the risk. When doing something new, our calculations of how successful it will be are based on fancy market analyses and understanding of what has been successful in the past. But when dealing with an entirely *new* product or process, these models can't fully capture the likelihood of success. Further, people are not great at forecasting long-term futures even with existing, routine events. This is in part because we fail to expect market and environment changes. Consider COVID-19 as an example. Most, if not all, new business owners or new product launches in late 2019 did not consider a raging pandemic in their forecasts. And if you want to see how bad our forecasting with new things really is, consider that when COVID-19 first closed businesses and educational institutions, we speculated that the change would last 2 weeks. One year later, many businesses and schools remained closed or entirely online. At 2 years in, we had fundamentally changed the way we work; hybrid work was widely accepted, and the idea of coming to an office became a reason to leave your job!

In addition, new products and services often have no standards and regulations to guide development and execution. Consequently, standards by which to evaluate a new idea have not yet been established. The evaluating-ideas step is therefore both incredibly important and obnoxiously hard.

Not only does a lack of standards lead to difficulty in assessing risk, potential success, and consequences, but research on biases and decision making also tells us that these conditions allow for *more biased* judgments.

The more ambiguity in a situation, the more likely our biases are to creep into our decision making.

For women, this means a double-edged sword for being different. While we may have more leeway to act differently because we don't fit the traditional mold, we will simultaneously experience more sexist and biased judgments. For instance, in 2022, the media released footage of the 36-year-old Finnish Prime Minister Marin drinking and dancing with her friends at a party. As a woman in her 30s, Marin goes against both gender- and age-related norms. (Although Finland's parliamentary statistics out-perform those of many other countries, a majority of politicians are still middle-aged men.) As a result of the video, many demanded she explain herself, and some even called for a drug test. She complied. Completed the drug test. Tested negative. Still, some called for the dancing queen's resignation. In the days following this video, many came to her aid, with famous politicians such as Hilary Clinton even posting videos of them-selves dancing "on the job." Others were quick to point out the gendered double standard. Former UK Prime Minister Boris Johnson, for example, had held several parties in his office while the United Kingdom was under strict COVID-19 laws banning—you guessed it—parties. Rules that Johnson himself established, I might add. When called out on it, Johnson suggested that the country "move on."[24] In response, many were willing to brush off his behavior; some people even argued that "boys will be boys." It wasn't until many months after the revelation about these par-ties, that a formal investigation was conducted, and many members of his Johnson's own cabinet resigned in protest. Eventually, Johnson himself resigned from his role in 2022. By comparison, Marin received immediate pressure for behaving transparently: drinking legally, dancing legally, and enjoying her friends on her own time, *not* in her office. *I guess girls will be girls!*

Despite the inherent risk in taking on a leadership role as a woman, women are still perceived to be more risk averse than men. That is, we still expect women to play it safe and to take fewer chances than we expect men to. Women's perceived risk aversion is often cited as a reason for women's *un*fitness for leadership roles. Decision making in leadership requires risk—risk that women won't take (or so it is assumed).

As we've done throughout this book, let's now see how research proves this view wrong, shall we?

A recent study investigated gender differences in risk aversion and any underlying causes.[25] Across five studies with more than 2,000 participants, the researchers found no gender differences in risk-taking.

Case closed.

But the researchers were also interested in the cyclical nature of risk-taking and how responses to taking risks influence men's and women's future behavior. A survey study of approximately 500 working adults in the United Kingdom asked participants to report whether or not they had engaged in the risks listed. Risks included speaking up about bullying, asking for a pay raise, and taking on a task they didn't know how to complete. For risks they had taken, participants then reported the outcomes of those risks. For risks they had *not* taken, participants shared what they expected the outcomes of taking that risk would be.

When men and women hadn't taken the risk described in their lives, they did not differ in the consequences they expected to follow from taking the risk.

However, their lived experiences significantly differed from their expectations. Men reported experiencing more positive reactions to risk-taking than did women. As a result, men were also more likely than women to report engaging in the same risk-taking activity again at a later time.

The conclusion? Women are *conditioned* to take fewer risks. When women take fewer risks, it is because they have received negative reactions to risk-taking—a response that suggests engaging in risky behavior in the future is not a good idea. In comparison, we react positively to men who take risks (likely because it aligns with our stereotypes). In the same way women learn to not take risks, men learn through experience that risk-taking is encouraged and rewarded.

However, the types of risk that men and women take may differ. To date, most research investigating risk-taking has relied on masculine definitions of risk. For example, measures of risk-taking often ask participants to report how likely they are to ride a motorcycle without a helmet. While women certainly own and ride motorcycles, the activity is stereotypically male. Conversely, risks more stereotypically related to women, such as reporting sexual harassment at work or having elective surgery, are not included. As such, there is an inherent male bias baked into the research.

Interested in this idea, the same researchers who investigated the gender-driven consequences for risk-taking also explored whether men and women differed in the types of risks they took at work. They presented participants with a list of both stereotypically masculine and stereotypically feminine risks and asked them to select which risks they had engaged in at work.

Although men were likely to engage in both types of risks, women were significantly more likely to engage in stereotypically feminine risks than in stereotypically masculine risks. Further, men reported positive outcomes for engaging in both types of risks, meaning contrary to the idea that men are punished for engaging in stereotypically feminine behavior, men in this study did not report experiencing backlash for taking more feminine risks.

To summarize,

1. Men and women do not fundamentally differ in their amount of risk-taking.
2. Women are more likely to take "lady risks."
3. When men take risks, we say YAY!
4. When women take risks, we say "Behave yourself."
5. As a result, men may be more likely than women to repeat risky behavior.

In the context of COVID-19, discussions of risk largely centered on women's risk aversion being an advantage. Women in leadership generally took more stringent and decisive actions more quickly than did their male counterparts in response to the emerging virus.

In light of the research on risk-taking, there are arguably two reasons why we saw women choose this response pattern. The first, and arguably the most popular defense to date, is that women took the less risky decision. As a result, commentators argued that their decision making proved that risk-taking is not always beneficial. This is certainly a viable conclusion and one that should not be downplayed. Undoubtably, crises such as the 2008 financial crash, which resulted from excessive risk-taking in financial markets, have taught us that lesson before.

However, an alternative explanation could be that women in leadership took *different* risks in response to COVID-19. Perhaps their risks were more "lady-like" than those of men in leadership. Take, for example, the notion of locking down an entire country and closing its borders. Call me crazy, but that seems risky to me. The outcomes were unknown—never in modern history had a country asked its citizens to not leave their homes for weeks, to not go to work, and to not travel. The idea was preposterous. Even today, as I reflect on the reality of what occurred, the idea that I left my house for only 1 hour a day for 6 months feels like a different life (*also a good reminder of why I gained 10 pounds last year*).

If we consider women's responses from this perspective, we might argue that they prioritized different types of risks than did male leaders. Perhaps the women, in line with our expectations of them, immediately prioritized human lives. And perhaps the men, similarly in line with our expectations of them, immediately prioritized economic consequences. That's an empirical question, an answer to which may be too late, but one that seems to flow from recent research. In a recent scientific paper, for example, OG gender researcher Alice Eagly discussed the ways in which women take personal risks to protect others.[26] For example, in the United States, woman donate live kidneys more frequently than men do (and this kidney gender gap is growing!). Live kidney donation comes with risks, including several health-related complications. In the US Peace Corp, members are often exposed to health risks such as malaria, yet, women make up 65 percent of the Peace Corp. During the Holocaust, more single women in Poland, the Netherlands, and France participated in rescue activities compared to single men. If caught, this offense was punishable by death or placement in a Nazi concentration camp.

The idea that men make better leaders because they take more risks is foundationally flawed. Men and women take different kinds of risks. The question each of us needs to answer then becomes, which types of risks do we want our leaders to take?

Actions for Change

"CHAMPAGNE!" yell my friends through the narrow hall of our London flat.

In my friend group, whenever someone accomplishes something (literally anything—we will take any excuse after COVID-19 to celebrate), we pop a bottle of bubbles and cheer to the success. We do this for wins both big and small. When I signed a contract for this book, we popped the champagne. When I finished writing the book, we popped the champagne. Even when my nasty skin infection healed by itself with little effort from me, we popped that champagne!

(This sounds like a very expensive habit, so I'd like to clarify that it is often sparkling wine and not actual champagne that we pop. My friend Jamie even once celebrated my tenure by putting chardonnay in the soda stream.)

It's a fun tradition that allows us to commemorate the small and big wins. When working on big tasks, like writing a book, for example, celebrating the little wins along the way helps make the progress feel more tangible and keeps motivation high.

In that spirit, we should take a moment and celebrate the movement that has been made and the outstanding examples set by the women discussed in this book. They represent progress and provide outstanding models of leadership for us to look to.

In honor of these women, CHAMPAGNE!

These women have shown us that their leadership characteristics, characteristics so often seen as flaws, are actually their strengths. Their preparation, and often *over*preparation, makes them worthy competitors in any room. Their empathy and focus on the collective gain means more of their followers are heard and can win. And their willingness to learn helps them continuously grow into better leaders.

What an amazing set of leadership skills! Why would we want women to be anything other than their already outstanding selves? And certainly, why would we encourage women to be more selfish, risky with the lives of others, less caring, or more stuck in their ways? Despite what 1990s pop culture books on leadership tell us, we shouldn't.

We should celebrate these women, and the women in our own lives, who show us how to lead differently, how to lead outstandingly. As I said at the beginning, we should be shouting, "YOU GO, GIRL" from the rooftops.

Celebrating their successes, however, doesn't ignore the fact that there remains plenty more work to be done to help them and other women succeed in these roles. What can we do to help?

We must dismantle our stereotypes and create a new meaning of leadership.

In the words of Elle Woods, "What, like it's hard?"

In reality, dismantling our stereotypes *is* hard work, and scientists aren't entirely convinced of how to best do it. For example, corporate leaders often tout their diversity and bias trainings as reflections of their efforts to combat negative stereotypes. But the science on how effective these trainings are is mixed. A review of the research in this area, for instance, found that these trainings are often poorly designed.[1] In addition, the way we measure the success of these trainings is inherently flawed, obscuring their real value. Some research even suggests that workplace training aimed at reducing biased behavior such as sexual harassment can have a backlash effect, further engraining existing attitudes.[2]

But it is important to bear in mind that our understanding of the effectiveness of bias or diversity trainings depends on how they are evaluated. Given that bias and implicit diversity-related attitudes are extremely difficult to measure, our understanding of these trainings and their effectiveness is inherently limited. In contrast, when it comes to personal, actionable steps that we can each take to help more women attain leadership positions, research provides several paths forward.

What does all this science tell us about what *you and I* can do?

To see real change, we need radical transformation in our systems, practices, and mindsets. Until we see such a revolution, however, we must recognize that leadership continues to exist in a male-dominated landscape. To make progress, we must dismantle the systems that hold women back, while simultaneously working within them to fight our way to the top. With this in mind, I offer a range of ideas for moving forward depending on your leadership aspirations or position.

WOMEN ASPIRING TO LEAD

If you are a woman aspiring to become a leader, you have a difficult road ahead—a road that is different and more difficult than the road the men in your life will take. However, the world is changing. There is more space for women, more attention being paid to women, and more growth opportunities for women than ever before. There is reason for hope and to go after what you want.

Go for It, Girl!

I'm not a fan of a cheesy quotes, but some are worth their while despite the cheddar. One of these quotes comes from Wayne Gretzky (and then famously repeated by Michael Scott):

"You miss 100 percent of the shots you don't take."

It's true. When it comes to women occupying leadership positions, part of the issue stems from women's preference for preparation and men's willingness to wing it. Research repeatedly finds that men are more likely to apply for leadership positions that they are not fully qualified for than are women.[3] By simply putting themselves in the running more frequently than women put themselves in the running, men are more likely to hold leadership positions.

The first step, then, is for women to apply. If you're interested in a leadership position but don't meet *all* of the requirements, go for it. Take the shot. Don't count yourself out when you're not the one making the decision.

When you do earn your spot, it's then up to you to continue to reward those who apply and are *most prepared* for the role. You can then help change the system by hiring and promoting new leaders based on the skills and values important for effective leadership rather than on confidence and flash.

Learn to Communicate Your Value

Until the strengths of women become more widely recognized and valued, we must communicate those strengths to those who need to hear them. We must be our own advocates. Few people will spend time searching for what you have to offer them. Rather, it's human nature to make judgments based on initial impressions and our biases. Bearing this in mind, when you go for that well-deserved job, you must be able to sell your skillsets.

Although this holds true for everyone, the stereotypes held about women mean that many will automatically count women out. Until this changes, it falls on women to communicate their specific skills and why they are valuable to leadership.

If you find it difficult to shout about your greatness from the rooftops, you're not alone. Women have been told for centuries that we must be humble. We must be modest. So it comes as no surprise that many of us find it difficult to talk about our accomplishments—an act that could be seen as boastful. In many cases, our discomfort with self-advocacy is justified. Research repeatedly demonstrates that violating expectations of modesty by "bragging" about one's accomplishments results in a backlash effect for women. Women who self-advocate are viewed more negatively than men who engage in the same behavior.[4,5]

However, women are also great champions of one another. Think about the hype women in your life. Those women who have your back no matter what. The women who praise your every accomplishment. The women who yell CHAMPAGNE! when your skin infection heals. In their study on overcoming the modesty challenge in women's self-advocacy, researchers at Montana State University recounted a story about a magazine feature for women on their campus.[6] They asked women to share their successes in their work and family life. But they received no such stories. Instead, they received several submissions from women writing about other women's successes. While women may be taught to remain modest about themselves, the same is not true about our friends. We feel much more comfortable talking about others' successes than we do about our own.

If you need to talk yourself up (which you inevitably will), here are two action items to consider. First, if you feel that the environment you're in would welcome a little self-promotion but you're out of practice, try this. Write out your list of accomplishments, your list of skills, everything that makes you a badass woman. Look at that list. Now imagine that your very best friend wrote that list. What would you say about her? How would you promote her? When you go into that meeting or that call to talk about your own successes, imagine you're talking about your best friend rather than about yourself. Talk her up!

Maybe you're less certain about how your boss or coworker will respond to you promoting yourself. If that's you, find someone who can advocate for you. This could be a coworker or mentor or even your boss. Find someone, or better yet, find several someones whom you feel comfortable speaking about yourself with. Then ask that person, or those people, to talk you up. You don't have to limit this to the women in your office. Find men to be your allies as well.

Build a Supportive Network

Women's journey to power is plagued with obstacles. These obstacles are debilitating and require that you maintain a certain amount of reslience. When it all seems too much, having a supportive network of people whom you can ask for help or simply vent to can help sustain your energy to keep going amid the obstacles and make you feel less alone. Support can come from anywhere—friends, family, coworkers, mentors. But importantly, they should be people you trust. People you trust to give advice. People you trust to not judge you when you just need to complain. People you trust to be real with you.

These people should be your biggest cheerleaders. As you will inevitably face obstacles along your leadership journey, having support to back you up when you lose steam will help you persist.

Choose a Champion

Many of the women discussed in this book also talk about the people who championed them early in their career. Angela Merkel, for example, was mentored by Helmut Kohl. As her mentor, he not only shared his advice and wisdom, but he also gave her opportunities and opened doors for her that might have been harder for her to open on her own.

If you want to grow into a position of leadership, then find someone who can similarly champion you and your progress. This can be someone you already know or someone you reach out to blindly and invite for coffee to discuss their journey to leadership. Ask questions. Learn from them. Soak up what you can and let them know what you want from the relationship and in your career.

Find Your Mantra

As an academic, I regularly sit on expert review panels. Our goal on these panels is typically to review grant proposals and make recommendations for which proposals should be funded. The first time I received an email inviting me to participate, I emailed back and said, "Are you sure?" I was convinced they had sent the email to the wrong person. *The imposter syndrome was real.*

When I entered the room on the first day of the panel, I was visibly nervous. I barely slept the night before, couldn't eat any of the free breakfast (very unusual for me), and couldn't imagine speaking up in a room full of people I looked up to. I was by far the youngest person in the room, which only added to my feeling that I shouldn't be there.

Before the meeting began, I turned to the woman next to me and asked a question—about what, I don't remember. However, I do remember qualifying my question by saying, "Sorry, this is my first time, and I'm really nervous."

She looked me dead in the eyes and, gesturing to the men who occupied a majority of the seats, said, "You belong here. You belong here as much as I do. As much as they do. Your voice is just as important as anyone else's in this room."

Those words have stayed with me in every aspect of my life. Whenever I feel that I should stay quiet because my opinion differs from that of others, or when I feel out of my depth in a room at work, I remind myself, "You belong here, and your voice is just as important as anyone else's in this room."

As you begin your leadership journey, find your mantra. What will you tell yourself, or what will you do, when you feel out of your depth? How will you pump yourself up when you're the only woman in the room and sexist remarks are made at you? Have a mantra that you can repeat in your head to remind yourself that you belong in that room. Because you do.

CURRENT LEADERS

For those already in leadership, your to do list should focus on helping others achieve their goals and change the system.

Support Women

Sometimes when we go through hardships to reach our own success, it is tempting to believe it is those hardships that made us and that others must face those same hardships to be as successful as we are. Some of this thinking stems from perceptions of fairness: "It's only fair that, because I had to walk through hell to get here, so should you."

In reality, the existing systems that hold women back from leadership are not necessary. Do you build skills and a thick skin from going through them? Probably. But are there also less toxic ways of building those skills? Yes. And are there downsides to those experiences, such as trauma and burnout, that could otherwise be avoided if taking a different route? Yes. The road through hell need not be taken if another route exists!

As a woman in a position of power, it is your job to make the road better for the women who follow you. You can do this in many different ways: by serving as a mentor and sharing your experience, by championing the outstanding women on your team, and by changing the inequitable system that holds women back in the first place.

Be Open to Different

Stereotypes about leadership are held by both men and women. Meaning that even as a woman in leadership, you still have gender-driven biases that influence how you view a job candidate or a woman on your team. Even if not explicit, there's likely a part of you that associates leadership with men. Being a woman does not exempt you from being gender biased.

Bearing this in mind, you must constantly challenge your own beliefs. Ask yourself, why do I perceive that woman to be less qualified than that man? Or, why am I annoyed by my female teammate trying to lead the meeting? Would I be similarly annoyed if a male teammate did the same? In some instances, the answer may be that the woman is less qualified than the man or that the woman shouldn't be taking over the meeting. But in other instances, you might realize that your biases need a check in. Once you recognize how these biases are influencing your perceptions, you can begin to change your actions.

Challenge Others

As someone in a position of power, others are looking to you for guidance. They are looking to you to signal what is acceptable and unacceptable behavior. If someone makes a sexist comment and you let it go, it sends a signal to others that such language is acceptable. But if you call out or challenge that person who made a sexist comment, it shows the opposite: that language (and sexism) is noticed and is not acceptable here. Over time, calling out this behavior will reinforce that it isn't tolerated and will begin to push to extinguish it.

Along these lines, just as you need to continuously challenge yourself and your own beliefs, you can create change by challenging others' beliefs and encouraging them to do the same. As a leader, you can challenge ideas and ask *why* a team member or fellow leader thinks what they do. If you force them to vocalize their reasoning, they will have to justify it. And if stereotypes and biases are at play, then this will quickly become apparent. Similarly, as a leader, you can encourage your team to reflect on their own thinking and build in time to allow them to challenge their own biases.

Review the Systems

Our biases are baked into our practices. They are codified in our systems. We have formalized our biases into policies and procedures that perpetuated a sexist world that continues to hold women back. For instance, job advertisements are often written in an inherently male-leaning manner. This is particularly true in male-dominated industries.[7] Words such as *ambitious, go-getter*, and *rockstar* are all stereotypically associated with men. Other male-centric words, such as *dominant* and *ninja*, have similarly been found rampant in job advertisements in the tech industry.[8] Simply changing how we word our job advertisements to make them more gender neutral can influence who applies for a job. Check your word choices.

When it comes to job advertisements, we also know that women are less likely than men to apply for a job that they are not 100 percent qualified for. Adding an endless laundry list of required skills and qualifications in your job advertisement will increase the likelihood that women will find a skill they don't have and opt out of applying.[8] In reality, many of those skills and qualifications you deem necessary can be quickly learned on the job or may not be essential to the job at all. Keeping job advertisements tidy can help increase your applicant pool. You can then advance those who may have more of the desired skills later in the process. But don't limit your choice of job candidates by overcomplicating your job advertisement.

Hiring practices that emphasize particular backgrounds or traits can similarly influence who becomes a leader and who doesn't. For instance, some companies filter their job candidates on the basis of where they went to school. If the applicant did not attend an Ivy League university, then they are eliminated from the applicant pool. As these institutions are historically white, this means that these companies are systematically filtering out racial minorities. Their evaluation system produces racist outcomes.

When it comes to women who are mothers, we often see that inflexible work environments similarly filter women out of the workforce. As women are still largely viewed as primary caretakers, having flexibility in their schedules to work from home when a child is sick or to leave early when necessary can keep them from advancing and succeeding. Of course, the underlying problem here is much larger and raises the issue of gender imbalances within the home. From a leader's perspective, you don't have control over what happens in the home. You do, however, have control over the systems within your organization that can make it a more conducive place for women to grow.

ALLIES

The importance of male allies to women's success is well documented. As men remain the dominant group in leadership, they are the gatekeepers of power. They still largely control the system. If you're a man, or if you know a man who wants to be an ally, the tips for women in leadership apply to you as well. But here are some additional steps you can take to support women who are in, or who aspire to, leadership.

Bystander Interventions

In 2022, the mayor of London, Sadiq Khan, ran a campaign focused on reducing street harassment of women. In a series of advertisements, the campaign depicted "mates" out on the town when one begins to harass a visibly uncomfortable woman. The campaign shows the internal monologue of one of the bystanders debating whether or not he should intervene. In the end, the friend chooses to simply say to the person harassing the woman, "Hey man, that's not cool. Let's go." They then leave and the woman is left to get in her cab unharmed.[9] Each campaign advertisement focuses on our personal responsibility in these types of situations. We can't just sit back and let it happen. We must intervene.

In the scientific literature, researchers refer to this as "bystander intervention." When someone on the outside of a situation, a bystander, intervenes, they can change the course of an event. In the case of the mayor's commercial, the woman is left alone. When it comes to gender-biased thinking and explicit or implicit sexism at work, in your family, or with your friends, bystander interventions can work similarly. When you hear someone make a sexist comment about a woman in leadership, step in. When you hear someone put down a job candidate because they are a woman, speak up. When a woman asks you for advice on preparing for a leadership interview, help her! (Please note the word choice here: she has *asked* you. This is not an endorsement to mansplain).

Challenge Yourself and Others

Gender bias influences everyone. No matter how "woke" or "unwoke" you might believe yourself to be, you are susceptible to making a biased decision. Accepting that you might be biased is the first step in making better, unbiased decisions. You see, if we don't recognize our own propensity for bias, we may not look out for it when it comes time to make a decision or take action. We must therefore be consciously aware of our susceptibility to bias and challenge ourselves to make objective, unbiased decisions. Check in with yourself regularly and reflect on your past and current decisions. What criteria did you use when making them, and how did gender bias play a role? Then, consider how you can make a better decision in the future.

Being a man in today's world means that you are granted a gender-driven power that is not similarly granted to women. Consequently, you possess a power to create change by being an example to others and by challenging others' behavior and judgments. For those in formal positions of power, this is especially important, as your actions send a signal about what is and is not acceptable. By challenging others' views, you can wield your power—formal or informal—to create an environment where sexist behavior won't be tolerated.

Recent research looked at the impact male allies have on women's advancement and the progression of gender equity initiatives in the work-place.[10] When looking across thousands of responses about gender equity movements at work, the researchers found that women-only groups lacked "issue legitimacy." Others in the organization didn't believe that their issue was important. In contrast, men-only groups lacked "coalition legitimacy." They weren't viewed as the appropriate people to be speaking out about these issues. However, mixed-gender groups possessed both types of legitimacy. When men and women work together to advance gender equity initiatives in the workplace, they have the potential to create real change.

How will you help be part of the change?

WHAT'S NEXT?

As I sat down to type this conclusion, a BBC alert flashed across my screen—Nicola Sturgeon, the First Minister of Scotland has just resigned. Her decision follows a few weeks after the resignation of Jacinda Ardern, Prime Minister of New Zealand. Public reaction to both announcements is largely marked by surprise. Why are these women leaving office early? Why are they giving up power? Both leaders made their rationale clear—they could no longer give the job their very best. Sturgeon noted, "Giving absolutely everything of yourself to this job is the only way to do it. The country deserves nothing less. But, in truth, that can only be done, by anyone, for so long. For me, it is now in danger of becoming too long."[11] And for Ardern, "I'm leaving, because with such a privileged role comes responsibility—the responsibility to know when you are the right person to lead and also when you are not. I know what this job takes. And I know that I no longer have enough in the tank to do it justice. It's that simple."[12] In resigning, these women leave as they led—putting others ahead of themselves.

Their resignation also puts the treatment of women in leadership back in the spotlight. Although their male counterparts were certainty not without their criticisms during their time in office, these women, and the countless other women holding leadership positions around the globe face a unique labyrinth of criticisms and challenges that make their job especially difficult. It is difficult then, to decouple the resignation of these women from the many challenges they faced during their time in power— challenges not encountered by men in the same positions.

We have work to do. We must make leadership a safer, a more inclusive space for women. For everyone along the gender spectrum. If we each play our part, we can help more women advance into leadership. From a moral perspective, we have an obligation to create a more equal and just society in which men and women can equally pursue and attain their dreams. But if you aren't convinced by the moral argument, will the idea of a world with fewer bad leaders, fewer lions, convince you? The more we expand leadership opportunities for women, as well as for people of color and of different sexual orientations and gender identities, the more we open our talent pool to new ways of leading. In doing so, we can usher in a new, more effective, era of leadership—the era of the Painted Wolf.

Acknowledgments

So many people contributed to the ideas shared in these pages and to my energy to continue writing. I'd like to say a special thank you to a few of those people who went above and beyond to do so.

Chris, my husband, this book would have taken at least five times longer without your constant support and encouragement to continue writing, editing, and making decisions. Thank you for reminding me that while starting the book is a good accomplishment, finishing the book makes a better one. And for helping me finish writing by listening to me read paragraphs out loud again and again, as well as even typing a few while I finished my hair before a night out. Your near daily mantra that I am a "strong, powerful woman" kept my imposter syndrome in check and regularly encouraged me to just open the document and keep writing. More than just keeping me working on this, however, our conversations about leadership helped challenge my thinking and put shape to many of the ideas discussed in these pages. Your determination, willingness to learn, and leadership inspire me daily. I love you mucho.

To my hype women, Jenn Griffith and Jamie Wagner, who read the early "shit drafts" of each chapter and helped make them "less shit." Your feedback helped improve the stories told and the ideas shared. Your endless enthusiasm for this project made what was, at times, an isolating process, far more fun than it would have been without you two. And your fire for loudly yelling about the patriarchy and the unequal treatment of women at work (and everyone else) with me over the phone, Zoom, and wine reminded me of the importance of this message and fueled my energy for this project.

An extra thank you to Jenn for fighting all the lady fights with me since our first brunch at Syrup in 2015.

And a special shout out to Jamie for the homemade "champagne."

My Council—Amanda, Paige, and Laura—your love and support have never wavered. Thank you for being my biggest cheerleaders since our drama room days. Although I'm bad at chiming in to the group chat, your messages never go unread. Many of the chats sparked ideas shared in this book to help women navigate the patriarchal world in which we find ourselves. More importantly, your unwavering support throughout the years gave me the confidence and support I needed to write this. When I got scared or thought maybe it was too risky, your I-would-cut-a-bitch level of support reminded me that no matter what happens, I always have you. Thank you for being uniquely you and for always keeping the witch-like rage burning.

Although she didn't contribute much when it came to content, I must thank my dog, Luna, for her excellent emotional support animal work. Your underbite smile, googly eyes, and stinky cuddles always made the difference when I felt like giving up.

Hi mom! I did it! I wrote a book! Thank you for your constant positivity and belief that I can do anything. Throughout my life, you have been such an inspiring example of a woman who knew what she wanted and went out and got it. I know that came with its challenges, and it certainly came with a great deal of whining from me, but I hope you know that I recognize your commitment, your drive, and your fight. Those traits inspire me to fight for a better, fairer world for you, me, and all other women.

Sam Hunter, when I joined your lab at Penn State, I didn't expect it to lead me here. All I wanted was an extra-curricular activity, and instead, you helped me find a passion and a career. Thank you for suggesting that this California girl go to Oklahoma, for continuing to mentor me all of these years, and for always believing in me. The first time I asked you a question in your creativity seminar and you turned the tables asking for *my* view, you taught me the value of my own voice. Your continued belief in me served as a reality check each time I thought about giving up because my voice "didn't matter." In our chats, you regularly reminded me that my voice, opinion, and expertise deserve its own space. Thank you.

Thank you to my sister, Paigey, for providing your Gen Z perspective on life, leadership, and work. I can't wait to see what leadership lessons you teach me in the years to come as you continue your journey to becoming a "real doctor."

Dad, thank you for telling your Uber passengers about the book—even before it had a title. I always enjoyed sharing my book updates with you your traffic-jammed drives back from LAX.

Heather, how lucky I am to have such a thoughtful and intelligent mother-in-law. Thank you for all your encouragement and discussions throughout the writing process. Our chatty walks provided a great source of feedback and for the construction of thoughtful ideas about women in leadership. Thank you for being so open with me.

Big shoutout to Zara and Will who provided CHAMPAGNE!, encouragement, and thoughtful (and usually heated) discussions from day one. Thank you for the intellectual debates, booze, coffee dates, and the many sweet treats throughout the process.

Thank you to Susie for always asking about the book despite having nine million and one other things to think about with your growing family. Your encouragement and thoughtfulness helped keep my energy up!

Thank you to Pip and James for the many dinner discussions about Elon Musk that served as a secondary motivation for writing about these women. Our debates inspired and challenged my thinking. And thank you for being so enthusiastic about the book that you started planning a book launch party before I finished writing (even if you don't remember that offer).

Thank you to Elder Press Café for letting me consistently break the rules and work on my laptop downstairs so I could work on this book with my dog Luna and a lovely iced soy latte.

To the editors and copyeditors, thank you for your wordsmithing and suggestions for better communicating my message. Thank you to Christine for regularly checking in on me and being a source of accountability during the editing process.

And finally, thank you to the Hogan team for giving me the opportunity to publish this book. Thank you for believing in the idea and in me from the start.

References

PREFACE

1. Bhuiyan, Johana. 2022. "SpaceX employees say they were fired for criticizing Elon Musk in open letter." November 17, 2022. *The Guardian*. https://www.theguardian.com/science/2022/nov/17/spacex-employees-file-unfair-labor-practice-charges-elon-musk.

2. Smith, Allen. 2022. "Elon Musk Faces Lawsuits at Twitter and Tesla." November 8, 2022. *Society for Human Resource Management*. https://www.shrm.org/resourcesandtools/legal.

3. BBC, 2019. "Ana Brnabić: Gay Partner of Serbian PM Gives Birth." February 20, 2019. *BBC*. https://www.bbc.co.uk/news/world-europe-47312826-and-compliance/employment-law/pages/elon-musk-twitter-tesla.aspx.

4. Stolberg, Sheryl Gay. 2021. "'This is Politics.': Dr. Rachel Levine's Rise as Transgender Issues Gain Prominence." May 8, 2021. *The New York Times*. https://www.nytimes.com/2021/05/08/us/politics/rachel-levine-transgender.html.

5. Al Saidi, Ahmen Mohammed Obaid, et al. 2020. "Decisive Leadership is a Necessity in the COVID-19 Response." *The Lancet* 396(10247): 295–298. https://doi.org/10.1016/S0140-6736(20)31493-8.

6. Alwan, Nisreen A., et al. 2020. "Scientific Consensus on the COVID-19 Pandemic: We Need to Act Now." *The Lancet* 396 (10260): 71–72. https://doi.org/10.1016/S0140-6736(20)32153-X.

PAINTED WOLVES VS. LIONS

1. WWF, 2023. "African Wild Dog." https://www.worldwildlife.org/species/african-wild-dog.

2. Discovery UK, 2022. "How much does a lion weigh?" April 22, 2022. https://www.discoveryuk.com/big-cats/how-much-does-a-lion-weigh/.

3. Thornybush, 2020. "African Wild Dog vs. Domestic Dog - What's the Difference?." January 21, 2020. https://www.thornybush.com/difference-wild-domestic-dogs/.

4. Lion Alert, 2020. "Predatory Behaviour." January 8, 2020. https://lionalert.org/predatory-behaviour/.

5. Shields, Laura G. 2019. "Painted Wolves: The Colorful Carnivores of the African Wild." February 28, 2019. https://www.livescience.com/64889-painted-wolves-the-colorful-carnivores-of-the-african-wild.html.

6. Viegas, Jen. 2017. "African Dogs Vote by Sneezing." September 7, 2017. https://www.livescience.com/60335-african-dogs-vote-by-sneezing.html.

7. Hogan, Joyce, Robert Hogan, and Robert Kaiser. 2011. "Management Derailment." In *APA Handbook of Industrial and Organizational Psychology*, vol. 3, edited by Sheldon Zedeck, 555–75. Washington, DC: American Psychological Association.

8. Keller, Scott. 2018. "Successfully Transitioning to New Leadership Roles." *McKinsey Quarterly*, May 23, 2018.

9. Training Industry. 2021. "Size of the Training Industry." Last modified March 29, 2021. https://trainingindustry.com/wiki/learning-services-and-outsourcing/size-of -training-industry/.

10. Antonakis, John. 2011. "Predictors of leadership: The usual suspects and the suspect traits." *SAGE Handbook of Leadership*: 269–285.

11. Bousquet, Jean, et al. (2020). "Cabbage and fermented vegetables: From death rate heterogeneity in countries to candidates for mitigation strategies of severe COVID-19." Allergy 76(3): 735–750.

12. Labmate Online. 2020. "How Germany Has Led the Way on COVID-19 Testing." Last modified May 2, 2020. https://www.labmate-online.com/news/ laboratory-products/3/breaking-news/how-germany-has-led-the-way-on-covid-19 -testing/52141.

13. Walker, Andrew. 2020. "Coronavirus Pushes German Economy into Recession." BBC News, May 15, 2020. https://www.bbc.co.uk/news/business-52673727.

14. Pannett, Rachel, and Stephen Wright. 2020. "Both New Zealand and Australia Contained Coronavirus, but One Is Set to Pay a Heavier Price." *Wall Street Journal*, April 29, 2020. https://www.wsj.com/articles/both-new-zealand-and-australia -contained-coronavirus-but-one-is-set-to-pay-a-heavier-price-11588158002.

15. Graham-McLay, Charlotte. 2020. "Ardern urges New Zealanders to 'act like you have Covid-19' as lockdown looms." The Guardian, March 25, 2020. https://www.theguardian.com/world/2020/mar/25/ardern-urges-new -zealanders-to-act-like-you-have-covid-19-as-lockdown-looms.

16. Fifield, Anna. 2020. "New Zealand Isn't Just Flattening the Curve. It's Squashing It." *Washington Post*, April 7, 2020. https://www.washingtonpost.com/ world/asia_pacific/new-zealand-isnt-just-flattening-the-curve-its-squashing-it/ 2020/04/07/6cab3a4a-7822-11ea-a311-adb1344719a9_story.html.

17. Griffiths, James. 2020. "Taiwan's Coronavirus Response Is among the Best Globally." CNN, April 5, 2020. https://edition.cnn.com/2020/04/04/asia/taiwan -coronavirus-response-who-intl-hnk/index.html.

18. Klein, Alice. 2020. "Australia Seems to Be Keeping a Lid on COVID-19— How Is It Doing It?" *NewScientist*, April 8, 2020. https://www.newscientist .com/article/2240226-australia-seems-to-be-keeping-a-lid-on-covid-19-how-is-it -doing-it/.

19. Wittenberg-Cox, Avivah. 2020. "What Do Countries with the Best Coronavirus Responses Have in Common? Women Leaders." *Forbes*, April 13, 2020. https://www .forbes.com/sites/avivahwittenbergcox/2020/04/13/what-do-countries-with-the -best-coronavirus-reponses-have-in-common-women-leaders/?sh=4732b3c23dec.

20. Taub, Amanda. 2020. "Why Are Women-Led Nations Doing Better with COVID-19?" *New York Times*, May 15, 2020. https://www.nytimes.com/2020/ 05/15/world/coronavirus-women-leaders.html.

21. Henley, Jon, and Eleanor Ainge Roy. 2020. "Are Female Leaders More Successful at Managing the Coronavirus Crisis?" *The Guardian*, April 25, 2020.

https://www.theguardian.com/world/2020/apr/25/why-do-female-leaders-seem
-to-be-more-successful-at-managing-the-coronavirus-crisis.

22. Persaud, Raj. 2020. "Why Women Make Better Crisis Leaders." *Japan Times*,
May 17, 2020. https://www.japantimes.co.jp/opinion/2020/05/17/commentary/
world-commentary/women-make-better-crisis-leaders/.

23. North, Anna. 2020. "Are Women Leaders Better at Fighting Coronavirus? It's
Complicated." *Vox*, May 21, 2020. https://www.vox.com/2020/5/21/21263766/
coronavirus-women-leaders-germany-new-zealand-taiwan-merkel.

24. Mathers, Matt. 2020. "Coronavirus Belgium: 'Outraged' Medics Turn Their
Backs in Protest at PM's Handling of Pandemic." *Independent* (US edition),
May 18, 2020. https://www.independent.co.uk/news/world/europe/coronavirus
-belgium-medics-protest-hospital-sophie-wilmes-a9519686.html.

25. Bremmer, Ian. 2020. "The Best Global Responses to the COVID-19
Pandemic, 1 Year Later." *Time*, June 12, 2020. https://time.com/5851633/best
-global-responses-covid-19/.

26. Kristof, Nicholas. 2020. "What the Pandemic Reveals About the Male Ego."
June 13, 2020. *The New York Times*. https://www.nytimes.com/2020/06/13/
opinion/sunday/women-leaders-coronavirus.html?smid=tw-share.

27. Eagly, Alice, and Steven J. Karau. 2002. "Role Congruity Theory of Prejudice
Toward Female Leaders." *Psychological Review* 109 (3): 573–98. https://doi.org/
10.1037//0033-295X.109.3.573.

28. Eagly, Alice and Linda L. Carli. 2007. "Women and the Labyrinth of
Leadership." Harvard Business Review. September 2007. https://hbr.org/2007/09/
women-and-the-labyrinth-of-leadership.

29. Ryan, Michelle K., and Haslam S. Alexander. 2005. "The Glass Cliff: Evidence
That Women Are Over-Represented in Precarious Leadership Positions." *British
Journal of Management* 16 (2): 81–90. https://doi.org/10.1111/j.1467-8551.2005
.00433.x.

30. Consultants 500 Team. n.d. "The MBA Reading List According to the Top
Business Schools in the World." Consultants 500. Accessed October 21, 2022.
https://www.blog.consultants500.com/consulting/mba-reading-list-according-top
-business-schools-world/.

31. Oliver, John. 2019. *Last Week Tonight with John Oliver*. Season 6, episode 170,
"Bias in Medicine." Aired August 18, 2019, on HBO.

32. Criado Perez, Caroline. 2019. *Invisible Women*. New York: Harry N. Abrams.
chap. 14. New York: Routledge.

33. Lebowitz, Shana. 2018. "When People Are Asked to Draw What a Leader
Looks Like, Almost Everyone Draws the Same Thing—And It's a Disturbing
Picture of How Little Progress We've Made." *Business Insider*, March 19, 2018.
https://www.businessinsider.in/When-people-are-asked-to-draw-what-a-leader
-looks-like-almost-everyone-draws-the-same-thing-and-its-a-disturbing-picture-of
-how-little-progress-weve-made/articleshow/63370097.cms.

34. Beaman, Lori, et al. 2012. "Female leadership raises aspirations and education
attainment for girls: A policy experiment in India." *Science* 335 (6068): 582–586.
https://doi.org/10.1126/sciecne.1212382.

35. Latu, Ioana, et al. 2013. "Successful female leaders empower women's
behavior in leadership tasks." *Journal of Experimental Social Psychology* 49 (3):
444–448. https://doi.org/10.1016/j.jesp.2013.01.003.

36. Clinton, Hilary. 2016. "Hilary Clinton's Concession Speech—Full Transcript." *The Guardian*, November 9, 2016. https://www.theguardian.com/us-news/2016/nov/09/hillary-clinton-concession-speech-full-transcript.

MYTHS ABOUT WOMEN IN LEADERSHIP

1. Loden, Marilyn. 2017. "100 Women: 'Why I Invented the Glass Ceiling Phrase.'" BBC News, December 3, 2017. https://www.bbc.co.uk/news/world-42026266.

2. Lang, Cady, and Anna Purna Kambhampaty. 2020. "'People Are Going to Take My Daughters Seriously Too.' For Women of Color Who See Themselves in Kamala Harris, Her Historic Win Is Personal." *Time*, November 10, 2020. https://time.com/5910084/kamala-harris-historic-win-women/.

3. Geiger, A. W., and Lauren Kent. 2017. "Number of Women Leaders around the World Has Grown, but They're Still a Small Group." Policy Commons, March 8, 2017. https://policycommons.net/artifacts/617998/number-of-women-leaders-around-the-world-has-grown-but-theyre-still-a-small-group/1598895/.

4. UN Women. 2022. "Facts and Figures: Women's Leadership and Political Participation." Last modified September 19, 2022. https://www.unwomen.org/en/what-we-do/leadership-and-political-participation/facts-and-figures.

5. Hinchliffe, Emma. 2021. "The Female CEOs on This Year's Fortune 500 Just Broke Three All-Time Records." *Fortune*, June 2, 2021. https://fortune-com.cdn.ampproject.org/c/s/fortune.com/2021/06/02/female-ceos-fortune-500-2021-women-ceo-list-roz-brewer-walgreens-karen-lynch-cvs-thasunda-brown-duckett-tiaa/amp/.

6. Okahana, Hironao, and Enyu Zhou. 2017. "Graduate Enrollment and Degrees: 2006 to 2016." Council of Graduate Schools, September 2017. https://legacy.cgsnet.org/publication-pdf/4642/CGS_GED16_Report_Final.pdf.

7. Bryant, Jessica. 2022. "Women Continue to Outnumber Men in College Completion." Best Colleges, July 8, 2022. https://www.bestcolleges.com/news/analysis/2021/11/19/women-complete-college-more-than-men/.

8. Matias, Dani. 2019. "New Report Says Women Will Soon Be Majority of College-Educated U.S. Workers." NPR. June 20, 2019. https://www.npr.org/2019/06/20/734408574/new-report-says-college-educated-women-will-soon-make-up-majority-of-u-s-labor-f.

9. Moran, Gwen. 2015. "Women Now Make Up 40% of Students at Top MBA Programs." *Fortune*, November 9, 2015. https://fortune.com/2015/11/09/women-mba-40-percent/.

10. Dill, Kathryn. 2019. "More Women Pursue MBA as Elite Schools Step Up Recruiting." *Wall Street Journal*, November 6, 2019. https://www.wsj.com/articles/more-women-pursue-m-b-a-as-elite-schools-step-up-recruiting-11573036204.

11. Folkman, Joseph, and Jack Zenger. 2015. "A Study in Leadership: Women Do It Better Than Men." In *Real Women, Real Leaders: Surviving and Succeeding in the Business World*, edited by Kathleen Hurley and Priscilla Shumway, 165–69. Hoboken, NJ: Wiley.

12. Zenger, Jack, and Folkman, Joseph. 2019. "Research: Women Score Higher Than Men in Most Leadership Skills." *Harvard Business Review*, June 25, 2019. https://hbr.org/2019/06/research-women-score-higher-than-men-in-most-leadership-skills.

13. Abouzahr, Katie, Matt Krentz, Frances Taplett, Claire Tracey, and Miki Tsusaka. 2017. "Dispelling the Myths of the Gender 'Ambition Gap.'" BCG Perspectives. http://www.yasargil.co.uk/public/upload/ckeditor/files/bcg-dispelling.pdf.

14. Grandey, Alicia, Allison Gabriel, and Eden King. 2019. "Tackling Taboo Topics: A Review of the Three Ms in Working Women's Lives." *Journal of Management* 46 (1): 7–35. https://doi.org/10.1177/0149206319857144.

15. McFarlane, Jessica, Carol Lynn Martin, and Tannis MacBeth. 1988. "Mood Fluctuations: Women versus Men and Menstrual versus Other Cycles." *Psychology of Women Quarterly* 12 (2): 201–23. https://doi.org/10.1111/j.1471-6402.1988 .tb00937.x.

16. Sommer, Barbara. 1992. "Cognitive Performance and the Menstrual Cycle." In *Cognition and the Menstrual Cycle*, edited by J. T. E. Richardson. New York: Springer-Verlag.

17. Ni Meng, Joseph Hazzard, Pamela Smith. 2018. "Balance Performance Maintained during Dual-Task Condition with a Cognitive Task across Menstrual Cycle." *Neurology* 91 (23). https://doi.org/10.1212/01.wnl.0000550632.95899.61

18. Small, Deborah A., Michele Gelfand, Linda Babcock, and Hilary Gettman. 2007. "Who Goes to the Bargaining Table? The Influence of Gender and Framing on the Initiation of Negotiation." *Journal of Personality and Social Psychology* 93 (4): 600–613. https://doi.org/10.1037/0022-3514.93.4.600.

19. Bowles, Hannah Riley, Linda Babcock, and Kathleen L. McGinn. 2005. "Constraints and Triggers: Situational Mechanics of Gender in Negotiation. *Journal of Personality and Social Psychology* 89 (6): 951–65. https://doi.org/ 10.1037/0022-3514.89.6.951.

20. Artz, Benhamin, Amanda H. Goodall, and Andrew J. Oswald. 2018. "Do Women Ask?" *Industrial Relations* 57 (4): 611–36.

21. Eagly, Alice H., and Mary C. Johannesen-Schmidt. 2002. "The Leadership Styles of Women and Men." *Journal of Social Issues* 57 (4): 781–97. https://doi .org/10.111/0022-4537.00241.

22. Martell, Richard F., Christopher Parker, Cynthia G. Emrich, and Marnie Swerdlin Crawford. 1998. "Sex Stereotyping in the Executive Suite: 'Much Ado about Something.'" *Journal of Social Behavior and Personality* 13 (1): 127–38.

23. Rudman, Laurie A., and Peter Glick. 2001. "Prescriptive Gender Stereotypes and Backlash toward Agentic Women." *Journal of Social Issues* 57 (4): 743–62. https://doi.org/10.1111/0022-4537.00239.

24. Eagly, Alice H., Christa Nater, David I. Miller, Michéle Kaufmann, and Sabine Sczesny. 2020. "Gender Stereotypes Have Changed: A Cross-Temporal Meta-Analysis of US Public Opinion Polls from 1946 to 2018." *American Psychologist* 75 (3): 301–15. https://doi.org/10.1037/amp0000494.

25. Hentschel, Tanja, Susanne Braun, Claudia Peus, and Dieter Frey. 2018. "The Communality-Bonus Effect for Male Transformational Leaders – Leadership Style, Gender, and Promotability. *European Journal of Work and Organizational Psychology* 27 (1): 112–25. https://doi.org/10.1080/1359432X.2017 .1402759.

26. Hall, Lauren J., and Ngaire Donaghue. 2012. "'Nice Girls Don't Carry Knives': Constructions of Ambition in Media Coverage of Australia's First Female Prime Minister." *British Journal of Social Psychology* 52 (4): 631–47. https://doi .org/10.1111/j.2044-8309.2012.02114.x.

27. Martinez, Anthony, and Cheridan Christnacht. 2021. "Women Are Nearly Half of the U.S. Workforce but Only 27% of STEM Workers." US Census Bureau, January 26, 2021. https://www.census.gov/library/stories/2021/01/women-making -gains-in-stem-occupations-but-still-underrepresented.html.

28. Catalyst. 2022. "Women in Science, Technology, Engineering, and Mathematics (STEM) (Quick Take)." Research, August 23, 2022. https://www.catalyst.org/ research/women-in-science-technology-engineering-and-mathematics-stem/.

29. Connley, Courtney. 2020. "New Report Shows It Could Take 12 Years to Reach Equal Representation of Women in Tech." CNBC, September 29, 2020. https:// www.cnbc.com/2020/09/29/it-could-take-12-years-to-reach-equal-representation -of-women-in-tech.html.

30. Tiku, Nitashu. 2019. "For Young Female Coders, Internship Interviews Can Be Toxic." *Wired*, August 22, 2019. https://www.wired.com/story/for-young-female -coders-internship-interviews-can-be-toxic/.

31. Streitfeld, David. 2015. "Ellen Pao Loses Silicon Valley Bias Case Against Kleiner Perkins." *New York Times*, March 27, 2015. https://www.nytimes.com/ 2015/03/28/technology/ellen-pao-kleiner-perkins-case-decision.html.

32. Shu, Catherine. 2019. "Meredith Whittaker, AI researcher and an organizer of last year's Google walkout, is leaving the company." *Tech Crunch*. July 16, 2019. https://techcrunch.com/2019/07/15/meredith-whittaker-ai-researcher-and-an -organizer-of-last-years-google-walkout-is-leaving-the-company/.

33. O'Connor, Pat, et al. 2021. "Organisational characteristics that facilitate gender-based violence and harassment in higher education?" *Administrative Sciences* 11 (138): 1-13. https://doi.org/10.3390/admsci11040138.

34. Williams, Christine L. 1992. "The Glass Escalator: Hidden Advantages for Men in the 'Female' Professions." *Social Problems* 39 (3): 253–67. https://doi.org/ 10.2307/3096961.

35. Ryan, Michelle K., and S. Haslam Alexander. 2005. "The Glass Cliff: Evidence that Women Are Over-Represented in Precarious Leadership Positions." *British Journal of Management* 16 (2): 81–90. https://doi.org/10.1111/j.1467-8551.2005 .00433.x.

36. Eagly, Alice H., Steven J. Karau, and Mona G. Makhijani. 1995. "Gender and the Effectiveness of Leaders: A Meta-analysis." *Psychological Bulletin* 117 (1): 125–45. https:doi.org//10.1037/0033-2909.117.1.125.

37. Judge, Elizabeth. 2003. "Women on Board: Help or Hindrance?" *The Times*, November 11, 2003. https://www.thetimes.co.uk/article/women-on-board -help-or-hindrance-2c6fnqf6fng.

38. Morgenroth, Thekla, Teri A. Kirby, Michelle K. Ryan, and Antonia Sudkämper. 2020. "The Who, When and Why of the Glass Cliff Phenomenon: A Meta-analysis of Appointments to Precarious Leadership Positions." *Psychological Bulletin* 146 (9): 797–829. https://doi.org/10.1037/bul0000234.

39. Tabrizi, Behnam. 2015. "Carly Fiorinia's Legacy as CEO of Hewlett Packard." *Harvard Business Review*, September 25, 2015. https://hbr.org/2015/09/carly -fiorinas-legacy-as-ceo-of-hewlett-packard.

40. Chapman, Madeleine. 2020. *Jacinda Ardern: A New Kind of Leader.* Cheltenham, United Kingdom: History Press.

PREPARATION

1. Northouse, Peter G. 2021. *Leadership: Theory and Practice (Ninth Edition)*. California: Sage.

2. Anderson, Cameron, Sebastien Brion, Don A. Moore, and Jessica A. Kennedy. 2012. "A Status-Enhancement Account of Overconfidence." *Journal of Personality and Social Psychology* 103 (4): 718–35. https://doi.org/10.1037/a0029395.

3. Price, Paul C., and Eric R. Stone. 2003. "Intuitive Evaluation of Likelihood Judgment Producers: Evidence for a Confidence Heuristic." *Journal of Behavioral Decision Making* 17 (1): 39–57. https://doi.org/10.1002/bdm.460.

4. Sah, Sunita, Don A. Moore, and Robert J. MacCoun. 2013. "Cheap Talk and Credibility: The Consequences of Confidence and Accuracy on Advisor Creditability and Persuasiveness." *Organizational Behavior and Human Decision Processes* 121 (2): 246–55. https://doi.org/10.1016/j.obhdp.2013.02.001.

5. Carpenter, Shana K., Miko M. Wilford, Nate Kornell, and Kellie M. Mullaney. 2013. "Appearances Can Be Deceiving: Instructor Fluency Increases Perceptions of Learning without Increasing Actual Learning." *Psychonomic Bulletin & Review* 20: 1350–56. https://doi.org/10.3758/s12423-013-0442.z.

6. Rudman, Laurie A. 1998. "Self-promotion as a risk factor for women: The costs and benefits of counterstereotypical impression management." *Journal of Personality and Social Psychology*, 74 (3): 629–645. https://doi.org./10.1037/0022-3514.74.3.629.

7. Criado Perez, Caroline. 2019. Invisible Women: Exposing data bias in a world designed for men. New York: Harry N. Abrams.

8. Medeiros, Kelsey E., Jennifer A Griffith, Stephan D. Shipe, Matthew P. Crayne, Rachel Campagna, and Tristan McIntosh. 2022. "Minding the ($500,000) Gap: Accounting for the Gender-Driven Gap in Executive Severance Agreements." *Journal of Business and Psychology* 37: 1065–77. https://doi.org/10.1007/s10869-021-09785-w.

9. Marko, Matthew David, et al. 2020. "Leadership lessons from the Titanic and Concordia disasters." *Journal of Management History* 26 (2): 216–230. https://doi.org/10.1108/JMH-09-2018-0050.

10. Khamsi, Roxanne. 2006. "Overconfidence is a disadvantage in war, finds study." *New Scientist*. June 21, 2006. https://www.newscientist.com/article/dn9374-overconfidence-is-a-disadvantage-in-war-finds-study/.

11. Hilts, Phillip J. 1986. "Excess of confidence and complication." *The Washington Post*. August 22, 1986. https://www.washingtonpost.com/archive/politics/1986/08/22/excess-of-confidence-and-complication/194cc4f9-6054-4ba5-ba93-f2422399b77e/.

12. Qvortrup, Matthew. 2016. *Angela Merkel: Europe's Most Influential Leader*. New York: Harry N. Abrams.

13. Miller, Saskia. 2020. "The Secret to Germany's COVID-19 Success: Angela Merkel Is a Scientist. *The Atlantic*, April 20, 2020. https://www.theatlantic.com/international/archive/2020/04/angela-merkel-germany-coronavirus-pandemic/610225/.

14. Jamison, Dean T., Lawrence J. Lau, Kin Bing Wu, and Yanyan Xiong. 2020. "Country Performance against COVID-19: Rankings for 35 Countries." *BMJ Global Health* 5 (12). https://doi.org/10.1136/bmjgh-2020-003047.

15. France24. 2021. "Bolsonaro's Most Controversial Coronavirus Quotes." *France24*, June 19, 2021. https://www.france24.com/en/live-news/20210619 -bolsonaro-s-most-controversial-coronavirus-quotes.

16. Risse, Leonora. 2018. "The Gender Qualification Gap: Women 'Over-invest' in Workplace Capabilities." *The Conversation*, November 19, 2018. https:// theconversation.com/the-gender-qualification-gap-women-over-invest-in -workplace-capabilities-105385.

17. Moss-Racusin, Corrine A., John F. Dovidio, Victoria L. Brescoll, Mark J. Graham, and Jo Handelsman. 2012. "Science faculty's subtle gender biases favor male students." *PNAS* 109 (41): 16474–79. https://doi.org/10.1073/pnas .1211286109.

18. Chapman, Madeleine. 2020. *Jacinda Ardern: A New Kind of Leader.* Cheltenham, United Kindgom: History Press.

19. Hiebert, Paul. 2016. "It's Not Just Hilary: Women Value Preparation More than Men." *YouGov*, October 13, 2016. https://yougov.co.uk/topics/politics/ articles-reports/2016/10/13/prepare-hard-work-natural-talent-women-men.

20. Chamorro-Premuzic, Tomas. 2021. "The Dark Side of Having Confidence: Why the Toxic Cult of Self-Belief Needs to Stop." *Psychology Today*, July 29, 2021. https://www.psychologytoday.com/gb/blog/mr-personality/202107/the-dark -side-having-confidence.

ISSUE-DRIVEN FOCUS

1. Bromwich, Jonah E., and Alexandra Alter. 2019. "Who Is MacKenzie Scott?" *New York Times*, January 12, 2019. https://www.nytimes.com/2019/01/12/style/ jeff-bezos-mackenzie-divorce.html.

2. Bayers, Chip. 1991. "The Inner Jeff Bezos." *Wired*, March 1, 1991. https:// www.wired.com/1999/03/bezos-3/.

3. Chang, Kenneth. 2021. "Jeff Bezos' Rocket Company Accused of Toxic Culture and Safety Issues." September 30, 2021. *The New York Times.* https:// www.nytimes.com/2021/09/30/science/jeff-bezos-blue-origin-safety.html#:~:text= The%20Lioness%20essay%20describes%20a,planet%2C%E2%80%9D%20 the%20essay%20says.

4. Kantor, Jodi, and David Streitfeld, 2015. "Inside Amazon: Wrestling Big Ideas in a Bruising Workplace." August 15, 2015. *The New York Times.* https://www .nytimes.com/2015/08/16/technology/inside-amazon-wrestling-big-ideas-in-a -bruising-workplace.html.

5. Scott, MacKenzie. 2020. "116 Organizations Driving Change." July 28, 2020. *Medium.* https://mackenzie-scott.medium.com/116-organizations-driving-change -67354c6d733d.

6. Sandler, Rachel. 2022. "Here's How Much More MacKenzie Scott has Donated to Charity than Ex-Husband Jeff Bezos." October 26, 2022. *Forbes.* https://www .forbes.com/sites/rachelsandler/2022/10/26/heres-how-much-more-mackenzie -scott-has-donated-to-charity-than-ex-husband-jeff-bezos/?sh=131db8741e28.

7. Simonetti, Isabella, and Nicholas Kulish. 2022. "Jeff Bezos Says He Will Give Away Most of His Fortune." November 14, 2022. *The New York Times*. https://www.nytimes.com/2022/11/14/business/jeff-bezos-charity.html.

8. Sandler, Rachel. 2022. "The Top Richest Women in the World 2022." April 5, 2022. *Forbes*. https://www.forbes.com/sites/rachelsandler/2022/04/05/the-top-richest -women-in-the-world-2022/?sh=730dc9be446a.

9. IUPUI Women's Philanthropy Institute. 2015. "Do Women Give More?" IUPUI Women's Philanthropy Institute, September 2015. https://scholarworks.iupui.edu/bitstream/handle/1805/6984/Do%20Women%20Give%20More%20-%20 Working%20Paper%201%20-%20Sept%202015.pdf.

10. Mesch, Debra J., Melissa S. Brown, Zachary I. Moore, and Amir Daniel Hayat. 2011. "Gender Differences in Charitable Giving." *International Journal of Nonprofit and Voluntary Sector Marketing* 16 (4): 342–55. https:doi.org/10.1002/nvsm.432.

11. Kulish, Nicholas. 2020. "Giving Billions Fast, MacKenzie Scott Upends Philanthropy." *New York Times*, December 20, 2020. https://www.nytimes.com/2020/12/20/business/mackenzie-scott-philanthropy.html.

12. Kristof, Nicholas D., and Sheryl WuDunn. 2010. *Half the Sky*. London: Virago.

13. Chapman, Madeleine. 2020. *Jacinda Ardern: A New Kind of Leader*. Cheltenham, United Kingdom: History Press.

14. Abend, Lisa. 2020. "Finland's Sanna Marin, the World's Youngest Female Head of Government Wants Equality, Not Celebrity." *Time*, January 16, 2020. https://time.com/collection-post/5764097/sanna-marin-finland-equality/.

15. Nichols, John. 2018. "Meet Katrín Jakobsdóttir, Iceland's Left-Wing, Environmentalist, Feminist Prime Minister." *The Nation*, March 8, 2018. https://www.thenation.com/article/archive/meet-katrin-jakobsdottir-icelands-left-wing -environmentalist-feminist-prime-minister/.

16. Kapur, Sonia, and Rajinder Kaur. 2004. "Gender Differences in Need for Power and Its Psychological Correlates." *Journal of the Indian Academy of Applied Psychology* 30 (1–2): 1–9.

17. Crayne, Matthew P., and Kelsey E. Medeiros. 2021. "Making Sense of Crisis: Charismatic, Ideological, and Pragmatic Leadership in Response to COVID-19." *American Psychologist* 76 (3): 462–74. https://doi.org/10.1037/amp0000715.

COLLECTIVE LEADERSHIP

1. Ordoñezm, Lisa D., and David T. Welsh. 2015. "Immoral Goals: How Goal Setting May Lead to Unethical Behavior." *Current Opinion in Psychology* 6: 93–96. https://doi.org/10.1016/j.copsyc.2015.06.001.

2. Prentice, Chris, Pete Schroeder, and Imani Moise. 2020. "Wells Fargo to Pay $3 Billion to US, Admits Pressuring Workers in Fake-Accounts Scandal." *Reuters*, February 21, 2020. https://www.reuters.com/article/us-wells-fargo-scandal-deal -idUSKBN20F2KN.

3. Alleman, Karl, and Julie Kalt. 2019. "We Need More Humble Leaders. Here's How to Get Them." *Fast Company*, June 3, 2019. https://www.fastcompany .com/90351437/we-need-more-humble-leaders-heres-how-to-get-them.

4. Hyman, Jeff. 2018. "Why Humble Leaders Make the Best Leaders." *Forbes*, October 31, 2018. https://www.forbes.com/sites/jeffhyman/2018/10/31/humility/?sh=685830c61c80.

5. Wang, Yanfei, Jiequiong Liu, and Yu Zhu. 2018. "Humble Leadership, Psychological Safety, Knowledge Sharing, and Follower Creativity: A Cross-Level Investigation." *Frontiers in Psychology* 19. https://doi.org/10.3389/fpsyg.2018.01727.

6. Ali, Mudassar, Li Zhang, Syed Jamal Shah, Salim Khan, and Adnan Muhammad Shah. 2020. "Impact of Humble Leadership on Project Success: The Mediating Role of Psychological Empowerment and Innovative Work Behavior." *Leadership & Organization Development Journal* 41 (3): 349–67. https://doi.org/10.1108/LODJ-05-2019-0230.

7. Ding, He., Enhai Yu, Xixi Chu, Yanbin Li, and Kashif Amin. 2020. "Humble Leadership Affects Organizational Citizenship Behavior: The Sequential Mediating Effect of Strengths Use and Job Crafting." *Frontiers in Psychology* 11. https://doi.org/10.3389/fpsyg.2020.00065.

8. Owens, Bradley P., and David R. Hekman. 2015. "How Does Leader Humility Influence Team Performance? Exploring the Mechanisms of Contagion and Collective Promotion Focus." *Academy of Management Journal* 59 (3): 1088–1111. https://doi.org/10.5465/amj.2013.0660.

9. Bharanitharan, Darren K., Kevin B. Lowe, Somayeh Bahmannia, Zhen Xiong Chen, and Lin Cui. 2021. "Seeing Is Not Believing: Leader Humility, Hypocrisy, and Their Impact on Followers' Behaviors." *The Leadership Quarterly* 32 (2). https://doi.org/10.1016/j.leaqua.2020.101440.

10. Chandler, Jeffrey A., et al. 2022. A meta-analysis of humble leadership: Reviewing individual, team, and organizational outcomes of leader humility. *The Leadership Quarterly*. https:/doi.org/10.1016/j.leaqua.2022.101660.

11. Kelemen, Thomas K., Samuel H. Matthews, Michael J. Matthews, and Sarah E. Henry. 2022. *Journal of Organizational Behavior.* https://doi.org/10.1002/job.2608.

12. Blackwell, Debra L., Jacqueline W. Lucas, and Tainya C. Clarke. 2014. *Summary Health Statistics for US Adults: National Health Interview Survey, 2012.* US Department of Health and Human Services, series 10, no. 260. https://www.cdc.gov/nchs/data/series/sr_10/sr10_260.pdf.

13. Courtenay, Will H. 2000. "Constructions of Masculinity and Their Influence on Men's Well-Being: A Theory of Gender and Health. *Social Science & Medicine* 50 (10): 1385–1401. https://doi.org/10.1016/S0277-9536(99)00390-1.

14. Williams, David R. 2003. "The Health of Men: Structured Inequalities and Opportunities." *American Journal of Public Health* 93 (5): 724–31. https://doi.org/10.2105/ajph.93.5.724.

15. Wang, Yingying, Kate Hunt, Irwin Nazareth, Nick Freemantle, and Irene Petersen. 2013. "Do Men Consult Less than Women? An Analysis of Routinely Collected UK General Practice Data." *BMJ Open*, 3. https://doi.org/10.1136/bmjopen-2013-003320.

16. Nam, Suk Kyung, Hui Jung, Mi Kyoung, Ji Hee Lee, Nuri Kim, and Sang Min Lee. 2010. "A Meta-analysis of Gender Differences in Attitudes toward Seeking Professional Psychological Help. *Journal of American College Health* 59 (2): 110–16. https://doi.org/10.1080/07448481.2010.483714.

17. Juvrud, Joshua, and Jennifer L. Rennels. 2017. "'I Don't Need Help': Gender Differences in How Gender Stereotypes Predict Help-Seeking." *Sex Roles* 76: 27–39. https://doi.org/10.1007/s11199-016-0653-7.

18. Rosette, Ashleigh Shelby, Jennifer S. Mueller, and R. David Lebel. 2015. "Are Male Leaders Penalized for Seeking Help? The Influence of Gender and Asking Behaviors on Competence Perceptions." *Leadership Quarterly* 26 (5): 749–62. https://doi.org/10.1016/j.leaqua.2015.02.001.

19. Eagly, Alice, and Steven J. Karau. 2002. "Role Congruity Theory of Prejudice Toward Female Leaders." *Psychological Review* 109 (3): 573–598. https://doi .org/10.1037//0033-295X.109.3.573.xf.

20. Rudman, Laurie A., and Stephen E. Kilianski. 2000. "Implicit and Explicit Attitudes toward Female Authority." *Personality and Social Psychology Bulletin* 26 (11): 1315–28. https://doi.org/10.1177/0146167200263001.

21. Rudman, Laurie A., Corinne A. Moss-Racusin, Julie E. Phelan, and Sanne Nauts. 2012. "Status Incongruity and Backlash Effects: Defending the Gender Hierarchy Motivates Prejudice against Female Leaders." *Journal of Experimental Social Psychology* 48 (1): 165–79. https://doi.org/10.1016/j.jesp.2011.10.008.

22. Shan, Shelley. 2020. "International visitor numbers rose 7% in 2019." January 7, 2020. *Taipei Times.* https://www.taipeitimes.com/News/front/archives/2020/01/07/2003728830.

23. Hernández, Javier C., and Chris Horton. 2020. "Taiwan's Weapon against Coronavirus: An Epidemiologist as Vice President." *New York Times*, May 21, 2020. https://www.nytimes.com/2020/05/09/world/asia/taiwan-vice-president -coronavirus.html.

24. Wang, C. Jason, Chun Y. Ng, and Robert H. Brook. 2020. "Response to COVID-19 in Taiwan: Big Data Analytics, New Technology, and Proactive Testing." *JAMA Network*, March 3, 2020. https://jamanetwork.com/journals/jama/fullarticle/2762689.

25. Ing-wen, Tsai. 2020. "President of Taiwan: How My Country Prevented a Major Outbreak of COVID-19." *Time*, April 16, 2020. https://time.com/collection/finding-hope-coronavirus-pandemic/5820596/taiwan-coronavirus-lessons/.

26. Jang, Seulki, Tammy D. Allen, and Joseph Regina. 2021. "Office Housework, Burnout, and Promotion: Does Gender Matter?" *Journal of Business and Psychology* 36: 793–805. https://doi.org/10.1007/s10869-020-09703-6.

27. Williams, Joan C. 2014. "Sticking Women with the Office Housework." *Washington Post*, April 16, 2014. https://www.washingtonpost.com/news/on -leadership/wp/2014/04/16/sticking-women-with-the-office-housework/.

28. Guarino, Cassandra M., and Victor M. H. Borden. 2017. "Faculty Service Loads and Gender: Are Women Taking Care of the Academic Family?" *Research in Higher Education* 58: 672–94.

29. Mitchell, Sara McLaughlin, and Vicki L. Hesli. 2013. "Women Don't Ask? Women Don't Say No? Bargaining and Service in the Political Science Profession." *PS: Political Science and Politics* 46 (02): 355–64. https://doi.org/10.1017/S1049096513000073.

30. Cullinan, Renee. 2018. "In Collaborative Work Cultures, Women Carry More of the Weight." *Harvard Business Review*, July 24, 2018. https://hbr.org/2018/07/in-collaborative-work-cultures-women-carry-more-of-the-weight.

31. Hauschildt, Jürgen, and Edgar Kirchmann. 2002. "Teamwork for innovation—The 'Troika' of Promoters." *R&D Management* 31 (1): 41–49. https://doi.org/10.1111/1467-9310.00195.

32. Rawlins-Bentham, Julia. 2021. "Prime Minister Calls for Coordinated Response." Barbados Government Information Service, April 6, 2021. https://gisbarbados.gov.bb/blog/prime-minister-calls-for-coordinated-response/.

33. Pan American Health Organization. 2020. "Barbados: An example of government leadership and regional cooperation in containing the COVID-19 virus." Pan American Health Organization, August 26, 2020. https://www.paho.org/en/documents/barbados-example-government-leadership-and-regional-cooperation-containing-covid-19-virus.

WILLINGNESS TO LEARN

1. Lee, Bruce Y. 2017. "Bill Gates Warns of Epidemic That Could Kill Over 30 Million People." *Forbes*, February 19, 2017. https://www.forbes.com/sites/brucelee/2017/02/19/bill-gates-warns-of-epidemic-that-will-kill-over-30-million-people/?sh=5b8f1161282f.

2. Netflix. 2020. *Pandemic: How to Prevent an Outbreak*. Documentary series. https://www.netflix.com/title/81026143.

3. Knight, Victoria. 2020. "Obama Team Left Pandemic Playbook for Trump Administration, Officials Confirm." PBS News Hour, May 15, 2020. https://www.pbs.org/newshour/nation/obama-team-left-pandemic-playbook-for-trump-administration-officials-confirm.

4. Beecham, Amy. 2022. "Why Jonathan Van Ness's Reminder on Embracing Solitude and Being Patient with Your Mental Health Journey Is So Important." *Stylist*, February 16, 2022. https://www.stylist.co.uk/entertainment/celebrity/jonathan-van-ness-i-weigh-jameela-jamil/623784.

5. Francis, Donald P. 2012. "Deadly AIDS Policy Failure by the Highest Levels of the US Government: A Personal Look Back 30 Years Later for Lessons to Respond Better to Future Epidemics." *Journal of Public Health Policy* 33 (3): 290–300. https://doi.org/10.1057/jphp.2012.14.

6. Low, James. 2020. COVID-19 Crisis Management: An Early Look. Civil Service College–Singapore, June 3, 2020. https://www.csc.gov.sg/articles/covid-19-crisis-management-an-early-look.

7. Tan, Kevin Y. L. 2020. "Singapore's Regulatory Response to COVDI-19." *Regulatory Review*, June 15, 2020. https://www.theregreview.org/2020/06/15/tan-singapore-regulatory-response-covid-19/.

8. Aravindan, Aradhana. 2020. "Analysis: Vaccinated Singapore Shows Zero-COVID Countries Cost of Reopening." *Reuters*, October 22, 2021. https://www.reuters.com/world/asia-pacific/vaccinated-singapore-shows-zero-covid-countries-cost-reopening-2021-10-22/.

9. Navarro, Vicente. 2021. "Why Asian Countries Are Controlling the Pandemic Better Than the United States and Western Europe." *International Journal of Health Services* 51 (2): 261–64. https://doi.org/10.1177/0020731421999930.

10. Qvortrup, Matthew. 2016. *Angela Merkel: Europe's Most Influential Leader*. New York: Harry N. Abrams.

11. Bandura, Albert. 1971. *Social Learning Theory.* New York: General Learning Press.

12. Kaplan, Robert S. 2011. "Top Executives Need Feedback—Here's How They Can Get It." *McKinsey Quarterly*, September 1, 2011. https://www.mckinsey.com/featured-insights/leadership/top-executives-need-feedback-and-heres-how-they-can-get-it.

EMOTION MANAGEMENT

1. Newman, Andy, and Ray Rivera. 2010. "Fed-Up Flight Attendant Makes Sliding Exit." *New York Times*, August 9, 2010. https://www.nytimes.com/2010/08/10/nyregion/10attendant.html.

2. Kramer, Adam D. I., Jamie E. Guillory, and Jeffrey T. Hancock. 2014. "Experimental Evidence of Massive-Scale Emotional Contagion Through Social Networks." *PNAS* 111 (24): 8788–8790. https://doi.org/10.1073/pnas.1320040111.

3. Clymer, Adam. 2001. "Book Says Nixon Considered a Woman for Supreme Court." *New York Times*, September 27, 2001. https://www.nytimes.com/2001/09/27/us/book-says-nixon-considered-a-woman-for-supreme-court.html.

4. Clinton, Hilary Rodham. 2016. "The Hilary Clinton Conversation Special." Conducted by Amanda de Cadenet. January 12, 2016. https://www.amandadecadenet.com/shows/special.

5. Milligan, Susan. 2019. "Women Candidates Still Tagged as Too 'Emotional' to Hold Office." *US News*, April 16, 2019. https://www.usnews.com/news/politics/articles/2019-04-16/women-candidates-still-tagged-as-too-emotional-to-hold-office.

6. Barrett, Lisa Feldman, Lucy Robin, Paula R. Pietomonaco, and Kristen M. Eyssell. 1998. "Are Women the 'More Emotional' Sex? Evidence from Emotional Experiences in Social Context. *Cognition and Emotion* 12 (4): 555–78. https://doi.org/10.1080/026999398379565.

7. Weigard, Alexander, Amy M. Loviska, and Adriene M. Beltz. 2021. "Little Evidence for Sex or Ovarian Hormone Influences on Affective Variability." *Scientific Reports* 11 (20925). https://doi.org/10.1038/s41598-021-00143-7.

8. Salerno, Jessica M., Hannah J. Phalen, Rosa N. Reyes, and N. J. Schweitzer. 2018. "Closing with Emotion: The Differential Impact of Male versus Female Attorneys Expressing Anger in Court." *Law and Human Behavior* 42 (4): 385–401. https://doi.org/10.1037/lhb0000292.

9. Rasinski, Heather M., and Alexander M. Czopp. 2010. "The Effect of Target Status on Witnesses' Reactions to Confrontations of Bias." *Basic and Applied Social Psychology* 31 (1): 8–16. https://doi.org/10.1080/01973530903539754.

10. Smith, Alexis Nicole, Marla Baskerville Watkins, Jamie J. Ladge, and Pamela Carlton. 2019. "Making the Invisible Visible: Paradoxical Effects of Intersectional Invisibility on the Career Experiences of Executive Black Women." *Academy of Management Journal* 62 (6): 1705–34. https://doi.org/10.5465/amj.2017.1513.

11. Motro, Daphna, Johanthan B. Evans, Aleksander P. J. Ellis, and Lehman Benson III. 2022. "Race and Reactions to Women's Expressions of Anger at Work:

Examining the Effects of the 'Angry Black Woman' Stereotype." *Journal of Applied Psychology* 107 (1): 142–52. https://doi.org/10.1037/apl0000884.

12. Zahn-Waxler, Carolyn, JoAnn L Robinson, and Robert N. Emde. 1992. "The development of empathy in twins." *Developmental Psychology* 28 (6): 1038–1047. https://doi.org/10.1037/0012-1649.28.6.1038.

13. Rogers, Carl. 1951. *Client-Centered Therapy: Its Current Practice, Implications and Theory.* London: Constable.

14. Bas-Sarmiento, Pilar, Martina Fernández-Gutiérrez, María Baena-Baños, Alba Correro-Bermejo, Pablo Sergio Soler-Martins, and Soniade la Torre-Moyano. 2020. "Empathy Training in Health Sciences: A Systemic Review." *Nurse Education in Practice* 44 (102739). https://doi.org/10.1016/j.nepr.2020.102739.

15. Rochat, Magali Jane. 2022. "Sex and gender differences in the development of empathy." *Journal of Neuroscience Research*, 101 (5): 718-729. https://doi.org/10.1002/jnr.25009.

16. Van Bommel, T. 2021. "The Power of Empathy in Times of Crisis and Beyond." *Catalyst*, 2021. https://www.catalyst.org/reports/empathy-work-strategy-crisis.

17. France24. 2019. "Compassion, Grit Takes 'Jacindamania' to New Heights after Mosque Attack." France24, March 21, 2019. https://www.france24.com/en/20190321-new-zealand-jacindamania-ardern-popularity-mosque-attack.

18. Fifield, Anna. 2019. "New Zealand's Prime Minister Received Worldwide Praise for Her Response to the Mosque Shootings." *Washington Post*, March 18, 2019. https://www.washingtonpost.com/world/2019/03/18/new-zealands-prime-minister-wins-worldwide-praise-her-response-mosque-shootings/.

19. Nagesh, Ashitha. 2019. "Jacinda Ardern: 'A Leader with Love on Full Display.'" *BBC*. March 21, 2019. https://www.bbc.com/news/world-asia-47630129.

20. Friedman, Uri. 2020. "New Zealand's Prime Minister May Be the Most Effective Leader on the Planet." *The Atlantic*, April 19, 2020. https://www.theatlantic.com/politics/archive/2020/04/jacinda-ardern-new-zealand-leadership-coronavirus/610237/.

21. Blackwell, Geoff. 2020. "Jacinda Ardern: 'Political Leaders Can Be Both Empathetic and Strong.'" *The Guardian*, May 30, 2020. https://www.theguardian.com/world/2020/may/31/jacinda-ardern-political-leaders-can-be-both-empathetic-and-strong.

22. Reuters Staff. 2020. "Here's How Norway Is Reassuring Children over COVID-19 Fears." *World Economic Forum*, March 17, 2020. https://www.weforum.org/agenda/2020/03/norway-pm-tells-kids-it-is-ok-to-feel-scared-during-coronavirus.

23. Teding van Berkhout, E., and J. M. Malouff. 2016. "The Efficacy of Empathy Training: A Meta-analysis of Randomized Controlled Trials." *Journal of Counseling Psychology* 63 (1): 32–41. https://doi.org/10.1037/cou0000093.

24. Waytz, Adam. 2016. "The Limits of Empathy." *Harvard Business Review*, January-February 2016. https://hbr.org/2016/01/the-limits-of-empathy.

25. McRae, Kateri, and James J. Gross. 2020. "Emotion Regulation." *Emotion* 20 (1): 1–9. https://doi.org/10.1037/emo0000703.

26. Webb, Thomas L., Eleanor Miles, and Paschal Sheeran. 2012. "Dealing with Feeling: A Meta-analysis of the Effectiveness of Strategies Derived from the Process

Model of Emotion Regulation." *Psychological Bulletin* 138 (4): 775–808. https:// doi.org/10.1037/a0027600.

27. McRae, Kateri. 2016. "Cognitive emotion regulation: A review of theory and scientific findings." *Current Opinion in Behavioral Sciences* 10: 119–124. https:// doi.org/10.1016/j.cobeha.2016.06.004.

28. McRae, Kateri, Kevin N. Ochsner, Iris B. Mauss, John D. Gabrieli, and James J. Gross. 2008. "Gender Differences in Emotion Regulation: An fMRI Study of Cognitive Reappraisal." *Group Processes and Intergroup Relations* 11 (2): 143–62. https://doi.org/10.1177/1368430207088035.

29. Goleman, D. 2012. *Emotional Intelligence: Why It Can Matter More Than IQ.* New York: Bantam.

30. Salovey, Peter, and John D. Mayer. 1990. "Emotional Intelligence." *Imagination, Cognition and Personality* 9 (3): 185–211. https://doi.org/10.2190/ DUGG-P24E-52WK-6CDG.

31. Mayer, John D. and Peter Salovey. (1997). What is emotional intelligence? In P. Salovey & D. Sluyter (Eds.), *Emotional development and emotional intelligence: Implications for educators* (pp. 3–31). New York: Basic Books.

32. Antonakis, John. 2004. "On Why 'Emotional Intelligence' Will Not Predict Leadership Effectiveness Beyond IQ or the 'Big Five': An Extension and Rejoinder." *Organizational Analysis* 12 (2): 171–182. https://doi.org/10.1108/eb028991.

33. Carreyrou, John. 2018. *Bad Blood: Secrets and Lies in a Silicon Valley Startup.* Evansville, IN: Vintage Publishing.

RISK TAKING

1. Lüfkens, Matthias. 2022. "The Most Followed World Leaders on Social Media 2022." Medium, May 4, 2022. https://medium.com/digital-diplomacy/ the-most-followed-world-leaders-on-social-media-2022-193bb9d89d8d.

2. BBC. 2021. "New Zealand PM Jacinda Ardern's Live Stream Interrupted by Three-Year-Old Daughter." BBC News, November 10, 2021. https://www.bbc .co.uk/news/av/world-asia-59230846.

3. Kale, Sirin. 2022. "Sanna Marin: Finland's Prime Minister Who Just Wants to Be Herself." *The Guardian*, August 24, 2022. https://www.theguardian.com/ world/2022/aug/24/sanna-marin-finland-prime-minister-who-just-wants-to-be -herself.

4. Furnham, Adrian, and Hua Chu Boo. 2011. "A Literature Review of the Anchoring Effect." *Journal of Socio-Economics* 40 (1): 35–42. https://doi.org/ 10.1016/j.socec.2010.10.008.

5. Tversky, Amos, and Daniel Kahneman. 1974. "Judgment Under Uncertainty: Heuristics and Biases." *Science* 8: 1124–1131. https://doi.org/10.1126/science .185.4157.1124.

6. Thorsteinson, Todd J. 2011. "Initiating Salary Discussions with an Extreme Request: Anchoring Effects on Initial Salary Offers." *Journal of Applied Social Psychology* 41 (7): 1774–1792. https://doi.org/10.1111/j.1559-1816.2011 .00779.x.

7. Gudina, Esayas Kebede, Dabesa Gobena, Tessema Debela, Daniel Yilma, Tsinuel Girma, Zeleke Mekonnen, Mirkuzie Woldie, Dereje Abdena, et al. 2021. "COVID-19 in Oromia Region of Ethiopia: A Review of the First 6 Months' Surveillance Data." *BMJ Open* 11 (3): 1–9. https://doi.org/10.1136/bmjopen -2020-046764.

8. Berg, Justin M. 2014. "The Primal Mark: How the Beginning Shapes the End in the Development of Creative Ideas." *Organizational Behavior and Human Decision Processes* 125 (1): 1–17. https://doi.org/10.1016/j.obhdp.2014.06.001.

9. Wegener, Duane T., Richard E. Petty, Brian T. Detweiler-Bedell, and W. Blair G. Jarvis. 2011. "Implications of Attitude Change Theories for Numerical Anchoring: Anchor Plausibility and the Limits of Anchor Effectiveness." *Journal of Experimental Social Psychology* 37 (1): 62–69. https://doi.org/10.1006/jesp.2000.1431.

10. Mumford, Michael D., Erin Michelle Todd, Cory Higgs, and Tristan McIntosh. 2017. "Cognitive Skills and Leadership Performance: The Nine Critical Skills." *Leadership Quarterly* 28 (1): 24–39. https://doi.org/10.1016/j.leaqua.2016.10.012.

11. Mumford, Michael D., Michele I. Mobley, Roni Retier-Palmon, Charles E. Uhlman, and Lesli M. Doares. 1991. "Process Analytic Models of Creative Capacities." *Creativity Research Journal* 4 (2): 91–122. https://doi.org/10.1080/10400419109534380.

12. Medeiros, Kelsey, et al. 2018. "Timing is Everything: Examining the Role of Constraints Throughout the Creative Process." *Psychology of Aesthetics, Creativity, and the Arts* 12(4): 471–488. https://doi.org/10.1037/aca00000148.

13. Haught-Tromp, Catrinel. 2017. "The *Green Eggs and Ham* Hypothesis: How Constraints Facilitate Creativity." *Psychology of Aesthetics, Creativity, and the Arts* 11 (1): 10–17. https://doi.org/10.1037/aca0000061.

14. Mayer, Marrisa. 2006. "Creativity Loves Constraints." February 13, 2006. *Bloomberg.* https://www.bloomberg.com/news/articles/2006-02-12/creativity -loves-constraints#:~:text=Creativity%20thrives%20best%20when%20 constrained,obvious%2C%20unconventional%2C%20or%20unexplored.

15. Stone, Biz. 2015. *Things a Little Bird Told Me: Creative Secrets From the Co-Founder of Twitter.* Grand Central Publishing.

16. Piscopo, Jennifer M., and Malilga Och. 2021. "Effective, Decisive, and Inclusive: Women's Leadership in COVID-19 Response and Recovery." UN Women. https://www.unwomen.org/sites/default/files/Headquarters/Attachments/ Sections/Library/Publications/2021/Effective-decisive-and-inclusive-Womens -leadership-in-COVID-19-response-and-recovery-en.pdf.

17. Ethiopian Airlines. 2018. "Addis Ababa Airport Sees Record Upsurge in Number of Passengers, 18 July 2018." July 18, 2019. https://corporate.ethiopian airlines.com/Press-release-open-page/addis-ababa-airport-sees-record-upsurge-in -number-of-passengers-addis-ababa-18-july-2019.

18. Oqubay, Arkebe. 2020. "Ethiopia's Unconventional COVID-19 Response." *World Economic Forum,* June 5, 2020. https://www.weforum.org/agenda/2020/06/ ethiopia-covid19-response/.

19. Soudan, François. 2021. "Ethiopia's President Sahle-Work Zewde Saw That 'Abiy Was Dragging His Country into an Infernal Spiral.'" *Africa Report,* November 24, 2021. https://www.theafricareport.com/149465/ethiopias-president- sahle-work-zewde-saw-that-abiy-was-dragging-his-country-into-an-infernal-spiral/.

20. Sirleaf, Ellen Johnson, Presidential Center for Women and Development. 2022. "COVID-19 Heroine: Minister Lia Tadesse." https://www.ejscenter.org/covid-19/spotlight/minister-lia-tadesse/.

21. Department of Health and Social Care, Maggie Throup MP, and The Rt Hon Sajid Javid MP. 2022. "One Year Anniversary of UK Deploying Oxford -AstraZeneca Vaccine." January 4, 2022. https://www.gov.uk/government/news/one-year-anniversary-of-uk-deploying-oxford-astrazeneca-vaccine#:~:text=To%20date%20the%20UK%20government,early%20manufacturing%20of%20the%20vaccine.

22. UN Women. 2021. "Effective, Decisive, and Inclusive: Women's Leadership in COVID-19 Response and Recovery." September 2021. https://www.unwomen.org/sites/default/files/Headquarters/Attachments/Sections/Library/Publications/2021/Effective-decisive-and-inclusive-Womens-leadership-in-COVID-19-response-and-recovery-en.pdf.

23. Pilling, David. "No Lockdown, Few Ventilators, but Ethiopia Is Beating COVID-19. *Financial Times*, May 27, 2020. https://www.ft.com/content/7c6327ca-a00b-11ea-b65d-489c67b0d85d.

24. Merrick, Rob. 2022. "Boris Johnson Tells Public to 'Move On' from Partygate Despite Unanswered Questions." *The Independent*. May 25, 2022. https://www.independent.co.uk/news/uk/politics/boris-johnson-partygate-sue-gray-b2087431.html.

25. Morgenroth, Thekla, Michelle K. Ryan, and Cordelia Fine. 2022. "The Gendered Consequences of Risk-Taking at Work: Are Women Averse to Risk or to Poor Consequences?" *Psychology of Women Quarterly* 46 (3): 257–77. https://doi.org/10.1177/03616843221084048.

26. Eagly, Alice H. 2022. "Women Take Risks to Help Others to Stay Alive." *Behavioral Brain Sciences* 25 (135). https://doi.org/10.1017/S0140525x22000437.

ACTIONS FOR CHANGE

1. Bezrukova, Katerina, Chester S. Spell, Jamie L. Perry, and Karen A. Jehn. 2016. "A Meta-analytical Integration of Over 40 Years of Research on Diversity Training Evaluation." *Psychological Bulletin* 142 (11): 1227–74. https://doi.org/10.1037/bul0000067.

2. Steele, Logan M., and Joseph A. Vandello. 2019. "When Training Backfires and What Can Be Done About It." *Industrial and Organizational Psychology: Perspectives on Science and Practice* 12: 30–33. https://doi.org/10.1017/iop.2019.3.

3. Mohr, Tara Sophia. 2014. "Why Women Don't Apply for Jobs Unless They're 100% Qualified." *Harvard Business Review*, August 25, 2014. https://hbr.org/2014/08/why-women-dont-apply-for-jobs-unless-theyre-100-qualified.

4. Moss-Racusin, Corinne A., and Laurie A Rudman. 2010. "Disruption in Women's Self-Promotion: The Backlash Avoidance Model. *Psychology of Women Quarterly* 34: 186–202. https://doi.org/10.1111/j.1471-6402.2010.01561.x.

5. Rudman, Laurie A., and Peter Glick. "Feminized Management and Backlash Toward Agentic Women: The Hidden Costs to Women of a Kinder, Gentler Image of Middle Managers." *Journal of Personality and Social Psychology*, 77 (5): 1004–1010. https://doi.org/10.1037/0022-3514.77.5.1004.

6. Smith, Jessi L., and Meghan Huntoon. 2013. "Women's Bragging Rights: Overcoming Modesty Norms to Facilitate Women's Self-Promotion." *Psychology of Women Quarterly* 38 (4): 447–59. https://doi.org/10.1177/0361684313515840.

7. Gaucher, Danielle, Justin Friesen, and Aaron C. Kay. 2011. "Evidence That Gendered Wording in Job Advertisements Exists and Sustains Gender Inequality." *Journal of Personality and Social Psychology* 101 (1): 109–28. https://doi.org/10.1037/a0022530.

8. Nobel, Carmen. 2016. "How to Take Gender Bias Out of Your Job Ads." *Forbes.* December 14, 2016. https://www.forbes.com/sites/hbsworkingknowledge/2016/12/14/how-to-take-gender-bias-out-of-your-job-ads/?sh=59271a8a1024.

9. Degun, Gurjit. 2022. "Mayor of London Addresses Male Bystander Behaviour to Tackle Violence Against Women." March 14, 2022. *Campaign.* https://www.campaignlive.co.uk/article/mayor-london-addresses-male-bystander-behaviour-tackle-violence-against-women/1749496.

10. Hussain, Insiya, Subrahmaniam Tangirala, and Elad N. Sherf. 2022. "Signaling Legitimacy: Why Mixed-Gender Coalitions Outperform Single-Gender Coalitions in Advocating for Gender Equity." *Academy of Management Journal.* https:doi.org/10.5465/amj.2021.0174.

11. Stacey, Kiran. 2023. "Nicola Sturgeon in Her Own Words: Key Moments From Resignation Speech." February 15, 2023. *The Guardian.* https://www.theguardian.com/politics/2023/feb/15/nicola-sturgeon-in-her-own-words-key-moments-resignation-speech.

12. McClure, Tess. 2023. "Jacinda Ardern Resigns as Prime Minister of New Zealand." January 19, 2023. *The Guardian.* https://www.theguardian.com/world/2023/jan/19/jacinda-ardern-resigns-as-prime-minister-of-new-zealand.

Printed in Great Britain
by Amazon

27850796R00116